No Regrets

No Regrets

Patricia Haley

BET Publications, LLC
http://www.bet.com

NEW SPIRIT BOOKS are published by

BET Publications, LLC
c/o BET BOOKS
One BET Plaza
1900 W Place NE
Washington, DC 20018-1211

ISBN: 1-58314-299-1

First Printing: June 2002
10 9 8 7 6 5 4 3 2

Printed in the United States of America

I joyfully dedicate this book to my role model, my friend, my childhood disciplinarian, my encourager, my faithful supporter, and dear mother: Fannie Haley.

Through each challenge in your life, of which there have been many, you have triumphed and managed to land on your feet with something funny to say on your lips and a few more scars on your back. Even without a formal education, you have proven to be one of the wisest people that I know. You truly are my hero. I recognize the hard work, sacrifice, and love that you have faithfully, consistently, and unselfishly given to me throughout my life.

I remember the times in my youth when you walked to work with holes in your shoes. You always held down at least two jobs to support Fred, Erick, and me, checking on us every break you got, because so many times you couldn't find a reliable baby-sitter. I can't forget all the times that you dug down in your purse and gave us the last few dollars you had, just so we could have spending money on our school field trips. I know there were many times that you denied your own needs, only to press on for the sake of your children. You showed tremendous love and courage in caring for Erick during his illness. To go even further, you tirelessly took incredible care of our daddy, your ex-husband, Fred "Luck" Haley, for eight years during his bout with Alzheimer's, while simultaneously getting up at the crack of dawn for nearly two years to go visit your sister, Arletha, at the nursing home.

Yes, Ma, you are irreplaceable to me. You are what it's all about, one who has generously used her life to make this world a more loving place for someone else. Even if you never do another thing for me in my life, I have already received enough support and love from you to carry me on. You have drenched me with love, and the warm sweet shower of your affection floods my heart daily. Truly God has blessed me with a phenomenal mother. Well done.

I love you, Ma. Always and always.

ACKNOWLEDGMENTS

Why do I have such a long acknowledgments section? It's simple—none of us show up in this world on our own. We are all linked to somebody, and it's the only way to realize certain accomplishments. God has blessed me with an entourage of people who have each played a role in helping me to write and get published. So, my honor and gratitude to God is expressed through my appreciation of His children, and I take the time and space to acknowledge them.

To my beloved Jeffrey—my confidant, my ace, my best friend, and my true love—thank you for being such a supportive dream of a husband. You have brought so much fun to my writing. I'm glad that we're able to share this project together. Thank you for helping with the editing and for reading it over and over, only to always come back with a wealth of excitement and suggestions. You made me want to write more and to willingly make changes. You are an absolute blessing in my life—a gift beyond imagination. Every day you are a constant reminder to me of how merciful and gracious God is to me. You are undoubtedly my soul mate, and I love you.

Thanks to the other encouraging men in my life, which include my big brother Fred, one of my fathers—Bob Thomas, my younger brother Freddy, and always to the memory of my brother Erick for showing me unconditional love and always making me feel special.

To Rena Burks—thank you, sis, for always supporting me. You were the first one to read the sample pages of *Nobody's Perfect* and the first to say go for it. I love you dearly. Special thanks and love to my other "sisters"—Dr. Leslie Walker for the medical input; attorneys Tammy and Renee Lenzy for the legal and editorial advice; Dorothy Robinson for the spiritual perspective; Diedre Campbell, Kirkanne Moseley, Patricia Hill, and Bonnie Hargrove for the unwavering support. Although I don't have any biological sisters, I've never missed out, having known each of you for so much of my life.

To my other advance readers—thank you for being awesome. The depth of your comments, candor, enthusiasm, and encouragement helped me to write a better story. I am grateful to each of you—Emma and John Foots, Pam and Andre Seals, Laurel Robinson, and Ada Tennin. Thanks to my other volunteer, Elaine Kellam.

I have to honor my friends whose battle with breast cancer was the inspiration behind my needing to tell this story. I honor the memory of Dorcas Latchison. I praise those that have been challenged with the illness, yet press on—Rev. Roxanne White and Michelle Keene.

Thanks to my family, which includes the Haleys, Tennins, Moormans, Glasses, Donald and Mary Bartel, and Joan and Frances Walker. I appreciate each of you for showing up at events and promoting my works every chance you get.

To my agent, Claudia Cross—thank you. You hung in there and kept relentlessly shaking the bushes to find the right deal. From the first moment we talked, I knew that God had given us a connection. You believed in my writing when others were hesitant. Thank you.

I am grateful to Victoria Christopher Murray, a special author and friend. Your generosity and support is overwhelming. You went as far as rallying prayer groups together to encourage me through the book deal process. Thank you my dear sorority sister, friend, fellow believer, and, as you say, "my literary twin." You are truly a blessing to me in this arena, and I am thankful to God for you. May you be abundantly blessed with your novels, *Joy* and *Temptation,* for your unselfishness and your display of tremendous courage and faith.

Ms. Glenda Howard-King, you have been a dream of an editor. It has been nice knowing that you respect my input while also being able to offer your recommendations and insight in a very receptive fashion. Thank you for helping me to tell a more powerful story. To my publisher, Linda Gill, I am grateful to you for taking on this project.

Special thanks to the Iowa summer writing classes of 2001. I learned so much about the craft of writing. Specifically, I want to thank Hans, Tom, Charlie, Robbie, Heidi, Lee, Alan, Fedor, Gary, Steve, Eileen, Geoff, and Sands for the feedback that you gave me on my writing samples. It is greatly appreciated.

Thanks to Dorothea Kalra, the warriors at New Covenant Church (Trooper, PA), and Dominion Christian Center (Rockford, IL) for constantly covering me in prayer during my writing and traveling.

Thank you to those who helped me cross the self-publishing bridge. You enabled me to get to this point with *No Regrets.* Ms. Audrey Williams, you were sensational with the promotion of *Nobody's Perfect.* Thank you for your creative, persistent, and effective efforts. I also have to thank Wanda Gates, Gazelle Robinson, Millicent Udeaja, Laurelle and Erik Williams, Emma Collington, Stephenson Clark, Philip Claycomb, and Michelle Mitchell.

With three pages of acknowledgments in *Nobody's Perfect,* I still managed to forget some people, like Richard and Brenda Wright, Monique Bernoudi, Evelyn Robison, and Michelle (Micki) Jacobs.

Special thanks to my Delta Sigma Theta sorority sisters who have gone the extra step to show themselves sisterly to me. Your support is tremendous. All of them deserve recognition, but I want to give special thanks to the alumnae chapters of Valley Forge (PA), Houston (TX), Harrisburg (PA), Schaumburg-Hoffman Estates (IL), Richmond (VA), Milwaukee (WI), Rockford (IL), Pontiac (MI), Baltimore County (MD), Beaumont (TX), San Francisco (CA), North Jersey, Alaska, Palo Alto Bay Area (CA), and Stanford University undergraduate chapter (Omicron Chi).

I also want to thank my sisters of Alpha Kappa Alpha, Zeta Phi Beta, and Sigma Gamma Rho for the support they've given me.

There are many authors with whom I have come in contact through this literary journey, each with their own aspirations. This arena is sometimes viewed as competitive, whereby not everyone extends a hand to help a new author just learning the ropes. So I give an extra special thank you to those who did just that without hesitation—Eric Jerome Dickey, Michael Baisden, Franklin White, Jacquelin Thomas, Meme Kelly, Monique Jewell Anderson, and Melvin Banks, Jr. Each of you unselfishly helped me in a different way and at different times, but all at pivotal points.

To my other literary buddies, thanks for helping me to maintain my sanity in this fast-paced business. Thanks to Vincent Alexandria, Nicole Bailey-Williams, Sharon Ewell Foster, Terrance Johnson, Stephanie Perry Moore, Bernadette Connor, Kim Lawson Roby, Trevy McDonald, Evelyn Palfrey, Veraunda Jackson, Troy Martin, Judith Griffie, Keena Parker, Jason West, and Maurice Gray.

No way can I leave out the host of supportive media personnel, booksellers, distributors, Waldenbooks, and B. Dalton. Special thanks to a long list of independent African-American booksellers and to Myrt Yarbrough with Waldenbooks. I am grateful to the book clubs—Millenium (MI), Sisterhood (MI), Tabahoni (CA), Extra Special Women (IL), Cover to Cover (PA), Expressions (PA), Ebony Expressions (DE), Sister Circle (PA), Ebony Girl Talk (TX), African-American Women (PA), Reading by the Dozen (MD), Sistahs with a Vision (NJ), Gateway Reading Group (PA), and Felicity Women's Discussion Group (PA).

I have attended many events and encountered many memorable groups that I value greatly. However, I want to especially acknowledge Sorority Sisters Thelma Gould, Myla Meeks, Karen Portis, Tanoa Ford, Ernestine Jolivet, Cynthia Bernoudi, George and Monica Lloyd, Dr. Lola Richardson and Will Evans with Paine College, Pearl Ings and Eddie Brown with St. Marks Church (Orlando, FL), Xinos (Beaumont, TX), and Estelle Black and Fayrene Muhammad with the Rockford Public Library. From the media I give special thanks to Willie Walker, Julie Snively at the *Rockford Register Star,* for so graciously writing articles highlighting each pivotal point in my literary development, Nicole Bailey-Williams and Tamlin Henry on WDAS radio in Philadelphia, and Joe Wilson with the *Black Suburban Journal.*

Last, but most certainly not least, I acknowledge you, the readers. Thank you for the encouragement and overwhelming E-mails and notes that you consistently send. My writing is for you.

I am grateful to each and every one of you who has given me so much assistance and support. If I have unintentionally left out your name, please forgive me. Know that God remembers and may He bless you abundantly for all that you have given to me.

My flesh and my heart may fail, but God is the strength of my heart. . . .

—Psalm 73:26

CHAPTER 1

"Home sweet home" was her unspoken motto, and Karen took pride in creating a happy haven for her family at any cost. She steadied herself against the mahogany fireplace mantel lined with family photos. Smiling faces captured at graduations, birthday parties, proms, and other special moments created a storybook picture. Among the memories was also a dusty Bible that had been received as a wedding gift eighteen years ago and a few other favorite trinkets collected from countless vacations including the annual trip to Martha's Vineyard. The Clarks had worked hard to get a slice of the American dream. One glance around the room showed that their efforts were paying off.

Head tilted down and eyes closed, she started from the center of her forehead and repeatedly spread her thumb and index finger forcefully slow across her brow like a butterfly struggling to stay in flight.

"Oh, God. Please help me."

Feeling a moment of relief, she meandered to the window, which was squeaky clean as far up as a step-ladder-assisted arm could reach. Beyond the beds of spring tulips, Karen could see their collie running around and around the sprawling well-manicured backyard. Going in circles wasn't a question of if, only a matter of when. She envied that the only dilemma their dog had was whether to chase his tail now or later. She stared into the evening wondering where the week had gone and what time her husband would be getting home.

"Mom, Dr. Costas is on the phone!"

Karen heard the teen yelling from upstairs. It was occasions like this when she regretted forgoing the intercom package eight years ago when they had the home built. She made her way back across the family room to take the call. She slipped into her favorite chaise longue and picked up the phone that was resting on the marble end table. She didn't bother to return the scream with a thank you. "I got it, Chelle-baby. You can put the phone down now. Thank you."

"Hi, Karen. Dr. Costas here. I got a message that you called. What's going on?"

"I've had a throbbing headache for the past few days. Nothing major."

"Hmmm"

"I didn't want to take any kind of medication without checking with you first."

"That's good. Under normal conditions, it would be fine, but we've come a long ways. It's been a tough fight and we don't want any setbacks in your remission."

"I know."

"Do you have any nausea or any problems with your bowels?"

"No. No fever, no fatigue, no chills either."

Karen knew the routine list of questions that Dr. Costas asked whenever there was potential trouble brewing. Each time Karen got sick, she didn't find it any easier. She wanted to be brave in facing her health challenges, but found herself more often afraid. She couldn't decide which was worse, knowing or not knowing.

"Good. There doesn't seem to be any need for alarm. Why don't you take a simple over-the-counter pain reliever, something like Extra Strength Tylenol? Let's try that first. If the headache persists, give me another call in a few days, and we'll get you in for a look. Karen, it's also going to be important that you keep your stress level down. Remember pressure really seems to take a toll on you and we don't want to wear your immune system down. So, take some time to relax over the weekend. That's the best medicine I can prescribe for you right now. Okay?"

"That's fine. Thanks, doctor."

The phone rang as Karen put it down. Caught off guard by the incoming call, she put the phone up to her ear to see who was on the line.

"Hey, Karen." A deep, authoritative voice greeted her.

"Oh, Johnny, it's you."

"Why? Were you expecting somebody else?"

Karen knew he wasn't really looking for an answer. She kept quiet.

"What a way to answer the phone. You answer it like one of the kids."

Early in his career he'd spent seven years as a production line supervisor before getting promoted to senior management. Barking out orders at work carried over into his personal life. Karen heard Johnny loud and clear, internalized his comment, and opted to say nothing in her own defense. His personality didn't accommodate timidity or shortcomings in others.

"I just got off the phone with Dr. Costas. She told me to take some Tylenol for my headache."

"Tylenol! That's it? See you should have taken the pain pills like I suggested a few days ago. You would have been over it by now."

"I didn't want to take anything without talking to the doctor, Johnny."

"No, you'd rather sit around and whine."

"The doctor's job is to give me medical advice. It's not like either of us went to medical school," Karen snapped.

"You don't have to go to med school to know you should take a painkiller when you have a headache. That's basic common sense. Not everything has to be dramatic, Karen."

She cut in and tried to change the subject. "Well, could you stop by the pharmacy on your way home and pick up some Extra Strength Tylenol for me?"

"I wasn't planning to come straight home. I'm going to make a quick stop, and I'll be in later."

"Later!" Karen sighed. She hesitated before voicing her frustration.

"What's the big deal, Karen? I asked Tyrone to meet me at Floods for a hot minute."

Silence fell over the line.

Karen hadn't been fond of Tyrone years ago, back when she saw him as a partying bachelor who had been married and divorced several times with no intention of settling down. Those were the times when she had viewed him as a bad influence on her husband. She now knew that the truth was that Johnny's strong personality didn't allow anyone too much influence in his life. He made up his own mind. Yet she found it more comfortable to blame her marital issues on outside factors. So long as it wasn't her fault, she didn't have to take responsibility for fixing it.

"What about the card game?"

"What card game?"

"The one the Burks are having."

Karen knew that she didn't feel up to going, but if that was what it took to get Johnny home, she was willing to go along.

"Oh, yeah, okay, the couple from your church. You didn't tell me anything about a card game."

Karen knew that telling him in advance would not have made a difference. Friday was turning out to be his night, and nothing interfered.

"I already have plans. Why don't you go on without me?"

"Why do I always have to go without you? Why can't you just come home after work on Friday, for a change?"

"There you go. I try to be considerate and let you know where I'm going. This is the thanks I get. You make a big deal out of my taking a few hours every now and then to wind down."

"Every now and then? You've been doing this every Friday night for the past three months."

"See, you're exaggerating. It hasn't been that long."

"Oh, yes, it has. It started right after New Year's, right after I closed the business."

She realized that it was still a sore topic with Johnny and didn't expect him to acknowledge the truth, but his silence was confirmation enough. He hadn't agreed with her decision to quit. Her interior decorating business was doing well, but she felt that it had become too stressful managing a household, children, her health, and a career. Despite Johnny's disapproval, she closed her business in hopes of finding something less demanding. So far nothing promising had come along.

"Before, you only went out once every couple of months. That was fine."

"No, it wasn't. You complained about that too."

"It was better than this. I'm here alone every Friday night."

"You're not alone. The girls are there."

"You know what I mean, Johnny. Your hanging out every Friday night is not fair to me."

"You're talking about fair! Don't I work hard all week, take care of the bills, and take care of you and the kids? Remember that I don't have all week to relax like you. Somebody has to work."

He took a deep breath.

"I can't believe you won't allow me to have a few hours to hang out without breathing down my neck with this guilt trip. I mean, it's not like I'm doing anything out here. I don't press you about going to church so much. Why do you always have something to say about the little bit of time that I take for myself?"

"I'm sorry, Johnny. I was just hoping we could do something together." A whisper was all she could manage. Eyes closed tightly, she pressed her forefinger against one temple to alleviate the pain.

"If you're really serious about doing something together, I have a few ideas."

Karen suspected that Johnny was talking about sex, and she wanted to avoid the topic. "Well, I'm tired and I don't really feel up to doing too much."

"That's what I thought. Look, I've already made a commitment for this evening, but we can do something tomorrow. Maybe I'll even go to church with you Sunday."

"Fine, Johnny."

Yet again, Karen had stirred the pot of emotions. She tried to perk up and get past her disappointment. She was feeling less and less guilty about questioning his time out. She wanted to trust Johnny but didn't know how. Doubting had become a natural state of being. He hadn't made it any easier.

Karen rested her eyes, pulled her knees into a tight fetal position, and allowed her thoughts, fears, and insecurities to drift away. For a fleeting moment, she was free.

CHAPTER 2

Johnny could still turn the heads of women when he walked into a room. His six-foot-two silhouette stood in the arched doorway of the large banquet room. He kept his slightly graying hair short to draw attention away from the fact that he was balding. He no longer had the trim body he sported in college. Over the years, extra pounds had taken up residence on his physique. His age had started showing, but his handsome demeanor was still winning out.

Dim lighting, stimulating music, a few appetizers, and a stiff drink provided just the right mix to set Johnny's evening into motion. Floods was known for attracting a professionally dressed and diverse after-work crowd.

Self-confidence, sometimes mistaken for arrogance, often oozed out of Johnny whenever he entered a room. Tonight was no different. A camel-colored, double-breasted suit rounded out any rough edges in his appearance. Normally, Friday was casual day at Tennin Automotive, where Johnny was executive vice president of manufacturing and plant manager of the metal products division. No casual clothes for him. Although he had neglected to share his plans with Karen, Johnny knew early in the morning that he was stopping by his favorite hangout after work and opted to dress the part.

He eased into the room like a warm knife slicing butter. There was the usual happy-hour crowd in the place. Johnny had been coming to this club for over eleven years, with more frequency in recent months. He knew all of the regulars and was on automatic alert for the newbies, which was his term for new faces in the place.

Floods was one place Johnny was glad Karen chose not to frequent. Her presence at his favorite nightspot would cripple his ability to flirt with the women the way he liked.

Standing next to the bar was Johnny's friend Tyrone. Johnny made his way through the crowded room and approached the bar.

"Hey, what's up, buddy?"

The two clasped hands, pulled toward their chests, and did their secret shake.

"You got it, chief," Tyrone responded between cigarette drags.

Tyrone still used the nickname he'd given Johnny at the onset of their friendship twenty-two years ago to reflect his take-charge attitude. They had initially met in college, pledged the same fraternity, and ended up in the same city ten years later. IBM had relocated Tyrone many times. The two had lost contact during Tyrone's frequent moves. But they both ended up in Detroit and had unexpectedly run into one another at Floods nearly ten years ago.

The two leaned on the bar and Johnny scoped the room.

"It's crowded in here." Tyrone took another drag on his cigarette.

Johnny spotted two empty seats amid the crowd. "There are a couple of seats over there, right next to those honeys."

Tyrone hadn't noticed and said to Johnny, "I don't mind sitting here at the bar." The club scene wasn't Tyrone's thing anymore. There was a time in his past when he could have settled in comfortably during an evening out. He had matured beyond his rambunctious twenties and thirties and had stopped chasing women after marrying Connie.

"Nah, come on, man. Let's ease on over. It won't hurt anything. It's just a little conversation with a couple of nice-looking ladies. It's not like we're trying to start a serious relationship with them. Come on, man."

Tyrone sighed and without much more resistance followed his friend toward a table in the middle of the room.

The two men casually strolled toward the young women.

"Good evening, ladies."

The women acknowledged them with a simple greeting.

"We noticed the empty seats. Do you mind if we sit with you?" Johnny asked.

While waiting for the okay to join the women, Johnny checked their ring fingers. He knew married men didn't always wear wedding bands, but women were more likely to wear theirs. There was no guarantee with men like himself.

"Not at all."

"I'm Johnny, and this is Tyrone." Johnny patted his friend on the back. Noticing the women's empty glasses, Johnny asked, "Can we get you another drink?"

The two ladies declined.

Unlike Johnny, Tyrone wasn't interested in sitting down for a warm-and-fuzzy get-to-know you conversation with the two ladies. He wanted to keep the encounter impersonal.

"Hey, look, I'm heading back over to the bar to pick up the pack of cigarettes that I left over there. Can I get anyone anything?" Tyrone asked.

One of the young ladies said, "I could use a cigarette. I'll walk over with you."

Tyrone wasn't expecting any company on his short trip to the bar. He was willing to let Johnny entertain both women. He politely led the way through the crowd to the bar, unable to make a clean break.

Johnny eyed the woman as she left the table. Her switching hips moved like sand being sifted from one hand to the other. He remembered how much of a hip man his friend used to be. Johnny found full-busted women a bit more attractive, which was why his acceptance of Karen's mastectomy two years ago had been such a surprise to himself.

Johnny was left at the table with the other lady. He was not shy about starting up a conversation.

"You work around here, uh . . . ?" He waited for her to give a name.

"Isabelle."

"What did you say?" Johnny wasn't sure if he had heard her correctly.

"My name is Isabelle."

Johnny leaned back in his seat and exhibited some discomfort. He picked up the book of matches from the center of the small table and twirled them between his fingers.

Isabelle noticed his behavior and asked, "What's wrong?"

He placed his elbow on the arm of the chair and covered his mouth for a moment.

"Oh, nothing really." He chuckled. "It's just your name, Isabelle. I had a close friend once named Isabelle. It's not a very common name. As a matter of fact, you're only the second person I've met named Isabelle."

"I hope that's good."

"Could be," Johnny flirted. "So, do you?"

"Do I what?"

"Do you work around here?"

"Not too far away."

Johnny stirred the small red straw in his drink, and said, "I haven't seen you here before."

"I don't come here often."

Bingo, he'd found a newby. They were his preference, the ones who presented a lower probability of knowing his routine flirtatious behavior. He was hoping Isabelle wasn't going to ask about his marital status too early in the conversation. If necessary, he was ready with the I'm-just-looking-for-a-friend-and-this-doesn't-have-anything-to-do-with-my-marriage line.

"Can I get you another drink?"

"Sure."

Johnny motioned for the cocktail waitress. He placed his hand lightly on Isabelle's hand. "What are you drinking?"

"Strawberry daiquiri."

"And I'll take a shot of Hennessy, straight up."

The waitress scribbled the order on a napkin and left.

Johnny leaned back in the chair, rested his wrist on the table, and gazed into Isabelle's eyes. She looked away before her smile completely manifested.

"So, if you don't come here much, what does a beautiful woman like you do for fun?"

Isabelle blushed from the compliment, giving Johnny the impression that she was easily flattered. That was when Johnny knew he had her. He felt safe with Isabelle, figuring that it was highly unlikely that she knew his wife, since Karen didn't frequent the club and Isabelle didn't get out much. It would be easy to work his magic. All of the indicators pointed to an easy rendezvous without fear of being caught cheating.

"Oh, I don't know."

Johnny was on alert. His game seemed to work best with a married woman or a pure party girl who was looking for fun without commitment. The nice, Goody Two-shoes type was too dangerous. Johnny didn't want to kick off a fatal attraction with a single, available, and searching woman. He wanted companionship without any strings attached. A shred of a good time away from his pressures was all he needed. He wasn't looking for a wife, seeing that he already had one of those at home. Isabelle was a red flag, but something about the game drew him in. There was still the possibility that she was married. He had to find out.

"Do you and your husband come here a lot?"

"Not now, but we used to come here."

Ah, Johnny thought, *she is married.* The hot and heavy pursuit was back on.

The waitress placed a small napkin in front of Johnny and Isabelle. She plopped the drinks down and asked for ten dollars. He pulled a fifty-dollar bill from his pocket and placed it on the waitress's small round tray. Tipping and spending were all part of the player's MO. Johnny had to look good from all angles: clean-cut, fine suit, sharp car, and fat, dollar-filled pockets.

"Keep five for yourself."

"Thanks."

Charm had top billing in his deliberate approach. Johnny took time to lay his trap. Now it was time to go in for the thrill.

"How can your husband let someone as beautiful as you come out by yourself?"

Johnny relied on his standard line, since it was quite effective in determining the condition of a potential candidate's marital relationship.

"My husband and I are separated."

Jackpot! Experience led Johnny to believe that "separated" generally meant "unavailable for a long-term relationship but suitable for short-term get-togethers." It was easy to take the game home from here.

"Ah, that's too bad," Johnny said. "I know how that goes."

"Why, you separated, too?"

"I guess you could say so. My wife and I have some differences. We mostly stay together for the kids. I do my thing, and she does hers."

He had already tested Isabelle's morality by exposing his marriage and letting the chips fall as they might. Even though he was married, she was still interested. Just the kind Johnny liked. The kind who knew he was unfaithful and liked him anyway.

"How many kids do you have?" she asked.

"Three."

He held his head down and stirred his drink again. As much of a ladies' man as he professed to be, questions about his children often penetrated his steel exterior. He was uninhibited when talking about Karen, but discussing his kids with another woman somehow felt wrong.

Tyrone had given the other woman no cause to hang around. He was sitting at the bar alone. He glanced at his watch and realized it was already a quarter to eight. He made eye contact with Johnny, who was knee-deep into flirting with Isabelle. Tyrone held up his wrist and pointed to his watch several times. He didn't mind meeting Johnny for a drink from time to time but always knew when it was time to go home.

Johnny got the message. "It's getting late. I'm going to head home. Can I give you a ride?" He stood up and rebuttoned his double-breasted jacket.

"If you don't mind. I live off the Lodge Expressway," Isabelle told him.

"No problem. I'm going that way. Tyrone, I'm heading out, man. I'm giving Isabelle a ride."

"All right, chief. I'll catch you later."

Tyrone gave Johnny a look that said, Yeah, partner, you'd better be careful.

Heading for the door, Johnny helped Isabelle put on her jacket.

Outside, he pulled the parking ticket from his pants pocket and handed it to the valet.

Isabelle's eyes widened as the car approached.

He peeled a ten-dollar bill from his pocket as the valet attendant drove the new Cadillac up to the curb.

He walked around to the passenger's side of the car and opened the door for Isabelle. He hadn't opened the door for Karen in ten years, but then she wasn't someone he had to impress.

"Hi, Johnny," a soft voice came from over his shoulder.

He turned to see who it was.

"Tina!" He went cold on the inside, but struggled to maintain his composure. Of all the people he could have run into, Johnny was wondering why it had to be Ms. Motormouth. Karen's nosy friend was the last person he wanted to see.

Tina flashed a cunning smile, knowing Johnny was caught in the act. She had him right where she wanted—squirming.

"How's Karen?" Tina asked while getting a good look at the lady sitting in her girlfriend's car.

He closed the door and walked toward the driver's side of the car. "She's fine."

"Tell her I said hello." Tina walked past the car and without looking back said, "No, better yet, I'll just call her myself."

"Will do." Johnny hopped into the car. He drove away as quickly and with as little drama as possible.

The twenty-minute drive was filled with small talk and moments of complete silence. The unexpected run-in with Tina had put a damper on Johnny's playboy routine.

He pulled up to Isabelle's house without much enthusiasm.

"I'll give you my number," Isabelle offered.

She took a small piece of paper from her purse and wrote her home number on it.

Johnny took it, glanced at the writing, and shoved it into his pocket. Glancing away from her eyes, he said, "It's been nice meeting you."

He didn't want to give Isabelle his pager number. But any other number was out of the question. He rattled off his number with the last two digits transposed. If he ever ran into her again, he could claim she wrote the number down incorrectly. For now, it was better to minimize contact.

Johnny and Karen's sexual connection had repeatedly deteriorated after her cancer recoveries. Her doctors had confirmed that there was no physical limitation. Johnny chalked it up to lack of interest on her part. Instead of trying to figure out how to rekindle the eighteen-year marriage, he found ways to survive.

He wasn't interested in developing a relationship. The women he pursued at the club were mostly for the thrill of the hunt, and on occasion went further during times when Karen had unofficially declared a sexual sabbatical. He liked playing the player's game from time to time. It did wonders for his ego.

Turning forty had been traumatic for him, although he wouldn't openly admit it. He had purchased a Porsche to stroke his aging ego.

He rarely got an opportunity to drive the sports car, since he was an executive working for an American auto supplier. He was expected to drive domestic vehicles. Still, Johnny got the car as an attempt to restore his youth. A man his size could barely get in and out of the car, but it suited him.

As soon as Isabelle got out of the car, he pulled off without extending any extra courtesies. Three blocks down the road, he was back in husband mode.

"Ooh," he blurted. He had neglected to schedule the home appraisal. His palm covered his mouth and his fingers scraped his chin. How could he have forgotten something so important? Finding a way to relieve the financial pressure was crucial with Karen out of work. Refinancing seemed to be the only answer. Most of their emergency money was gone, and his retirement plan was not an option. They had already tapped that enough. A few of the other homes in their suburban neighborhood had sold for well over four hundred thousand dollars. He was hoping that there was some equity left from the previous refinancing. They got fifty thousand out four years ago when Karen first got sick and was off work for months without warning. Two years ago all they could get was another forty to help out while she was laid up. He needed enough to cover the next three to six months, plenty of time for Karen to get back on her feet.

Johnny sat at the stop sign, turned on his cell phone, and dialed home to see if Karen still needed him to stop by the pharmacy and pick anything up. His best hope was that Tina hadn't told Karen about his escapade at Floods.

Karen answered the phone to hear Johnny on the other end.

"Hey, I'm on my way home."

"It's about time!"

"I told you I was going to be out."

"If I'd known you were going to take this long, I would have gotten the Tylenol myself."

"Look, I'm tired and your nagging is really starting to get on my nerves."

"Well, I'm sorry, Johnny, but I deserve a little more consideration."

"I'll be there when I get there. 'Bye." *Beep* went the sound of the disconnecting cell phone.

Johnny was feeling the weight of running a plant and taking care of a family. He was doing the best he could, but the only gratitude he got from Karen was suspicions and constant badgering. He thought more and more about what he'd been working for. He didn't want to give up living the American dream, but Johnny felt the installments were becoming too difficult to keep up. Something was going to have to give—and soon.

Karen heard the dial tone and put the receiver on the hook. When the phone rang again, she grabbed it.

"Johnny?"

"No, it's not Johnny. This is Tina, Karen. How you doing?"

CHAPTER 3

The morning light poked through the loosely closed window blinds. Karen wanted to talk. She rolled over next to her snoring husband. The drinks he had consumed the night before had ushered him into a deep sleep. Since he wasn't awake, she decided to get up and start the Saturday-morning chores.

For a while, the maid service had done all of the major cleaning. It was a godsend during her mastectomy and chemotherapy over two years ago, when she was too weak to do anything.

Johnny cut out the hundred-and-fifty-dollar weekly maid service. With a three-thousand-dollar monthly mortgage payment and one paycheck coming in, it was an easy decision for him. His perspective was, "You're at home all day. You should have plenty of time to clean."

Cleaning the huge house was too much for Karen to do single-handedly. Saturday morning was the only block of time when the children could help. It was officially deemed the Clarks' housecleaning time.

Karen entered the walk-in closet, which was equivalent in size to a small bedroom. An array of clothes filled the automated circular spindle, which resembled the kind found in dry cleaners'. She pulled the dirty clothes from the hamper and quietly pushed them down the chute. It was a modern convenience, which eliminated her need to lug baskets of clothes from the master bedroom to the basement.

With an empty basket in hand, she headed down the long hallway lined with photos. The first room she passed on the left was the guest room. The next sparsely decorated room on the left belonged to her eldest child, John Erick. Erick, as the family called him, had graduated high school one year early and was now completing a foreign exchange program during his freshman year at Stanford. She stuck her head into the room directly across the hall from his room.

"Chelle, are you up?"

"I'm getting up," the teenager responded.

The fifth bedroom belonged to eight-year-old Elizabeth, the baby of the family.

"Bethy," Karen colorfully called to her daughter. She had created affectionate play names for her daughters. She often said, "It's just an extra dose of motherly love."

"Umm," came from the mass covered up in the middle of the bed.

"Get up, sweetie."

"Already?"

"I told you about staying up so late. See, now you're tired. Get up before your daddy goes downstairs and sees that messy kitchen. Get your dirty clothes together, too."

Although Elizabeth was the youngest, she was given household responsibilities like the other kids. Johnny felt it important that they be able to carry their own weight from an early age.

Karen didn't stop until she got to the laundry room downstairs. She dumped the basket of clothes sitting under the chute and separated the laundry from those items needing dry cleaning. Routinely, she checked the pockets on garments before shipping them off to the cleaner's. It was common for her to find money and other miscellaneous items in the pockets of her family's clothes. She reached into Johnny's shirt and pulled out a piece of paper with the name Isabelle. On the note was scribbled, *Home phone.*

"What's this?"

The phone number threw her for a loop. Karen stood in the laundry room completely spellbound. Her heart raced, and she took a step back to maintain balance.

"Isabelle!"

The memories of six years ago flooded Karen's thoughts as though it were only yesterday. That was when she had found out about Johnny and Isabelle's affair. It had taken every bit of strength she could muster to get past that dark point in their marriage. Karen thought the thing with Isabelle was over and had been for years.

Why would Johnny have her number in his pocket?

"Here are my clothes," Chelle said, startling her mom back into consciousness.

"Separate the rest of these clothes and start the wash," Karen mumbled in her distracted state.

"Mom, I still need to finish my essay."

"That's because you were on that phone last night. All right, young lady, first go finish the essay and then come right back down here and do this laundry."

"Thanks, Mom." Chelle gave her mother a quick peck on the cheek. "I'm sure glad we have two washing machines. Otherwise this would take forever."

Johnny crept down the long corridor, noticing lights on in the bathroom and in the bedrooms. He headed down the back staircase, which let out between the family room and kitchen.

He yelled coming down the stairs, "Who has all of these lights on?"

The Hennessy shots that had helped Johnny wind down at Floods the night before had him in a foul mood. Anyone crossing his path this morning was bound to get their feelings hurt.

Elizabeth was coming up the basement stairs as her daddy was walking by.

"Elizabeth, get upstairs and turn off some of those lights," he demanded. "Where's yesterday's mail?"

"Johnny, it's on the dining room table." Karen pointed. Her nerves were in full bloom. She had many questions for Johnny, but didn't want to broach the subject with the girls present.

He poured a cup of coffee and glanced out the kitchen window. "Has anyone fed the dog?"

Neither Karen nor the two girls responded quickly enough.

He slammed the coffee mug down on the counter and belted out, "I said, did anyone feed the dog?"

His stern, commanding tone got the attention of everyone in the room.

"Did you guys feed the dog?" Karen asked Chelle and Elizabeth before Johnny blew a gasket.

She didn't normally interfere when he disciplined the kids. Johnny was a good father who stayed involved in his children's lives. He was proud to have all honor-roll children who were most likely headed for prestigious careers. However, there were times, like this morning, when she thought he was being a little too hard with the girls.

"I didn't," Chelle answered.

"It's Chelle's week," Elizabeth interjected.

"How many times do I have to tell you to feed the dog? Get out there right now."

Chelle fully intended to carry out her father's order, like a good soldier, just as soon as she finished writing a paragraph in her English essay.

Johnny tolerated no hesitation. "Didn't you hear me? *Do it now.*"

"Chelle, go feed the dog," Karen calmly reinforced. "Johnny, yelling at the kids doesn't help."

"Look, don't tell me how to handle the kids." He turned to Chelle, who was scooping the dry food into a bucket. "Next time, young lady, don't make me have to remind you. And when I say do something, I mean right away, not when you get ready. Got that?"

"Yes, Daddy." She sniffed.

Sipping his coffee, Johnny picked up the stack of mail lying on the dining room table.

"I need help around here," Johnny said. "Everyone knows what they're supposed to be doing."

"Elizabeth, honey, go out there and help your sister feed the dog. When you finish, both of you go back downstairs and finish washing the clothes, okay?"

"Yes, Mom."

Elizabeth gave her mom a hug and headed outside.

Karen and Johnny were left alone in the large, eat-in kitchen.

"You seem to be in a bad mood this morning."

Johnny continued opening the mail without response.

Before blurting out her question about why Isabelle's number was in his pocket, Karen wanted to let him calm down.

"Tina called me last night."

That got his attention. He didn't know how much she had told Karen about his choice of companionship at the club last night.

"Ooh, boy. Here we go. What did that meddling witch want?"

Before Karen could respond, an irritated Johnny spoke again.

"Nah, nah. Don't tell me." He slammed the cup down on the table and the warm coffee spurted all over the table. "Miss Meddling makes one call and next you'll be accusing me of cheating."

"Why, have you been?"

"You tell me. You're the one doing the talking." Feeling uncomfortable and cornered, Johnny got up to get another cup of hot coffee.

"I'm not accusing you of anything. I'm asking you a question."

"Karen, how can you listen to Tina after all we've been through? Why are you so determined to let your friend drive us to divorce court? You saw how she drove her man away, and she probably wants you to be in the same position."

He pulled a clump of napkins from the table holder and plopped them on top of the coffee mess. "Misery loves company."

"Johnny, it wasn't anything Tina said. She called about next Saturday's dinner."

"Then why did you ask me if I was cheating? Where did that come from?"

"You brought it up, not me. But since you did, maybe I can ask you about the phone number I found in your pocket this morning?"

Through several bad encounters, he had learned not to keep loose numbers in his pockets. It was an open invitation for Karen to find the number and create a less-than-pleasant marital scene. The run-in with Tina threw him out of sync. Now he was paying for his carelessness.

"So now you're snooping around in my pockets? The number you found belongs to a coworker who was nice enough to help me put together the business plan for my marketing idea."

Johnny knew every strategic maneuver in the book of Get-Out-of-Trouble-If-Caught. His tactic was to use the simple reverse-psychology strategy for the awkward predicament.

"Think about it. If it were someone I was seeing, do you think I would have left her number in a place so easy for you to find? She was kind enough to offer her services. It's not like you're offering to help me put the plan together."

"Johnny, I'm not going to let you put me down. Just because I'm not working doesn't mean that I don't want to help." Karen's voice escalated, even though it increased the throbbing pain in her head. "Why was Isabelle's phone number in your pocket? Are you seeing her again?"

"Isabelle! Come on, Karen."

"'Come on, Karen', what?"

"You think I'm seeing Isabelle! Give me some credit."

Johnny got up in a cloud of fury.

"Huh, Isabelle, of all people." He smirked. His reaction was as if the mere thought of Karen's suggestion was ridiculous and without any merit. He wanted Karen to let it go, but he knew that she wasn't ready to.

"When was the last time you talked with her?"

Johnny turned in Karen's direction and forcefully said, "How many times do I have to go through this, Karen? I said, Isabelle is a coworker. She's not the one you're thinking about."

"How do I know for sure?"

"Boy, I don't need this. I need some peace around here. I work hard all week. I want some peace on my weekends. You have all week to sit around here and worry about stuff that isn't even happening. I have apologized over and over. I have all but kissed your behind, and it's not good enough for you, is it? It's been six years and you still don't want to let it go."

Johnny pushed his chair back with full force, screeching along the way.

"Johnny, I'm trying to talk to you."

"No, I'm through talking. Since you have so much time to focus on what I'm doing, why don't you spend some time trying to help me out? If you would help a little, maybe I would be able to get home earlier. I work too hard to stand around here and let you accuse me of something stupid like seeing Isabelle again. Better yet, let's put it this way. Since you don't care enough to help me take care of this place, you shouldn't care about whatever else I do."

"How long am I supposed to put up with you?"

"Put up with me! Maybe that's something I should be asking you."

"I don't know what you mean. I've been a good wife to you."

"Good wife, huh. Would that be before or after you decided to stop having sex with me? Before or after you decided to close up shop when you know that we have a child in college and an extravagant lifestyle? Huh, what about that? When you can come up with those answers, then we have something to talk about."

"You're just letting the devil corrupt you. You're not even trying to hear God."

"No, you didn't! You need to quit with all that religious crap, Karen. God, God, God, holy, holy, holy. I am sick of your self-righteous holier-than-thou attitude. Trust me. You have some issues too, sweetheart."

Johnny and Karen both knew how to push each other's hot buttons. Karen felt a sense of power when she exposed his lagging religious convictions. Johnny would get the upper hand in the argument when he harped on her limited professional achievements. It was a weapon that both kept fully loaded and ready to fire off on short notice.

Karen ignored his implication and continued to speak her mind.

"What do you expect me to do, Johnny? Do you expect me to find a woman's home number in your pocket and just let it go without saying anything?"

"Honestly, I can't tell you what to do. You're good about making decisions on your own. You don't need my input. The best decision you can make at this moment is to leave me alone."

Karen and Johnny had been there before, many times, with the speculations, put-downs, and accusations. Like clockwork, this was the point in the argument when he would feel guilty and walk away. She would buckle under pressure and cry. He didn't budge. Her eyes were swollen but not a tear fell. This time was different.

CHAPTER 4

The atmosphere was thick and jaws were tight around the Clarks'. Karen was putzing around the kitchen, making her usual full-course Sunday-morning breakfast. She seemed to garner a special bit of joy when cooking for her family and bringing them all together, if only for one morning each week. The grits were simmering, turkey bacon popping, Johnny's pork sausage sizzling, pancakes browning, hash browns sautéing, and coffee brewing. The blended aromas drew in anyone who was within a whiff of the kitchen.

It wasn't status quo around the house.

Karen's mind was flooded. Saturday hadn't been such a good day for her and Johnny. How could he do this again? she wondered. Why? She put the fork down and stared out the window for a moment, as though the answer were scribbled across the lawn.

I know that's got to be Isabelle. What, does he think I'm that stupid? I just can't believe he would hurt me like this, not again.

The percolating anger gave her chopping fingers extra zeal. A pile of diced vegetables cut in record time was the evidence. Karen scooped the onions and green peppers up and slammed them into the skillet. Her hands were saturated with onion juice. She lifted her shoulder to brush a tear falling from the corner of her left eye. She sighed and let her head droop in discontent.

Usually it was one of the kids who reached the breakfast first on

Sunday, but today it was Mr. Clark. He entered the room, knowing that Karen was still mad. She had avoided him all Saturday afternoon and had gone to bed exceptionally early to ensure that she was asleep before he got in the bed. No one said a word. He picked up the newspaper Karen had previously laid on the table. Johnny was not big on the silent treatment. It was something he could dish out frequently, but he couldn't take it.

"So, what, are you going to go all day without saying anything?"

Karen continued ignoring Johnny for fear of getting into an unpleasant conversation in the presence of the girls.

"Karen, I know you hear me. How long are you going to keep up the silent treatment?"

"Johnny, I'm not giving you the silent treatment. I'm just cooking breakfast."

"Yeah, right. You think I can't tell that you're mad? What else do you want me to do? I told you that number belongs to a business colleague. Why can't you just believe that and let it go?"

"Humph. You know why I can't let it go."

"No, I don't."

Karen firmly put down the carton of juice and turned to Johnny with more conviction and guts than she was accustomed to showing.

"Johnny, you may think that I'm stupid and naive because I let you run around, hang out, and do what you want to do. Oh, but trust me, I'm far from being stupid. I let things go because I love what we have. But that doesn't mean that you can treat me like I'm a fool. You know that number belongs to Isabelle Jones. And here I am—after all this time, I thought she was long gone and you were over her."

"She is, and I am. I keep telling you, this isn't Isabelle Jones." Johnny chuckled because this time he was actually telling the truth and Karen didn't believe him. He sensed that no matter what the story was, when it came to Isabelle, Karen wasn't buying it.

"If you want, I will even introduce you to her."

"Okay, introduce me."

Johnny offered the introduction as a good-faith gesture to ease Karen's discomfort. He made great efforts to conceal his extracurricular activities. Under no circumstances did he actually plan to introduce his wife to a woman he was flirting with in the club. At least for now, it looked like Karen was softening.

Karen looked right through Johnny and knew he was lying. Yet it didn't sting as much as it did six years ago, when she had caught him cheating. The affair with Isabelle nearly cost them their marriage. It had taken every bit of the past years to recover from Johnny's ultimate betrayal of getting another woman pregnant. She had worked hard to hold the family and its image together. Although spiritually she didn't believe that it was right to rejoice in someone else's misery, she was relieved to know that Isabelle had miscarried Johnny's illegitimate baby. Somehow the unfortunate event had enabled Karen to stay in the marriage. Whatever peace she felt during the agonizing period was short-lived with the cancer coming a few years later.

Sensing that Karen was returning to serenity, Johnny relaxed a bit. "Don't forget that we have the executive banquet this afternoon."

Karen closed her eyes and let her three middle fingers press into her forehead. Up and down, up and down. Any gesture that could help relieve the stress was welcome.

"Is that today?" she asked.

"Yes, and I have to be there. The CEO and the SVP of manufacturing will be there. I have to go."

Karen had attended numerous black-tie affairs. It was the kind of life she'd grown accustomed to in his climb to the executive VP and plant manager position. She enjoyed the various social events. But today wasn't one of her best, and she was not thrilled about going.

"What time do I need to be dressed?"

"The program begins at three and the reception starts at two."

"Where is it?"

"In Detroit, at the Renaissance Center. So we should leave here by one in order to get downtown and get parked."

"One! Johnny, you know I don't get out of church until one."

"I know, but what's more important, Karen? Let's face it. I haven't seen Anointed Vision Christian Center on any paychecks around here. The only employer I see is Tennin Automotive. That ought to give you some hint of where our priorities should be."

Johnny attempted to soften his appeal once he realized that he was coming across in a condescending way. "Can't you miss one Sunday, or at least leave early?"

"You don't miss Floods on Friday, no matter what. Why do I always have to miss church because you have planned something else for me to do?"

"This isn't some trivial event, Karen. This banquet is important for my career. It should be important to you."

"Church is important to me, too."

"Come on, Karen. One Sunday won't kill you. Besides, you're so holy and perfect anyway," Johnny said in a semijoking fashion. "According to you, it's only the heathens like me who need to be up in the church every time the door flies open."

"Yeah, you do. So why don't you?"

"Look, let's not get too serious. I'm not getting into a heavy argument about the church and the God thing, Karen. This is not the time. Even God had a day of rest. Can't you give me one?"

"Whether you go to church or not is up to you, Johnny."

"That's right. It's up to me, and your pushing won't get me there any faster. Tell you what," he said, nuzzling up to Karen, "I'll go with you Mother's Day. How's that? Won't that be nice for us to go as a family?"

She had managed to get through much of the morning without a headache. It was the first time in a long time. The last thing she wanted to do was get one started by arguing with Johnny. Agreeing and keeping quiet seemed to be the path of least resistance and, ultimately, less pain.

"Sure, Johnny, whatever," Karen said, and pushed away from his affectionate gesture.

"In the meantime, I need you to go with me this afternoon."

Without any zeal, Karen looked at Johnny and said, "I'll be ready by one."

"Oh, yeah, I forgot to tell you. I looked over the budget for the next six months. We'll need to take out another equity loan for about eighty thousand dollars in order to make ends meet while you're off. The extra fifty thousand will give us enough to cover Erick's tuition for two quarters, plus be able to pay off one of the vehicles."

"We have to do that again? We've been taking out a loan every couple of years. We'll never get the mortgage paid off like that."

"That's because you're off work every couple of years."

"Like I can help it."

"I'm not saying that you can. I'm only stating the facts."

"We don't have to get the loan. We can make adjustments in our budget."

"Really! I don't see you trying to move out of your custom-built dream house or offering to give up one of the cars for a Geo. I don't see you tossing in any of your furs. You can't have it both ways. You can't quit work and want to keep living in the lap of luxury. Something has to give."

The alluring smell of breakfast traveled through the main floor.

Chelle hustled into the kitchen. "I'm hungry," she said, causing her parents to terminate their discussion.

"It's ready. Go get Elizabeth."

"She's on her way down. Oh, yeah, Mom, can I stay after church for the teen meeting?"

"Not today, Chelle, baby." Karen rolled her eyes at Johnny. "We can't stay for service."

"Why not?" the disappointed youth asked.

"Because, honey, we're only going to Sunday school and coming straight back afterward. Daddy and I have an important function to attend this afternoon." She added, "It's for Daddy's job, and that's more important than anything else around here."

CHAPTER 5

Karen's bubbly personality was a perfect fit with the warm hospitality exuding from the Anointed Vision Christian Center. She seemed to be happiest in an extended-family kind of environment, being an only child. Regardless of what she was going through, the church always seemed to lift her spirits.

The thousand-member congregation was a far cry from the fifty original members who were in attendance six years ago, when Karen and Johnny began going in hopes of saving their marriage. At that time, Karen knew it was critical to find a spiritual support group to help them get through her husband's infidelity. She had looked in the yellow pages and found the church.

The young minister and his wife had received the Clark couple with open arms. They went to counseling for about a month. When the discussions got too personal, Johnny began pulling back. It wasn't long before he stopped going to counseling and ultimately the church altogether, both to Karen's dissatisfaction.

Whenever Karen tried talking him into more counseling, his standard reply was, "I don't need some man all up in my business. How is he going to tell me what it takes to be a husband? You might be surprised to find that he's no better a husband than I am."

Johnny knew that Reverend Lane was aware of his indiscretions, and a part of him was embarrassed to let someone other than Karen know certain details about his life.

Karen stopped asking, figuring that if Johnny ever decided to go, it would be his own choice.

"Good morning, Mrs. Clark," a young lady greeted her, standing in the church entrance.

"Ooh, you're back. So how is married life, Mrs. Newlywed?" Karen gave the young lady a hug.

"Wonderful," the young admirer replied. "I want it to be as perfect as your marriage."

There were times when such a compliment would have generated a radiant smile from Mrs. Clark. Today wasn't one of those times.

Karen glanced at her watch and realized her Sunday school class would be starting in less than five minutes.

"Oh, my lesson."

In her distraction over the weekend, she'd forgotten to prepare for her married women's Sunday school class.

"Oh, phooey!"

Karen dug around in her tote bag to see if there was anything else she could use for the discussion. Striking out, she opened the door and saw forty or so women milling around the room.

Wouldn't you know it, she thought, *of all days a full class. Oh, well; God, you have to get me through this one.* At church, Karen was in her element. She was charming, knowledgeable, and most of all, confident in her abilities. It was the one place she felt respected.

"Good morning, ladies."

"Good morning."

After endless digging, Karen finally stumbled upon her lesson planner and turned it to the current lesson, titled, "When Is Enough Enough?" The words seemed to radiate off the page.

Karen sighed. Why this lesson today? She didn't feel like dealing with any deep relationship issues. She was barely getting by with the everything-is-happy-at-home image, knowing that really she was fed up with Johnny's mess. She had survived the first time around when Isabelle got a foothold in their marriage. A second encounter would be fatal. Perhaps she could find a way to get around the lesson, at least for today.

"How many people prepared for today's lesson?" She hoped that a low show of hands would warrant postponing the discussion.

Almost every hand in the room went up.

With no other way out, she said, "Okay, let's open with prayer and get started."

Karen knew that she was going to have to dig way down inside and pull out the strength needed to discuss and advise women on issues she was struggling with herself. She wanted to be honest and let the chips fall where they would, but decided that even though she and Johnny were going through a bad situation, the less outsiders knew, the better. Besides, what would people say?

CHAPTER 6

Fancy dresses, tailored suits, and linen and silk garments comprised her wardrobe. Whatever the function, from casual to formal, she was covered.

"I do not feel like going to this banquet," she mumbled with a sigh. "What can I throw on in a hurry?"

She pushed the button on the rotating closet rack and thumbed through some of the two-piece suits as they came around, looking for the peach one.

Karen was self-conscious about the few extra pounds she'd picked up while being off work for the past four months. Her well-proportioned five-foot-seven frame accentuated her golden-brown skin and engaging smile. It was one of the things that initially attracted Johnny to her. After the mastectomy, she struggled with her looks, and her self-esteem ended up taking a beating.

She stopped the rack and pulled out the plastic-covered silk tea-length dress with a matching short-waisted sequined jacket. She was hoping that it fit. She laid the outfit on the bed, removed her blazer, and began hurriedly unbuttoning her blouse. The dress was complete by itself, but Karen opted to wear a jacket to give her breast area extra coverage.

She wondered if there was time to take another hot shower. Karen looked at her watch. It was already after twelve. Running the risk of hearing Johnny's mouth was not worth an extra moment of solitude in the hot, soothing water. She decided not to chance it. She laid the blouse on the bed and unsnapped her bra.

Johnny eased into the bedroom like an uninvited guest who walked into the middle of a lover's quarrel and plotted how to retreat unnoticed.

Karen stopped at the full-length mirror with her loosely draped robe dangling open. Covered in protective emotional armor, she dodged the image that came hurling back at her. It was an ongoing battle. Her adversary had been put on the canvas time after time and wouldn't stay down. Her trembling hands glided over the leveled mounds and lingered at the jagged scar lines of where both of her breasts had once resided. She flicked a tear from her cheek before it made its way to the trail that had been carved from earlier downpours.

The cracking sound of the settling floorboard startled Karen back into the confines of the bedroom. Her eyes focused in on Johnny, and she instantly protected her body by clasping the robe tightly across her chest.

"Johnny, I didn't hear you come in!"

The bout with breast cancer had tested her faith in both God and Johnny's commitment. She was having difficulty applying her beliefs, religious pursuits, and godly conversations to her real-world situations. Fear had so often gotten the best of her over the past four years. She tortured herself with the same questions. Why hadn't she done self-exams sooner? What could she have done differently? What would have happened to her children if she'd died? Why did this happen to her? Before the cancer, it was easy talking about faith and hope. It was something totally different when she needed them to stay alive. Walking the walk hadn't been so easy for her.

If he could, Johnny would have eased back out of the room before Karen saw him. It was too late for a quick exit. He came in trying to pretend he hadn't noticed anything.

"So, you just about ready?" he asked, avoiding eye contact.

Karen was determined to believe he had a problem with her deformed breasts, despite his reassurances. She did everything to avoid the subject and, oftentimes, his sexual advances. All Johnny wanted was to get back to a normal level of intimacy.

"Why are you looking at me like that?"

"Like what?"

"You know, like that."

"Oh, boy," Johnny mumbled.

This was a time he hated. He knew Karen was in her feeling-sorry-for-herself mood, and there was no way out for him. Regardless of what he said or did to make her feel more comfortable about the appearance of her breasts, she didn't accept it.

"Karen," he relented, "I'm not looking at you in any particular way."

"Yeah, that's the problem."

Johnny tossed his arms loosely into the air and shook his head.

"What's the problem now, Karen?"

"Like I need to tell you!" Her anger trickled out like small bursts of steam being released from a pressure cooker.

"Yes, Karen, you do. You need to tell me. What is your problem?" His words were softly spoken but deliberate.

With her back to him, Karen looked at Johnny in the large full-length mirror.

"What happened to us, Johnny?"

She remembered how wonderful their intimacy was in the beginning. She chose to blame their latest round of sexual and marital problems on his inability to deal with her mastectomy, ignoring other looming issues.

"What do you mean, what happened to us?"

"I mean, what happened to all of the love and affection?" Pausing, she turned her eyes to the vanity tabletop. "And the lovemaking that we had when we first got married?"

Johnny scratched his head.

"Karen, we've gone through a lot since those school days."

Their eyes met, and both were at a momentary loss for words.

"But I still love you, Karen."

"Do you, Johnny? Do you really love me?"

"I said that I did."

"So is that it? You love me, but you don't find me attractive anymore?"

It was her constant allegations, and not the actual mastectomy, that forced Johnny to avoid being around Karen when she was nude. It was as if the more she falsely accused him of having a problem, the more he felt it becoming one.

"Gee, Karen, I've always found you attractive, and I still do."

She smirked in disbelief. "Then why?"

"Why what?"

"Why did you start seeing Isabelle?"

Johnny sighed. "Ah, man, is that what this is really about?" With his voice raised, he said, "When are you going to let it go?"

"When you let her go."

"I let Isabelle go years ago, and you know that."

"Do I? Do I really know that, Johnny? Maybe I just wanted to believe what you told me."

"Karen, you need to stop this."

Johnny sat on the corner of the sofa closest to the vanity table.

"Look, Karen, you either have to forgive me and let it go or let me go, because I can't continue to put up with you always holding the past over my head." He paced the room in a slow, tormented stroll. "You either need to step up to the plate or step off."

"I forgave you a long time ago." She turned to face him. "I did forgive you. It wasn't easy, but I did. I have to forgive you in order for God to continue forgiving me." Karen could feel the words on her lips but not in her heart. She turned back to the mirror and gently applied color to her lips.

Johnny whispered under his breath, "So you say."

Karen didn't hear him and so continued to express her feelings. "But don't think that I've forgotten the pain. With all of your cheating, I can't trust you."

"With all of my cheating, huh! Karen, it doesn't matter whether I cheat or not. You're going to accuse me regardless. When I go out you automatically assume that I'm cheating. When I used to come home right after work every night, you still thought that I was cheating. I'm starting to wonder if this is all because you're feeling guilty about not having sex with me for the last seven months. You say that you want to be married, but you don't act like a wife."

"Johnny, you know that I'm doing the best I can. I'm trying."

"Trying how? It happens over and over, every time you get sick. We have sex for a while, until you choose to cut it off. It's not your illness. It's all you."

Karen let her eyes slowly rise up to Johnny without response.

"Uh-huh, that's what I thought," Johnny said. "Well, I can't continue living like this. It's not working for me. Maybe it's time for a change."

"What do you mean?"

"I mean something like a separation. I think that's where we are," he stated.

"So that's where you think we are," Karen said, retracting the tube of lipstick.

Johnny stood up and headed for the door.

"Yeah, that's where we are." Leaning against the door frame with his back to Karen, he said, "See you downstairs."

CHAPTER 7

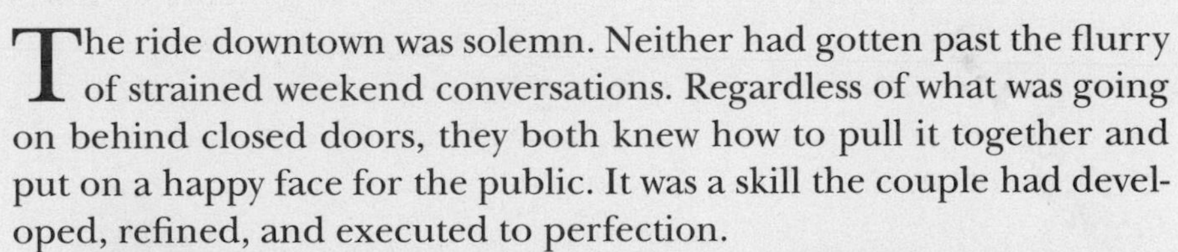

The ride downtown was solemn. Neither had gotten past the flurry of strained weekend conversations. Regardless of what was going on behind closed doors, they both knew how to pull it together and put on a happy face for the public. It was a skill the couple had developed, refined, and executed to perfection.

Cadillacs, Lincolns, and limos lined the Renaissance's circular drive. Johnny wheeled the Caddy into the valet line. Karen straightened his bow tie and brushed a piece of lint off his tuxedo.

"Karen, can you grab the valet key out of the glove compartment?"

The valet attendants opened the doors for the couple.

"Good afternoon, sir."

Johnny handed the man the valet key and a ten-dollar bill that he pulled from his pocket.

The glass elevators rising above the ten-foot crystal chandelier ushered them into the banquet room filled with corporate bigwigs. It was showtime for the Clarks.

"John and Karen," a tall, middle-aged man greeted them as they entered the room. "Glad you could make it."

Johnny was in his element. "To get where you want to be, you have to hobknob with the big boys," was his favorite saying. If moving to the top of the company required mingling and working a crowd, then Johnny was surely headed for the CEO position. No one did it better.

He was excellent at charming the ladies and equally effective at dazzling the executives.

"Good afternoon, Al," Johnny greeted the man with a firm handshake.

Turning to a gentleman standing next to him, Al continued with his introductions.

"John, this is Fred Suthers, the new VP of marketing. Fred, this is John Clark, the EVP of manufacturing."

The two men exchanged a handshake.

"And this is his lovely wife Karen." Al hugged her loosely. "Karen, you always look fabulous."

Her charming smile had not been hindered by the grim ride from home. Karen wasn't in full bloom, but knew how to play the executive wife routine down to a tee.

"John, you are a heck of a lucky man."

Johnny wouldn't normally tolerate any man randomly hugging or touching his wife, but this was one of the few exceptions. It was as though he wore his mentor's compliment as a badge of honor. He was quite pleased to have such a comfortable and personal rapport with the senior vice president. There were times when it had come in handy in his career, as evidenced by his frequent and substantial promotions.

Al's wife approached the group and the exchange of hellos continued.

"John, now that you're here, can you join Fred and me for a few moments? I'd like to discuss the third-quarter projections."

"Sure," Johnny anxiously agreed.

"Karen, would you mind if I borrowed your husband for a moment?"

"Absolutely not."

"Great."

"Excuse us, ladies. We'll only be a few minutes."

"Al, honey," Barbara spoke up and gently interlocked her arm with his, "you said no business today."

"I know, dear, I know. Just a few minutes." He kissed her on the forehead. "I promise."

With the men gone, the two women were left to carry on the conversation, as usual.

"So, Barbara, how are the kids?"

"Great."

Barbara spewed out the report card on her children's progress with unprecedented glee.

"Well, you know Constance is in medical school, Brian is completing his junior year at Harvard, and it looks like Angeline's high school gymnastics team is headed for national competition. So I have a full calendar keeping up with the children. How about your children? How's Erick's freshman year going at Stanford?"

"Erick is doing well." With pride, Karen added, "You know he's spending this quarter studying abroad in Europe."

"Ah, how intriguing. How about the girls? How are they?"

"Of course, Chelle is still on the honor roll. She decided not to skip tenth grade. Instead, she's going to use the time to brush up on her creative writing and take a few more advanced math and science classes."

"Really! I know a great-creative writing tutor. It's the one Brian used."

Karen wasn't really interested in the tutor. Swapping success stories about their children was one thing; adding another bill to the household budget was something else.

"How's that adorable little Elizabeth?"

"Fine." Karen smiled.

"You should bring her over to our gym sometime. I'm sure Angeline wouldn't mind working with her."

"Thanks for the offer. We'll try to work it into our schedule."

"Oh, boy, do I know how challenging a schedule can be. By the way, John mentioned that you are no longer doing the interior decorating."

"Yes, that's right. I stopped about four months ago."

"Well, good for you. Isn't it great?"

"What?"

"You know"—Barbara leaned in toward Karen and whispered as though her upcoming revelation were top secret—"not having to work. I don't know how you managed to take care of your children, plan parties for your husband, do volunteer work, and also hold down a job."

"Umm," was all the answer Karen could offer.

"We are so fortunate to be out of the workforce, don't you think?"

"Yeah, really fortunate," Karen pretended, knowing that a little extra income would come in handy around 712 Morning Glory Circle.

Karen enjoyed hobnobbing with the elite when things were good between her and Johnny. The social events were grueling otherwise.

"By the way, thanks for inviting us to your party next weekend."

"Hope you can make it."

"Al and I wouldn't miss it. We are thrilled to be included."

Barbara twirled the olive in her martini. Social drinking was an acceptable component of these gatherings. Even so, Karen never indulged.

"Tell me, it's your, what, twentieth anniversary?"

"No, our nineteenth." Karen engaged in a brief moment of reflection. "My, how fast the years have flown by for me and Johnny."

"Wonderful. We're celebrating our twenty-fifth this year."

"Congratulations."

"Thank you. It's been a wonderful twenty-five years for us."

Barbara was image-conscious and, much like Karen, the ideal executive wife, flattering, tolerant, and nonthreatening. Although she was painting the storybook twenty-five-year marriage, Karen knew better. She had heard through the grapevine that Al cheated on Barbara. Karen also knew that no matter how many skeletons were in the closet, wives in the executive circle were not about to give up the good life just because their husbands had a few marital indiscretions. "Doubt, deny, and deal with it" was the coping recipe.

To each his own, Karen thought. An afternoon of pretending was one thing, so long as it didn't continue to replace reality. Her headache was resurfacing. She'd had enough for one afternoon.

Johnny returned in time to rescue Karen. They headed for the hors d'oeuvres spread.

CHAPTER 8

Karen was submerged under the down-filled comforter when Johnny came out of the master bathroom.

"Are you taking me to the airport?"

The lump on the bed showed minimal sign of movement.

"Karen." Johnny spoke strongly. "Are you taking me to the airport or not? You said you wanted to talk."

"I forgot. Where are you going again?"

"I have to go to Tennessee for a production meeting. I should only be gone for the day. I expect to be back late tonight."

"Oh," Karen responded, with little confidence that he would be able to adhere to his proposed time of return.

"Look, it's almost seven-thirty. I have to get out of here in order to make the air shuttle. Are you getting up or not?"

"I don't feel well." Karen poked her head out from under the warm covers.

"What's wrong now?"

"I'm still feeling tired."

"So what's new?"

"Johnny, why can't you be more supportive and not make me feel bad about being sick?"

"I'm sorry, Karen. I'm not trying to make you feel bad. It's just that . . ." Johnny looked at Karen and hesitated before saying anything else.

"It's what?" Karen insisted.

"Nothing."

"What?"

"Nothing."

"It is something." She sat straight up in the bed and put some bass into her voice. "What were you going to say?"

"You're always sick with something. You're always complaining about something. If it's not me and some woman, it's your health."

Johnny sat down on the corner of the bed and used a shoehorn to slip his shoe on.

"You think I enjoyed having cancer and who knows what else?"

"No, I don't think you're happy about being sick, but I do think you enjoy using anything you can to get my attention." Johnny stood up facing Karen and adjusted his waistband.

"There's got to be a better way, Karen. This whining and manipulating can wear a person down after a while."

"It sure can!" she agreed ferociously.

Johnny straightened his tie in the full-length mirror and made eye contact with Karen in the background.

"So I guess you changed your mind about taking me to the airport?"

"Yeah, I don't feel like going now." She lay back down on the bed.

"No problem. I'll get the shuttle service. I'll call you later."

Johnny's departure was not filled with smooches and I-love-you-type innuendoes. The couple had long since passed the touchy-feely phase. The sporadic display of affection was an attempt to cover up Karen's distrust and Johnny's frustration.

Johnny left, and Karen climbed back under her fortress of pillows and bedcovers.

"Mommy, are you up?" Elizabeth poked her head into Karen's room, hoping to spend some time with her mom before school.

Karen rolled over.

"Hi, baby. Mommy's not up yet. I have a headache."

Elizabeth sat on the bed next to Karen and stroked her hair. Elizabeth was at the age where she could either be babied or given big-girl responsibilities. She seemed to enjoy both sides whenever convenient.

"Do you want me to stay at home with you today?"

"No, honey. Tell Chelle to help you get ready, and remind her to lock the door when you leave."

"Hope you feel better." Elizabeth gave her mother a gentle hug.

Karen lay in the bed a few more hours before getting up. She hadn't been able to keep her stress level down, as Dr. Costas had instructed. Karen had a headache from the surge of arguments that had begun on Friday, finding the phone number on Saturday, and attempting to keep up appearances at the banquet yesterday. She was paying for all of it this morning.

She eased down the stairs and found her way to a warm cup of tea. Phone calls were something Karen usually readily received. This morning she was not in the mood for chitchat. When the phone rang, she looked at the caller ID box before picking it up and recognized Tina's number. *Good timing.* Karen wanted someone to share in her distress. Her days of praying and talking to God were infrequent. It required too much energy and self-evaluation. She preferred talking to another person. It required less effort and virtually no self-development on her part.

"Hi, Tina."

"Hey, girl. I'm calling to let you know that I might bring this guy with me to your dinner party, if he doesn't get on my nerves between now and then. Oh, yeah, I keep forgetting to ask if you need any help with the party."

"What party?"

"Girl, what's wrong with you? Karen, don't tell me you forgot that I called you Friday night and asked if I could bring a friend to your anniversary dinner Saturday night."

"Anniversary! Oh, that. I almost forgot about the dinner."

"Forgot! That's not like you, Ms. Party Planner. Something has to be wrong if you're not knee-deep into preparing for this get-together. What's wrong?"

Karen paused before revealing her business to Tina. She knew Johnny would not like Tina's having a direct view into his home life, but Karen wasn't so concerned about how he felt. This time it was about how she felt. And Tina was on the short list of individuals whom she trusted enough to divulge some of her true feelings that were usually masked behind the storybook facade.

"I think Johnny's been seeing someone."

"And . . . ?"

"And!"

"And I assumed as much," Tina stated.

"Why?"

Tina hesitated before giving up the information that she'd been holding back. "I ran into Johnny Friday night at Floods and there was some little floozy sitting in your car."

With no regard for her throbbing temples, Karen elevated her voice. "Are you sure?"

"Positive."

"What did she look like?" She suspected that it was Isabelle Jones.

"I didn't get a good look at her. She was already in the car when I came up."

"I can't believe him."

"What did you expect?"

"What do you mean?"

"Come on, Karen. Don't tell me that it never crossed your mind that he was seeing someone."

"I have my suspicions but no real proof. Why didn't you tell me that you saw him?"

Karen had liked Tina's feisty and outspoken personality from the moment they had met four years ago at the oncologist's. Tina wasn't known for being timid or subtle. The friendship grew and so did Tina's candor.

"Why should I? It wouldn't have made a difference. You see only what you want to anyway. Let's be for real! It's probably not his first and won't be his last."

Tina was bitter toward men. Not only had her husband refused to be supportive during her struggle with cervical cancer, but he also left her before she fully recuperated. On top of it all, she couldn't have children. She felt robbed. The betrayal of her husband and the loss of a vital part of her womanhood left her angry, hurt, and distrustful. It didn't leave the door to her heart open for other men to enter. She dated a few and took none seriously. A safe arm's length away was as close as she let them get.

Karen was startled by Tina's reaction. "What makes you say that?"

"Karen, please. Your husband is out every Friday night. It had to have crossed your mind at least once."

Karen was silent, knowing that it had on many occasions.

"Girl, where have you been?"

"I don't know. I was hoping things would get better."

"I hate to say it, girlfriend, but you sure lead a sheltered life. I guess living in the backwoods of West Bloomfield has taken you out of touch with reality."

"Hmmm."

Tina considered herself to be a close friend, although her words were often piercing and insensitive. She found Karen to be too naive and Johnny to be too uppity. As much as she tried to be objective, her advice was often seasoned with envy.

"What are you going to do?"

An overwhelming surge of memories flooded Karen's soul. She hated to think that Johnny was cheating on her. But no matter how he would sneak around on Friday nights, he never expressed an interest in leaving the marriage—with one exception. She recalled the time Johnny had gotten caught with Isabelle Jones. She had been a true threat. She wasn't like the women Karen suspected Johnny had been messing around with since the cancer and their sexual problems began. Isabelle was different. From the little Karen had found out about her, it seemed that she was strong and smart, working as some kind of big shot in a company with all of those men. Karen didn't know where to turn. The emotional hurts she had endured from that affair felt like fresh wounds. He had put his marriage on the line for that relationship, and the mere thought of Isabelle resurfacing terrified Karen. She felt an emptiness deep inside, like a sickness she couldn't weed out. She knew from experience that the only way to get rid of a cancerous pain was to deal with it at the root.

"Karen, what are you going to do? You know men don't change."

"I don't know what to do. I know that I have to do something."

"You're always talking about having faith in God and letting Him work things out. At least that's what you're always telling me to do. But when push comes to shove, you can't follow your own advice."

"Tina, I'm tired of praying for the same old, same old. I know God can work things out, but I don't know what exactly it is I want him to work out."

"What exactly are you saying, Karen?"

"I'm saying I'm tired."

"Ump, you should have been tired a long time ago. Don't be nobody's fool."

"Tina, this doesn't have anything to do with being somebody's fool."

"Why not?"

"Believing things are going to work out and being a fool are two different things."

"If you say so. Look, you're my girl and I'm not calling you a fool. All I'm saying is that you can't let Johnny get away with this. You need to leave him before he tries to leave you for one of those little hookers he hangs out with."

"I don't know. I just might leave him. Wouldn't he be surprised?"

"Yeah, right, okay. That means about as much as when a man says he's leaving his wife. How many times have you threatened to leave?"

Karen had threatened to leave several times. Each had amounted to an empty emotional ploy.

Tina chuckled.

"What would happen if you told Johnny you were leaving? Let's see, most men would get mad, yell and scream, feel guilty, bring you flowers, buy you a nice diamond or fur or something expensive. Knowing you, humph, you'll soften, accept his apology, and believe him when he says it won't happen again."

Karen was silent.

"I gotta admit, for a couple with so much going on, you two sure do well."

"All that glitters isn't gold."

"Got that right."

As much material success as the Clarks appeared to have, it gave Tina a bit of comfort to know that their lives had as much struggle as her own.

Talking with Tina wore Karen down. In the end, it wasn't exactly the pep talk she was looking for. Then again, she wasn't exactly sure what she was looking for. Whatever it was, she didn't find it with Tina.

"Look here girl, I'm going to get off this phone so that I can start getting myself together for the day."

"Yeah, I better get going too. I'm sitting on this phone like I don't have any work to do around here. I'll catch up with you later. Be sure and let me know what you decide to do about Johnny. Inquiring minds want to know."

The wall clock displayed 9:45 A.M. as the call ended.

Karen shuffled around the kitchen in her robe with no intention of doing much of anything. *I wonder if Connie feels up to talking? Let me give her a call.*

Karen's two friends were quite different. When Karen wanted a reality check, she went to Tina. If it was compassion she was seeking, that required a chat with Connie. Her warm spirit had resonated with Karen the moment Tyrone had introduced them eight years ago. It had been hard for Karen to believe that he was attracted to such a soft-spoken and conservative woman. His type was more on the rambunctious side. It was even more shocking when he announced the marriage and exhibited signs of commitment and content. It was easy to see that he was hooked, and Connie adored him. Tina was not in the same place romantically. She wasn't interested in catering to a man. She was fine all by herself. Regardless of their idiosyncrasies, each of their individual bouts with life-threatening illnesses seemed to create an undeniable bond among the three women.

"Hi, Connie."

"Hey, lady. Where have you been? I didn't hear from you at all last week."

"I know, and I'm sorry. I had a headache most of the week, so I tried to take it easy," Karen answered.

"I know how that splitting headache can be. I was getting those all the time before I got the new herbs and vitamins. Thank goodness I got over those."

"The headache is bearable. Mostly I'm concerned about being tired."

"You know, you should have called me so that I could have come over and helped you out. Even though Tyrone tries to keep me from doing anything around here, I think that I still know how to cook and clean." She chuckled.

"Girl, please, you have it made. You haven't had to work, let alone cook or clean, in who knows how long." Karen laughed. "Anyway, how are you feeling these days? I know that you weren't doing too well the week before last."

"All is well."

It was often amazing and at times eerie. Karen couldn't believe that even in the advanced stages, Connie was still in denial about her inoperable brain tumor. The diagnosis was at least two years old. Karen had thought Connie was home free after the initial tumor was successfully removed during a sixteen-hour surgery and subsequent radiation. But she couldn't understand why Connie refused to acknowledge that the tumor had grown back. Even more astounding was Connie's ability to completely block it out.

"I know you probably don't want to go to the doctor," Connie stated.

"Well, I did talk to Dr. Costas before the weekend."

"At least you didn't have to go in. I get tired of going to the doctor. Every time I get a toenail ache, that husband of mine is rushing me off to the doctor or the hospital. Oh, my goodness, that man is too paranoid."

"He loves you. Can't complain about that." Karen longed for the kind of devotion and unwavering support that Tyrone gave his ailing wife.

Doctors had strongly recommended that Tyrone place Connie in a nursing home because she needed constant care. He had consistently refused for the past six months. Instead, he hired a full-time nurse to stay with Connie during the day and a part-time one to help out in the evenings and on weekends.

"No, I sure can't. I'm very blessed. Hey, maybe you can get the kind of vitamins I'm using for my headaches. They definitely work."

Karen downplayed the suggestion. She was into the more traditional approach to medicine versus the holistic one that Connie had embraced. After all of the medication, treatments, and surgeries that Connie had endured from the onset of her diagnosis, it was no wonder to Karen why her friend got tired of the traditional method and wanted to try a more natural approach. Medicine that was meant to fix one problem in the body generally had a side effect that broke down something else. Karen figured whatever juices and herbs Connie was taking were specifically related to the conditions associated with the brain tumor and not prescribed for a simple headache.

"I took some Tylenol for the headache and it seemed to work a little."

"What about the tiredness? What did she say about that?"

"I didn't tell her."

"Why not, Karen? I thought that was something you were always supposed to report?"

"I'm just a little tired. I probably need to get more rest. That's all. I figure a little rest and some leafy greens will get my energy level back up."

"You heard from Tina?"

"I just got off the phone with her."

"I need to give her a call. We should try to get together over the next week or two."

"Will you be able to come to our anniversary party?"

"Of course."

"Well, she's coming too. So we'll all be together then."

"I know, but I want us to get together by ourselves for some old-fashioned girl talk." Connie giggled.

Karen giggled too. When she was feeling down, things were always better after she talked to Connie.

"Well, then, lady, I'm going to take me a nap. I feel a little tired myself. Talk to you later this week."

"Okay, Connie. I'll call you later."

Karen set the cordless phone on the counter and took a moment to reflect on her friend. She shook her head in disbelief, perplexed at how Connie was dealing with the tumor. Karen understood constant pain and fear of the unknown. There were times when she felt like sticking her head in the sand. It wasn't the answer. If nothing else, she remembered that early detection of cancer was a key survival factor. She hadn't begun the self-exams in time, but Karen knew that it wasn't too late to be observant of the signals in her body now.

Without any hesitation, she picked up the phone and dialed Dr. Costas for an appointment. "Better safe than sorry" was her new-found perspective.

CHAPTER 9

Karen flipped through a magazine to pass the time. The sparsely colored waiting room was intimidating. It was a place she had to be only when necessary and not for a minute more.

The door leading to the examination rooms opened.

"Karen," the nurse called, standing behind the door, "you can come on back."

Karen neatly placed the magazine on the tabletop, collected her belongings, put on a brave face, and got up.

The nurse closed the door behind them.

"Let's get your weight."

Karen slipped off her shoes, not wanting to add any extra pounds.

"I've put on a few pounds since my last visit."

"Let's see." The nurse slid the weight to 150 and the scale didn't rise. She moved it back to a hundred and the scale flew up. She nudged the metal weight until the scale settled on 146. "Let me see where were you before. One thirty-five."

"I've gone from a six to a ten in four months."

"Still, for your height, your weight is fine. Five-seven is pretty tall for a woman. You can carry more weight than others without a problem."

"I just don't want to blow up now that I'm off work."

The nurse jotted down the weight. Karen followed her to the door marked *3*. White walls framed the room. Karen briskly rubbed her hands against her arms to generate a quick jolt of warmth. She sat on the edge of the examination table and took a deep breath. The nauseating smell of lanolin and medicated soap clogged her nostrils.

"Let me get your blood pressure."

Karen pushed her blouse sleeve above her elbow. It never failed. Every time she came to see Dr. Costas, her nerves would bounce out of whack. Her blood pressure would shoot up at the beginning of the appointment and drop back to normal by the end of the session.

The nurse wrapped the band around Karen's arm, put the cold metal end of the stethoscope in place, and pumped the meter.

Karen tried being calm, but the sterile environment hadn't brought the best of news in the past. She never felt totally at ease in the doctor's office. A thousand visits with a good report on each trip couldn't alter her disdain. She focused on the puffy cotton balls located a few inches past the tray of hypodermic needles.

"Done," the nurse said, and removed the band from Karen's arm.

"Is my pressure normal?"

"One forty-six over ninety-five; it's a little high," the nurse said.

"Yep, I know the routine by now."

The nurse told Karen on her way out, "Don't forget to strip down to your undies, unbutton your bra, and wrap up in one of the paper gowns on the counter. After Dr. Costas finishes up, I'll come back and retake your pressure."

"Thanks."

Karen undressed, wrapped herself in the paper robe, and sat on the examination table. She hummed, twitched her toes, and did anything she could to pass the time.

The door opened and a little lady with a headful of braids entered with a metal chart in her hand.

"Hi, Karen."

"Hello, Dr. Costas."

"So how are we doing?" She set the chart on the counter. "How's the headache?"

"I still have it."

"Did you take the Tylenol?"

"All weekend."

"And it didn't help?"

"Some, but not entirely."

"Lie back, please."

Dr. Costas opened the robe and placed her stethoscope in the center of Karen's chest.

"Breathe . . . again . . . and again." The doctor wrapped the stethoscope around her neck. "Have you been keeping up the self-exams with your underarms?" She checked Karen's breast area.

"Yes, I have. I check them practically every day while I'm showering."

"Good. It's a good habit to have. You can sit up."

Karen sat up and covered herself with the paper-thin wrinkled robe.

Dr. Costas sat on the tiny stool and wheeled it up to the counter. She made a few notes in the chart.

"Any other concerns, besides the headache?"

"Actually, I do," Karen reluctantly admitted. The longer she kept the complaint from Dr. Costas, the longer the symptoms could be suppressed.

"What?" Dr. Costas asked.

"I have been very tired. It's probably from having so much to do around the house with the kids and all. I thought I'd mention it, since I'm here."

Dr. Costas didn't show any alarm. She knew from years of treating Karen that it was best to minimize her concerns whenever possible. She pulled a flashlight from her pocket and a tongue depressor from the glass jar.

"Say 'aaah' and open wide."

Karen did as requested.

"You may be right about the stress. Let's order some blood work while you're here. I also want to make sure you're not suffering from anemia."

"Anemia! I haven't been anemic before."

"It's nothing to worry about. Between supplements and leafy green vegetables, that's pretty much all the remedy you need."

Dr. Costas wanted to put Karen at ease. She elected not to get into the medical aspects of anemia and how it tied in with blood loss. There was no reason to get her worried without more insight into what was going on. If it turned out that she was anemic, they could deal with the how and why then.

"I can handle that."

That was Karen's hope, something simple. She felt relieved about the examination. More medicine and treatment was the last thing she wanted to deal with.

"What about the headache?"

"I need to see the blood work first, and we'll go from there. If I don't get any hints from the lab work, I might have to schedule an MRI to get a look at what's happening."

Panic showed in Karen's eyes. The MRI was a test she would avoid if possible.

"An MRI! Do I really need one?"

The hair on her arms stood up. Claustrophobia was what she remembered about being in the confined space. Karen had freaked out four years ago when she needed it for the breast cancer. She was forced to go through with the closed MRI, since the accuracy and clarity of the images that it provided were critical for precise diagnosis of her condition.

Dr. Costas tried to ease her mind, sensing Karen's concern. "Karen, let's not focus on the MRI yet. Let me get the blood work back. I will call you tomorrow, and we'll go from there."

"Okay."

"In the meantime, keep that blood pressure down." She stood up and rubbed Karen's shoulder for reassurance. "Try not to worry. It never helps anyway."

"Thanks, Dr. Costas."

"I'll send the nurse back in to draw the blood."

CHAPTER 10

Karen was feeling jittery about the news that she'd received from Dr. Costas earlier in the day. She milled around the big house, feeling its emptiness. This was one evening she was looking forward to having Johnny around, even if she was still upset with him. When the phone rang, she grabbed it and found Johnny on the other end.

"Karen, the production tests ran overtime. I wasn't able to catch the corporate jet. I'm going to stay overnight and take the shuttle home in the morning."

"What a surprise."

"Come on, Karen. Let's not go there."

"Why not, Johnny? Why can't we talk about your job? It seems to be the most important thing to you."

"Look, you know how demanding this job can be. We've been over this a thousand times. When will you accept it?"

"When you show a little more interest in me and our family."

"Family!" His voice rose. "Family! Why do you think I work so hard? It's so that you and the kids can have it better than I did growing up. I bust my chops to give you everything you want and need. Don't I?" he yelled. "Don't I?"

"Yes, you do."

"I'm the only one working, and it takes a lot to keep what we have."

"I'm not trying to put extra pressure on you," Karen told him.

"Oh, no? I haven't seen you cut down on your spending. You're still signing the kids up for every after-school program that you can find. I don't see you jumping to get a smaller house. The only thing you were willing to give up easily was your job."

"What do you want me to say?"

"All I'm asking you for is a little support. I'm staying overnight," he bellowed.

Karen was out of sorts about her visit to the doctor. Although she didn't want to feel overly alarmed, she also didn't want to be unprepared.

"Fine, whatever."

He didn't feel up to having another blowout about where the marriage was going. Johnny made an effort to smooth the waters and find a less volatile subject.

"So what did the doctor say?"

Karen sighed. "Dr. Costas did some blood tests."

"Blood tests!" Having been with Karen during the cancer years, he'd learned those two words were an automatic barometer for concern. "What does blood work have to do with your headache?"

"I don't know. The only thing she said about the headaches was that I might have to get another MRI."

"MRI!" Although it was painless, he knew how much Karen dreaded the procedure. "Is it that serious?"

"Don't know yet. Dr. Costas didn't say I needed one for sure. We'll see what's going on after the test results come back."

"Yeah, so what's up with the blood work?"

"I've been feeling tired lately. I mentioned it to Dr. Costas, and I could tell she was a little concerned."

"You didn't tell me anything about being tired."

"I told you before you left."

"Yeah, but I thought that was . . . " he hesitated before finishing—"well . . ."

"Uh-huh. I told you I wasn't feeling well, but you didn't believe me. You thought I was begging for attention."

Sensing her edginess, Johnny decided to put an end to the conversation, at least for now.

"Stop it, Karen; I don't want to hear any more. We'll talk about it when I get back."

"That's it? That's the extent of your concern?"

"I'll be here if you need me."

"Thanks a lot for the support."

"What else can I do from here? I'm not a doctor." Johnny was irritated. "I'm only your husband, and that doesn't seem to be enough for you."

"I wonder why."

"That's it. I'll talk to you later."

Karen didn't feel up to carrying the conversation on either and chose to let it end on a sour note. She hung up the phone and wondered how she was going to spend the rest of the evening alone and disillusioned. Of all nights, the kids were going to be out late at the church's after-school spring event.

Karen realized the marriage was in trouble, but talking about leaving and actually doing it were worlds apart. She didn't know what to do. She tried to lift her spirits by reminiscing about the good years. Maybe going back to the beginning could erase some of the damage. She made her way downstairs to the media room. Karen could pick out the wedding tape in a few seconds, among hundreds of tapes. The smudged, barely legible label read, *Wedding—March.* The year had rubbed off long ago.

She sought out a few more sentimental videos for her pick-me-up party. She fumbled through the videos and pulled out a few labeled *Children's birthdays.* Back upstairs she went with an armful of memories. She inserted the wedding tape and pushed play after she settled back against the headboard. The first image on the screen was the smiling young couple in their simple living room ceremony accented by inexpensive daisy bouquets. She had been thrilled to find a dress big enough to cover her seven-months-pregnant stomach. Bliss abounded in the young couple.

The tape reminded Karen of how wide-eyed and in love they were in the beginning. They had met in their junior year of high school, become inseparable friends, and both ended up going to Wayne State. Johnny's pursuit of a law degree was cut short when Karen became pregnant their junior year in college. What they lacked in money, they made up for in romance.

The joy she had experienced in the marriage for many years was fading away. She pushed away the tears. The hopes, dreams, love, and experiences she and Johnny had once shared got sucked into a sea of distance and bitterness. It seemed that the possessions that they once talked about having had become more important than each other had.

The years hadn't been kind to her marriage or her spiritual stability. There was a time in the past when God had played a significant role in her life, and she would pray about everything. In the early years of the marriage, she grew in her faith and felt good about having a one-on-one relationship with the Lord. Twenty years ago she confidently believed in her heart that God knew her personally and made all things right.

Johnny never did get into the religious arena. His position used to be, "If it makes Karen happy, then I have no problem with it, so long as she doesn't push it on me."

Her religious pursuit slackened as their socioeconomic status grew. At times she felt guilty about putting God in the backseat. It was as if she had abandoned him during the surplus years.

Karen watched the tapes until she finally drifted into a deep sleep. She didn't budge when the girls poked their heads into her room around ten o'clock to let her know they were home.

The ringing phone startled Karen from her sleep the next morning. Half-awake and with no concept of time, she stretched out her arm and grabbed the phone without uncovering her head.

In a groggy, semiconscious voice, she answered the call, "Hello—umm."

"Karen Clark, please."

"This is Karen."

"Mrs. Clark, I'm calling from Dr. Costas's office."

That instantly got her attention. Wide-awake, she popped up in the bed.

"Dr. Costas wanted me to call you first thing this morning about your test results."

"Yes," Karen anxiously egged the nurse on for information.

"Your white blood cell count is high and the doctor wants some additional tests run."

Karen knew that her white blood cell count was high whenever the cancer was active. Her heart was racing and worry meter was in overdrive. "What do you mean, high?"

"There's no need to be overly concerned."

"Why shouldn't I be? I know that's an indication that my cancer might be back." Karen raised her voice. "How can you tell me not to be worried?"

"Mrs. Clark, please calm down. Dr. Costas is having the lab do some additional tests today."

"Do I need to come in to give more blood?"

"No. She ordered the test yesterday with the existing blood work. Some tests take longer than others do. She didn't want to wait for all of the results to come back before contacting you."

Karen tried to calm herself. She closed her eyes and rubbed her hand across the right side of her head.

"We will need you to go have an MRI done for the headaches."

"When?"

"If at all possible, we'd like for you to go early tomorrow morning. The doctor wants to get all of the tests and lab work done as soon as possible in order to get to the bottom of your discomfort. Do you think you'll be able to go?"

Karen wasn't up to the MRI or any other test. She had been through plenty. It was the last bit of information she wanted to get after such a strained weekend. A part of Karen wanted to stick her head back under the covers and sleep off the nightmare, to wake up and be back in the ideal household that she'd known years ago.

"I'll need to call you back after I check my schedule."

Karen covered her head and tried going back to sleep. Eleven-fifteen, read the digital alarm clock on the nightstand sitting next to the bed. Karen hadn't realized it was that late but wasn't ready to get up. It required too much energy, both physically and emotionally. She was hoping that a few more minutes underneath the warm confines of her blanketed fortress was going to do a world of good. All of a sudden she thought about the girls and popped up in the bed. Karen felt bad about not getting up in time to see them off. She was glad to know that Chelle was able to get herself and Elizabeth off to school, especially on days like today.

The bumping, thumping and running water coming from the bathroom woke her. She hadn't been out of bed all morning and didn't seem to care.

He was out of eye's view, but she knew that it must be Johnny and called out to him.

"Yeah," he yelled back.

"I didn't know you were here. When did you get in?"

Johnny walked from the bathroom and went into the closet.

"I took an early flight and got in about an hour ago."

Karen got up to go to the bathroom. Too much sleep was as tiring as too little. She was drowsy and tired from sleeping nearly five hours beyond her norm.

"You're not going to work today?"

Johnny walked out of the closet as Karen closed the bathroom door. He buttoned his starched white shirt.

"I'm on my way in now. I had to come home to get some clothes. I hadn't planned on spending last night in Springhill, so I didn't take anything with me."

She ran her fingers through her short hair. After losing her hair the first two times with chemo and radiation, she had opted to leave it short. Karen walked past Johnny and grabbed her robe off the bedroom sofa. Under her breath, she whispered, "At least something brought you home."

"Why aren't you dressed? What's wrong with you?" Johnny asked.

"The blood tests came back with some concerns."

It wasn't news he wanted to hear. He definitely knew it wasn't news Karen wanted to hear. Yet he didn't know how to react. As tense as their relationship had been over the past week, he was reluctant to step into a bigger can of worms. He decided, uncharacteristically, to let Karen lead the dialogue. The best he could hope for was to get his tie on and get out before another verbal explosion occurred.

"I also have to take another MRI."

She hung her head and twiddled her fingers. She rolled her head back, bit her lip, and stared at the ceiling in an effort to suppress the swelling tears.

Johnny knew how uncomfortable Karen had been in the past when she had to go for tests. He couldn't figure it out. There was no pain associated with the procedure. She had been through it in the past. What was the big deal?

"I don't want to do the MRI."

"Well, I mean, Karen, if it's something you have to do, you just have to do it."

"I'm not trying to get out of it, Johnny. I just wish I didn't have to do any more tests."

"Yeah, but you do. So there's no point stressing yourself out about it."

She was ready to cry.

"You don't understand. No matter how I try to share my feelings with you, you just don't get it."

"Ha, ha, ha, ha," Johnny belted out cynically. "I don't get it, huh? What exactly is it, Karen, that I don't get?" He let out another laugh.

"It's not fun going through illnesses, tests, pains, and—"

"And what, Karen? I am here for you. I've been here for you. I didn't leave you like Tina's husband did. So tell me, what is it that I don't understand?"

"I need you to show me more love and support, you know, like Tyrone does for Connie."

"Tyrone and Connie? They don't have anything to do with this. Look, I give up." Johnny threw his hands up in frustration. "Fine, Karen. I'm not getting into a deep discussion about my insensitivity. You've already told me enough times about that. Let's get back to the doctor. When is your test? I'll go with you."

"It's tomorrow morning." She perked up.

"Wednesday! Aaah." Johnny sighed. "I can't go tomorrow morning. I have an executive staff meeting."

"Can't you skip part of the meeting and go with me? You are the boss."

"Karen, this is a big meeting. The chief operating officer is coming down to go over the third-quarter projections. I have to be there."

"You can't miss one meeting?"

"Karen, come on. It's only a test. Don't try to make me feel guilty. If it were a life-threatening procedure, you know I'd be there."

"Life-threatening! I guess it's not enough for me just to want you there."

"Karen, my job is not easy. Not very many people get to work their way up from the line to senior management like I have. I've worked hard to get us where we are. So I'd appreciate it if you didn't try to make me feel guilty about doing what I have to do to take care of this family."

"I'm not talking about the family. I'm talking about me. You seem to be more committed to Tennin Automotive than you are to me."

"What's wrong with loving my job?"

"What's wrong with loving me?"

"I can't win with you. If I don't get out there and work to take care of my family, it means that I don't care about you. If I show commitment to my job, it means that I don't care about you. You're never happy, no matter what I do."

"Your career seems to be your one true love."

"Look, Karen, I don't expect you to understand where I'm coming from. When you got pregnant—"

Karen interrupted and asked, "When *I* got pregnant?"

"I'm sorry. I mean that when we got pregnant, you were in a position to graduate early, before Erick was born. I wasn't as fortunate as you were. I had to drop out and take a factory job. Did I complain? No. I did what I had to do. Every time I tried to go back to school, you know something came up. Between the children, our responsibilities, and you being sick, it took me thirteen years to finish my degree."

"So why do you make it seem like it's my fault?"

"I'm not saying that it's your fault. I'm not trying to blame you, Karen. I'm only asking you to understand where I'm coming from as a man. You always talk about my showing you some support. What about showing me some?"

Johnny grabbed his keys and walked out of the room, leaving Karen to sort out her raging emotions. In response, she returned to her safe haven underneath the bedcovers.

Before backing out of the driveway, Johnny placed a call on his cell phone.

"Hey, Tyrone. What's going on?"

"Not much happening. Trying to keep it together. What's going on with you?"

"I got a lot on my mind. I was wondering if you could hook up with me for a drink after work?"

"On a weeknight? What's up? What's going on?"

"I need to talk."

"Okay. Let me check on Connie first."

"I'm sorry, buddy. I didn't even ask. How's she doing?"

"This has been a good week for her."

"I don't know how you do it. Your wife has been sick for a couple of years. I have to give it to you, man. You got that."

"Karen has her share, too and you've been there for her. It's what husbands do."

"Nah, I haven't been able to stand as strong as you have."

"I'm only doing what I can. I love her, and that's all there is to it," Tyrone stated. "I'll have to get back with you about tonight."

Tyrone hadn't forgotten the years he'd played around. His world had changed when he met Connie. He couldn't explain what it was that drew him to her. Her big round eyes set against her honey-colored skin often caught the attention of men. But it wasn't her looks that drew Tyrone. He had had plenty of appealing women in his day. There was more to Connie. Something about her connected below the surface. Tyrone was proud to admit how she had managed to convert a player into a dedicated and faithful husband. He placed a call home.

"Hey, how you doing, babe?"

"I'm fine, same as I was when you called an hour ago. You know that you worry about me too much."

"If I don't, who will? I love you, girl. Johnny gave me a call. He wants to get together after work. If it's okay with you, I'm going to grab a drink with him right after work and then come on home."

"Is anything wrong?"

"I don't know. He seemed like there was something heavy on his mind."

"Go on with him. I'll be fine."

"Are you sure? Johnny is my buddy, but you are my first priority, no exceptions."

"I'm sure. Go on out and have a good time."

"I'll be in soon as I can."

"Take your time. I might invite the girls over for dinner, since both the cook and the housekeeper are here today."

"If you feel up to it. Don't overdo it, babe."

"I love you, honey. I don't know what I'd do without you," Connie said.

"That's something you don't have to worry about."

CHAPTER 11

Karen was spraying water on the leaves of the nine-foot tree that towered in the foyer. The housewarming gift had only been a few feet tall when they received it eight years ago. Thanks to the nurturing touch of Karen, the plant matured into full bloom like other things in her care. She heard the familiar sound of Chelle yelling for her to get the phone.

"It's Aunt Connie."

Karen walked down the hallway past Johnny's office and the back staircase into the family room, where she could relax in peace. She got situated on her chaise longue, excused Chelle from the phone, and greeted Connie.

"What are you doing tonight?" Connie asked.

"No plans."

"Good. You have to come over for dinner. I won't take no for an answer."

"I don't know, Connie. Johnny's out."

"I know. Tyrone told me they were going out for a drink."

"He did, huh?"

Karen didn't know where Johnny was going and felt embarrassed that Connie knew her husband's whereabouts better than she did.

"There won't be anyone here with the girls."

"What about the sitter down the street? Come on, Karen, no excuses. We haven't gotten together in a long while. I had the cook put together a nice dinner."

"I'll see what I can do. I'll check on the sitter. If she's available, I'll be over around seven."

"Great. I'm going to call Tina, too. I haven't seen her in a while either. It will be nice to have the three of us together."

Connie and Karen had been friends first. Tina came into the fold four years later. Karen was the linchpin in the trio, but Connie and Tina had managed to develop their own solid connection.

Maybe getting out of the house was exactly what Karen needed to shake the funk she was in.

"Mommy, what happened to you and Daddy last night?" Chelle wondered, since no one had been up when they had gotten home last night.

"I was tired, sweetie. I went to bed early. Daddy had to stay overnight in Tennessee. He didn't get back home until today."

"I came in to see you when they dropped us off from church," Elizabeth let her mom know. "You were already asleep by ten."

"You could have woken me up."

"Nah, Chelle wouldn't let me," Elizabeth tattled.

"Thanks for letting me sleep." Karen directed the comment to Chelle. "I did get up around ten-thirty to check on you. Both of you were sound asleep. Did you get all of your homework done last night?"

"Yes, and I got an A on my spelling test." Elizabeth was eager to share the good news with her mom.

"You did? Well, aren't I proud of you."

Elizabeth beamed from ear to ear.

"Chelle made me study all of the words over and over last night."

Karen smiled. She was so proud of her children. She was particularly grateful that Chelle was responsible and mature. She had been a vital component in the family's livelihood while Karen was sick. Many people helped out, but it was Chelle who got most of the meals together, took care of the laundry, and personally looked out for Elizabeth. Her grades never dropped below her standard As and Bs.

"Chelle, did you decide whether or not you are going to the Teen Redeem in D.C. next month? We have to turn in the enrollment form at church Sunday."

"I don't know if I want to go. It's right before finals. What do you think?"

"Well, it's only one weekend, and you deserve a break. I think you should go." Karen hugged her daughter. "It's not every day that you get to meet other Christian teens from all over the world."

"Will you get the deposit money from Daddy for me? I'll turn it in when we go to church." Chelle kissed her mom on the cheek. "Thanks, Mom. I love you."

Karen had strong relationships with all three of her children. Looking at the joy in her two beautiful daughters gave her reason to stay with Johnny. She couldn't imagine altering the children's lives by taking on a struggling single-parent status. It was hard enough nineteen years ago for two parents to get the family through tough financial times. Karen couldn't imagine doing it alone.

CHAPTER 12

Karen second-guessed herself during the twenty-minute drive to Connie's house. Did she feel up to being around others or not? Maybe she would go back home and nestle under her warm bedcovers and feel better in the morning. She slowly turned in to the subdivision off the main road, accepting that her opportunity to leave was escaping. She was startled by a horn blowing. Karen looked into the rearview mirror to see Tina waving. Too late to turn around; she had been spotted. She pulled the Lincoln Navigator into the circular driveway.

Tina pulled her five-year-old Chevy Cavalier into the driveway behind Karen. The two ladies gathered their belongings and got out.

"I wasn't sure if you were coming," Karen commented.

The women embraced.

"Why not? A single woman like me is always looking for a home-cooked meal. It's nice having rich friends like you all."

"There you go with that rich stuff." It was a comment Tina often made in jest, but Karen received it as a compliment. "We're struggling just like you and a whole lot of other people."

Connie came to the door with a walking cane. She didn't look as tired to Karen as she had the last time they were together. She was swollen, but visibly coming down. Karen recalled how Connie's weight had shot up seventy pounds from the steroids last year. The rashes were another side effect she suffered from her barrage of medication. It was the final factor in Connie's decision to switch from traditional to holistic medicine. Her skin had smoothed out around her cheeks and neck. Her hair was short and slicked back. Despite her cropped cut and heavy frame, Connie's warm personality overshadowed any shortcomings in her looks.

"Well, well, if it isn't the two strangers."

Both Tina and Karen hugged Connie on the way in.

"I'm so glad you both came."

"Something smells good," Tina said.

"Dinner is ready. Let's eat. We can talk later," Connie suggested.

Being in the midst of her two closest friends was rejuvenating to Karen. The trio had weathered physical battles, with each challenge weaving them a bit closer.

"I'm so glad you talked me into coming over. I really needed to get out," Karen admitted.

"Why, what's up?" Connie pressed.

"Oh, nothing."

"Come on, Karen. It's just us girls," Connie reassured her.

"Speak up, girl. What's on your mind?" Tina pushed.

At first Karen was reluctant to open up about the issues going on in her marriage. But after giving it some thought, she decided to go ahead. She needed a listening ear.

"Johnny and I are going through some issues."

"That's all? Oh, girl, please. You already went through that stuff. I thought you were leaving him?" Tina sighed.

"Maybe I will. I don't know."

"I knew that wasn't going to happen."

"It's not so easy to walk out after nineteen years, three kids, and a boatload of memories and bills. You're so eager for me to leave—are you willing to pay my bills?" Karen's voice was raised. "I'm not willing to just disrupt my children's lifestyle because Johnny and I can't get it together."

"Leave him! For what? What's going on?" Connie asked. She was trying to jump into the heated discussion, but no one was letting her get a word in edgewise.

"I don't want to get into it. It's a long story."

"I have nothing but time to listen," Connie offered compassionately.

"Humph. It's not a long story. It's the same old story women hear all the time," Tina contended.

"Tina, stop. You always have something to say. You are so quick to tell everyone else what they're doing wrong in their relationships," Karen yelled. "Where's yours?"

"I'm only being honest."

"Honest! Oh, please," Karen snapped. "You aren't even being honest with yourself."

"What does that mean?" Tina questioned.

"You always have something to say with that smart mouth of yours. Big Tina, the one who always has to set us straight, the one to tell it like it is. I am so sick of you always being so pushy. You want honesty?" She'd never spoken to Tina with such boldness. Her nostrils were pulsating and ready to spew fire. Her head was bobbing and weaving like a duck dunking for food. "How about this, Tina: you're a big hypocrite. You're a mean woman who needs to deal with the fact that your husband left you." Karen didn't know much about Tina's ex. She'd met him only a few times before he bolted.

"That wasn't my fault."

"It might not have been his fault either. Not everybody deals with illness the same way. Maybe he wasn't able to take it," Connie jumped in.

"It doesn't matter why he left. The bottom line is, he's gone. Because he left, it doesn't mean that every man out there is a dog," Karen suggested.

"Most are."

"See, that's what I'm talking about. You're an angry, bitter woman, and if you don't watch it, you'll be old and alone without any man, any children, and maybe any friends."

"Ooooh. Aren't you in a tizzy? Because you're mad at Johnny, don't take it out on me."

"I'm not taking out anything on you. I'm giving you back a dose of your own medicine. People like you have no problem dishing it out but don't do too well taking it." Karen looked away at the wall, as if that were to whom her conversation was directed. "And you have the nerve to talk about Johnny."

"That's right. I can talk about Johnny. He's not my husband. It's easy for me to see the dirt that he does."

"How? You don't sleep in his face every night. How do you know what my husband's doing other than what I've told you, and I regret that."

"I don't have to sleep with him to know that men are trifling, can't be trusted, self-centered, and uncaring."

"See what I mean? You need help," Karen reaffirmed.

"Me! I don't have a cheating man living under my roof."

"Cheating! Who's talking about cheating? Is that what this is about? Is Johnny cheating on you?" Connie was looking for a point to enter the heated dialogue.

"I didn't say he was cheating. Tina is the one who says he's cheating. I really don't know if he is or isn't."

"There you go making excuses. When are we women going to stop making excuses for these dogs?" Tina asked.

"When we feel that we are perfect enough to judge somebody else," Connie said.

"I'm not judging anyone. I'm merely telling the truth as I see it."

"It's not your place to judge her man. We feel awful about what happened to you. But Tina, not every woman has gone through the same thing that you did with your husband. Some husbands are very supportive to their women through sickness and in health," Connie calmly interjected.

"I'd expect you to say something like that." Without thinking about the ramifications, Tina said, "You live in denial about your own health."

"Tina!"

Karen jumped to her feet. She pointed her finger in Tina's direction but not right in her face.

"You have some nerve. That is cruel and cold, even for you. You're selfish and hard-hearted. You're really a trip."

As cutthroat as Tina could be, even she felt badly for what she'd said. She had let anger get the best of her and caused unnecessary hurt to someone she cared about.

Connie had always been the most timid among the three friends. Karen knew she'd be hurt by the piercing comment and went to comfort her. Connie sat up on the edge of the chair and pushed Karen away.

"I'm sorry. I shouldn't have said that," Tina admitted.

"You're right. You shouldn't have," Connie told her.

"Connie, you can talk, since you have a good man. Most women don't. I didn't."

"So what are you going to do about it?" Karen asked.

"What do you mean?"

"Are you going to keep walking around spitting venom or are you going to learn how to forgive?" Connie asked.

"I don't have anybody to forgive. Bobby is long gone and my cancer is over. That chapter is closed and behind me."

"The cervical cancer might be gone, but the cancer in your heart isn't. With all of that bitterness and hurt that you're carrying, you're going to have to forgive somebody before it eats you up. Your inability to forgive people is going to eat you alive. You're unhappy and hard to be around," Connie told Tina.

Tina kept unusually quiet. She had already overstepped her bounds and said more than was necessary.

"You need to find the Lord," Karen suggested.

"Yeah, I see what a great job he's done for you. A cheating husband, and you live in fear every day that your cancer is coming back."

"God didn't give me cancer, and he didn't make Johnny do anything."

"He didn't stop it either. I believe in God like everybody else. But if I'm going to end up like the two of you, no, thank you, about living on that faith stuff. I don't see anything between the two of you that would make me want to hang out there on a wing and a prayer."

"That's close to blasphemy."

"You two can say what you want. The doctors and medicine have done just fine by me. I'm in full remission, and I don't have relationship issues. I'm doing pretty good right now, if you ask me."

"So you don't think God has control over medicine and doctors? You really think that you are alive and well because of some hospital and some doctor?"

"Yes," Tina confidently acknowledged. "Yes, I do. I know that sounds terrible to the two of you Bible-thumpers, but God wasn't around for me. I was sick and alone and scared. I prayed night after night for God to let Bobby keep it together. I wanted children. I wanted the storybook family like everybody else. I begged God to let me have a child. I didn't feel God's presence when the doctor told me that I had to choose between living with a hysterectomy or dying with my uterus. All I felt was depression."

Karen and Connie didn't utter a word. Both knew that nothing they could say would reach Tina in her current emotional state. The best thing was to let her get it out. It was the first time she'd expressed to them some of her deep-seated feelings about her past medical challenges.

"I know Bobby wanted children. It was the one thing we talked about for years before getting married. He left. There was nothing that I could do, nothing that I could say—nothing. He never admitted it, but I know he blamed me for letting myself get the cancer. Once he found out that it could have been detected much sooner from my annual Pap smears, he freaked out. I trusted my doctor like everybody else. How was I supposed to know that he didn't read the results? I had no idea that I needed to call the doctor to make sure that he read my results. I bet most people don't." Refusing to be overcome by emotion, she cleared her throat and sat up in the chair. She flicked a tear from her eye as if to say, "Don't come back."

"It wasn't your fault. You can't blame yourself," Karen told her.

Tina was on a roll. She continued reliving the painful memories of her ordeal with cancer without hearing a word from Karen.

"Every year the doctor said that he'd call me if there was a problem with my Pap smear. I didn't hear from him. No news was good news. I assumed everything was fine."

Both Karen and Connie knew that Tina needed to vent and didn't interrupt any more.

Tina wiped her eyes and nose again.

"I didn't know Pap smears were that important. I relied on my doctor. I was young and dumb. The farthest thing from my mind was getting cancer of my cervix."

Tina gritted her teeth and held her head back.

"Where was God when my world was falling apart? There weren't any angels camped around my bed singing praises and hymns. I was alone, trying to decide if I wanted to live or die."

"You lived."

"Yeah, thanks to who? When Bobby first left me, I wasn't sure living was the best outcome."

"But you lived; that's the bottom line. You are alive, and whether you acknowledge God or not, he let you live."

Tina was sobbing softly.

Karen pulled a tissue out of her purse and moved next to Tina. She took the tissue and wiped her tears.

"You are alive," Connie said.

"You got past that time in your life," Karen added.

"Everybody has challenges, Tina. Some people are stronger than others. You just have to deal with it the best way you know how, without hurting other people along the way."

CHAPTER 13

The crowd at Floods was thin on weeknights. There wasn't the usual flow of attractive, unescorted women being admired by a host of flirtatious men. A few isolated conversations, piped-in easy-listening music, and sparse lighting set the ambiance.

The men arrived about the same time and took a small table near the bar. The mood was different but the drinks were the same. Johnny had his usual Hennessy straight up, and Tyrone had a gin and tonic.

Johnny stretched his right arm across his lap, propped his left elbow on top of the table, and covered his mouth with his open left hand.

"Hey, brother, you look stressed. What's up?"

"I don't know where this is going," Johnny said, shaking his head.

Tyrone had a confused look on his face. He wasn't accustomed to seeing his friend in such a worried state. Johnny exuded confidence and control in his walk and in his talk. That was his trademark. The attitude Johnny was sporting was new for Tyrone. It concerned him.

"Where is what going?"

"Me and Karen."

"What!" was all Tyrone could say in utter surprise.

He was expecting Johnny to open up about something job related, not about his marriage. Tyrone knew that all couples had their moments, but overall, he believed Johnny and Karen had what it took to go the distance. Johnny's comment seemed to come out of left field.

"We're struggling. No, I'm struggling."

Johnny believed that he still loved Karen, but he couldn't deal with the void in his relationship. Love didn't seem to be enough to get through the rough spots.

"I'm not getting what I need physically or emotionally."

Johnny saw himself as being strong-willed and confident in business. At home he needed unwavering admiration and constant appreciation. That was where his previous affair came into play. It gave him the ego boost that he desired, without pressure. It was as close to free love as he could get.

"I wonder what Isabelle is up to these days?"

"Isabelle? Man, you can't even think like that."

"Why not? Those were some good times. With Karen and I . . . well, you know."

Tyrone shook his head and tapped a cigarette out of the pack.

"Johnny, man, you just can't go there."

"Why not?"

"Because! It's one thing to go out for a drink. It's something else to get involved in a relationship. I'll tell you, that can lead to a lot of problems." Tyrone paused and reflected on his past mistakes. "The sacrifice might be too much."

"I know, I know. I'm not serious about Isabelle—or anyone else for that matter. But I might as well be, if you ask Karen. She won't stop dogging me about that. What happened with Isabelle was six years ago. I admit that what I did was wrong. I made a mistake. I've tried to patch things up, I really have, but it's not all on me. No matter what I say or do she thinks I'm cheating."

"Are you?"

"I'm at that point."

"Shoot, you have it made. You have a wife, a great job, smart kids, and a nice home. Most men only dream about having it as good as you."

"Tyrone, everything ain't always what it seems."

"Like what?"

As close as the guys were, Johnny was embarrassed about exposing certain aspects of his private life.

"I'm saying that we have some real issues."

"Who doesn't?"

"I mean real problems. Karen hasn't given it up in seven months, and it wasn't steady about a year before that. We were cool for about six months after she got out of the hospital the last time."

"Wasn't that a couple of years ago?"

"You got it."

"Do you know what the problem is?"

"I wish I did. All I know is that she started losing interest little by little. Seven months ago it dropped to none at all. At first I thought it had something to do with the chemo treatments, but the doctor says she's fine physically. I don't know what it is. What am I supposed to do? I'm sick of begging. I can't let things go on like this. It's not easy holding back. I have needs. I want some sex. No, I need some sex!"

"Wow. I had no idea. You really have to think this thing through. You don't want to get into a situation that could damage your marriage."

"I'm not sure that we still have a marriage. There's a lot of water under the bridge."

"Well, if you're not sure, take time to work it out."

"Time! That's the problem. It's been a long time since we both felt good about being together. I don't know what happened. I remember those big, beautiful brown eyes, contagious smile, and knockout body. She was easy to talk to and fun to be around back then. I guess we're not a couple of madly-in-love high school kids anymore."

He sat in silence for a few moments.

"We were so in love. We had the world by the tail twenty years ago. Everything was at our fingertips. I thought that everything would be wonderful for us after the baby came. Man, I have worked my butt off for Karen and the kids. That doesn't seem to be enough for her anymore." He took a swig of his cocktail. "Heck, it's not enough for me anymore."

Johnny sighed and leaned back in his chair, fumbling with the napkin. He gave a slight grin, remembering how intelligent she was. It was what had initially attracted him to her. At the time, he had thought she was the smartest, most attractive girl in high school.

"She used to be so"—he paused, searching for the right word—"sharp. I mean, man, she was on the ball."

"Karen is a sharp lady," Tyrone agreed.

"Nah, nah." Johnny shook his head. "No, man. She's changed. She's comfortable doing nothing. She sits around the house all day, and it seems to be good enough for her."

"I can't say anything. Connie stays at home."

"That's different; you can afford it. Don't get me wrong; it's all right to be at home. But I can't imagine that's what Karen really wants. She was headed to graduate school in college. Now she doesn't even bring it up anymore."

"It's hard to go back to school after you've been out for a while and have gotten into a routine."

"I did it, but it takes some motivation. She doesn't have it. I want someone more aggressive. I want to toss ideas around with her about work and career stuff. I need that. I hate to admit it, but that's how I got caught up with Isabelle. You don't run into too many women in manufacturing. She was sharp as a tack and ran a mean operation. I've never met a woman who was such a strong business match for me."

"I don't know what to tell you, Johnny. What are you thinking about doing?"

"I have no idea. Right now, I just want some peace in my house. Karen and I have been bickering ever since she found Isabelle's phone number in my shirt pocket Saturday."

"Jones?"

"No, not that one. I'm talking about that young lady we met at Floods the other night. You remember the one I gave a ride home? Well, turns out her name is Isabelle."

"Really! How weird is that? I didn't realize the two of you had gotten into anything Friday."

"We didn't. I ran into Tina right outside the club. After that, I dropped Isabelle off and went straight home. You know what a big mouth that cobra has."

Tyrone had seen Tina in action and didn't want to feel the wrath that she'd put on Johnny. All he could do was laugh at the predicament his buddy was in.

"That woman is evil. It's no wonder she got cancer. She hates all men. I'm surprised it hasn't eaten out more of her insides." Johnny spared no harshness when describing Tina.

Still chuckling, Tyrone interjected, "So you ran up on the player-hater." He shook his head in amusement.

"Man, that stuff isn't funny. By the time Karen let me know she'd found the number, she was ready to blow a gasket. She accused me of cheating, and who knows what else she's thinking."

"You know how women stick together." Tyrone chuckled.

"Get this—Karen swears that I'm seeing Isabelle Jones again. No matter what I say, she believes I'm lying."

"Are you?"

"No!" Johnny was somewhat insulted by the implication. "I honestly haven't talked to her since I broke it off six years ago."

"Don't get upset with me. You're the one who brought her name up half an hour ago."

"You're right. I guess I did."

"I'm telling you, Johnny, don't entertain the thought of another woman unless you're prepared to lay a lot on the line." Tyrone settled back in his seat. "Be careful, player. So what are you going to do about Karen's suspicions?"

"I offered to introduce her to the Isabelle I met Friday to prove it's not Ms. Jones."

Tyrone started laughing again. "You must be kidding. This is going from bad to worse."

"Now, you know I'm not going to introduce them, but I had to give Karen something to go on. Otherwise, man, she wasn't easing up. She was going for the jugular, and I had to toss her a bone."

"You need to settle down like me and stick with your girl. Back in the day, all of that messing around was fun. I'm too old for all of that lying and cheating. Too much drama for me."

"Look at you, Mr. Henpecked."

"Whatever. It's all good. All I know is that every night I go home to a woman who not only loves me, but also likes my company after eight years of marriage. I don't have any complaints. I'm telling you, Johnny, there is nothing like going home to a woman who you know loves you."

"What are you talking about? You still hang out with me from time to time."

"True, every now and then for a few drinks—that's it. But you better believe that there is no one with me when I leave Floods."

"Who would have thought it? Big, bad Tyrone has gone soft."

"Hey, call it what you will. I'm not messing this up."

Johnny knew his friend was sincere and truly did love his wife.

"Is Connie getting any better?"

"She's hanging in there. I wish there was more I could do to make things easier for her."

"Let Karen tell it, you are the star husband."

"Oh, yeah."

"Yeah, today she asked me why I'm not more supportive, like you are with Connie. She thinks you are the example to follow."

"Nah, not me, man. I just do what I can. You know I've done enough dirt in the past to last me a lifetime."

"So what changed you?"

"I can't explain it, man. I must have gotten tired of playing around and never really having anybody who was really in my corner. Then Connie came along. She was something special." His eyes lit up as he talked about her. "Finding the right woman to love will change a man."

Johnny reared back in the chair, sporting a smug grin. "Yeah, right. You sure your urge to settle down didn't have any connection with that woman who claimed you got her pregnant?"

Tyrone chuckled. "I can't believe you remember that."

"Yeah, I remember. Man, that kind of stuff will put fear into any man," Johnny said.

He couldn't forget when Isabelle got pregnant during the affair. An extramarital child would have jeopardized his reputation, his financial stability, and his family. He shrugged his shoulders and gave a sigh.

"Tyrone, that's the only reason that I keep out of real trouble. I'm not taking a chance on hooking up with one of those women and end up getting her pregnant."

"You can lie your way out of a few phone numbers and a boatload of late nights at Floods. You can't get away from DNA, not even someone as smooth as you, player," Tyrone stated.

Johnny sighed. "Seriously, I don't know if I still love Karen. We're different. Of course, I still care about her. I'll always take care of her financially, but my heart isn't there anymore. Man, it's gone. I see her as a social partner and the mother of my children. I see her as everything but my lover."

"I don't know what you're going to do, if you don't love her. That's the only thing that will keep you going. I guess that's where the new—or is it the old?—Isabelle comes in." Tyrone was being facetious.

"The new Isabelle is not an issue. Now, the old Isabelle, that was different. After all these years, I have to admit that she was quite a package. It's hard to find a woman who has beauty, brains, and is bold enough to stand up to me. I hate to admit it, but she was something special. That was the first time that I stepped out on the marriage. If I'd met her at a different time in my life . . . well, you never know how it might have turned out. Hey, maybe it wasn't the right time six years ago. Maybe this is the right time."

"You need to keep yourself together, Johnny. Don't do something you might regret."

"You're right. I'm not looking for anything serious. A little conversation and maybe . . . well, you know." Johnny pressed his lips together to restrain the smile. "A brother has needs."

"The grass is always greener," Tyrone pointed out.

"Right now, green grass sounds good to me. I'm tired of playing in the same spot where all of the grass has worn down."

"Sure, you say that now. Let someone else get interested in Karen and see how you feel about her. Your feelings will sober up quickly."

"Think so, huh?"

Tyrone had known his friend for enough years to speak candidly.

"Sure. As much as you don't think that you want her, I know that you don't want anyone else to have her either. That's the way it is, bro."

Johnny chuckled at Tyrone's implication that the age-old cliché had any merit with him.

"Nah, that's not me."

"Okay, if you say so. Just don't do anything that you might regret later," Tyrone advised. He looked directly into Johnny's eyes and spoke from his heartfelt experience. "You know, it can be hard to clean up certain kinds of messes." Tyrone sipped his drink. "Hey, partner, you know whatever you decide, I'm here for you."

"Thanks, man."

Tyrone patted Johnny on the back, intending to lighten the atmosphere.

"Just don't do anything crazy, if you know what I mean," he said with a smile.

It was eight o'clock. Johnny raised his hand to beckon the waitress.

"Yes, I do know what you mean. I'm heading out. I'll catch you tomorrow."

Johnny wasn't ready to go home. Instead, he went to the company's executive suite located on the mezzanine level of the Renaissance Center. He plopped down on the chair facing the ceiling-high windows. He was considering the warning that Tyrone had given. Should he or shouldn't he? His thoughts volleyed back and forth. At the end of the match, his desire for companionship had the stronger serve.

He turned on his cell phone and punched in a four-digit code to access the private directory. Names and numbers appeared. He hadn't used any of the seven phone numbers that he'd collected in the past three months, and couldn't place faces with each. He continued scrolling through the list until the name Annette appeared. He remembered her from a month prior—funny, sexy, and separated. He hesitated for a moment and then let the number dial.

She answered.

"Annette this is Johnny Clark. We met at Floods a few weeks ago and, well, I enjoyed our conversation. So I was wondering if you'd be interested in joining me for a drink at the lounge in the Pontchartrain?"

He stared at the glimmering lights lining the Canadian side of the river. He was pleased when Annette accepted his offer.

"Forty-five minutes sounds good to me. See you then," Johnny said.

He looked down at the floor while tapping on the cell phone in his hand. It was going to take more than one evening to sort out his problems. Tonight he was comfortable settling for an intoxicating drink, a relaxing view, and the friendly conversation of an attractive woman to whom he had no commitment.

CHAPTER 14

Johnny sat in his office and played his cell phone messages. The only people who were able to contact him on this phone were his family, Tyrone, Sonja, and a few designated business representatives.

"You have one new message to review. Please press two now." Johnny pressed the button and heard, "Hello, Mr. Clark. This is Mr. Lewis with E-Finance. Based on a rough approximation we can give you a new equity loan with sixty thousand dollars back at eight percent. I know you asked for eighty thousand dollars, but you need to maintain at least twenty percent of the appraised value of your house in order to avoid PMI. Let me know if you want to proceed. Thanks, Mr. Clark. Look forward to hearing from you."

Sixty thousand—that's it, Johnny repeated to himself. It would be tight, but what choice did he have? He shoved the dilemma into the back of his mind and shifted to an area where he had more success, his work.

Johnny was on top of his game at the office regardless of the shambles of his life at home. His career aspirations wouldn't allow him to settle for less than an office large enough to tastefully house an eight-foot-long cherry-wood desk, a ten-seat conference table, and a sofa and matching wing-backed chairs.

He twirled a pen in his hand while thinking about last night. He and Annette had left the Renaissance Center before ten-thirty and went for a bite to eat. He took her up on the offer to grab a nightcap at her place. When they arrived at her house just before midnight, she was in the mood. He wasn't relaxed because it had been a while for him. He didn't want to seem overanxious and unable to control himself. Her kisses and caresses had worn him down. Protection, coupled with the admission that her tubes were tied because she didn't want kids, enabled him to relax into the moment.

Thinking back on it, he didn't know if he felt more relieved or guilty that the encounter had taken place. He wanted to satisfy his physical needs, but it didn't make him feel good about cheating. At least he'd kept the six-year-old promise he'd made to himself, which was never to have sex with another woman while he and Karen were intimate. The only time that he'd ever had sex with two women concurrently was with Karen and Isabelle. After the fallout from the affair, the promise was a commitment he had to maintain.

"Mr. Clark, I have the production manager on the line. He says it's urgent."

"Okay, Sonja, put him through on the speakerphone."

"Jeff, hey, buddy. What's going on out there?"

"Johnny, we have a problem."

Johnny took his job seriously and prided himself on running a tight, award-winning operation.

"What kind of problem?" He sat up in his seat with anticipation.

"We got a set of bad blocks. We're having difficulty running them through without the line repeatedly crashing."

"Have you requested a new shipment of blocks?"

"I have, Johnny, but there's a backlog of about six weeks."

"Six weeks!" Johnny jumped up. "That won't do."

"I know."

"This is one of our biggest orders. We have got to get this shipment out by next week, no exceptions. The third-quarter numbers are in jeopardy if we don't."

"I don't know what else to do."

"I know that I can't go back to Al with this news." Johnny was adamant about finding a solution before accepting failure and telling the senior vice president.

"Well, you know I'll do whatever you want me to. I just wanted to keep you in the loop. I already put a call in to your assistant. I know he's supposed to start coming down for situations like this."

Normally Johnny would defer a production problem to his assistant VP. But he saw this as a prime opportunity to personally handle a critical problem while also being able to take a break from the home front.

"Yeah, thanks for filling me in, Jeff. This is critical. I'm going to follow up on this one myself."

"You're coming down yourself?"

"Yes, I will be there late this afternoon. In the meantime, get on the phone with the backup supplier and see what we can get. I also need you to check and double-check that line. Make sure it is fully functioning and that it is not the source of the problem."

"Will do, boss. I'm on top of it. I'll see you when you get here."

Johnny buzzed his secretary.

"Sonja, can you please check to see if the corporate plane is going to Tennessee this afternoon? If it is, get me on the list. If not, book me on a commercial flight."

"Okay, sir. I'll do it right away."

"Also, get me the most recent problem reports for the block lines. Yes, and, uh, get DeWayne on the line. I need to give him the update and to let him know I'm going down in his place."

"Anything else, sir?"

"Yes, hold my calls. I need to run home and grab a few clothes before the flight leaves. Call me on my cell phone and let me know which flight I'm taking."

Johnny had pressing issues at the top of his priority list. Smoothing the waters with Karen wasn't one of them.

CHAPTER 15

Karen would have given anything to have Johnny walk through the door. She sat in the waiting room trying to build up assurance.

The nurse eased the door open that led to the dressing rooms.

"Mrs. Clark, you can come on back."

Karen quickly gathered her belongings. She was anxious to get the procedure over with but in no hurry to get started.

"You need to take off all of your jewelry and clothes and leave them in one of the dressing room lockers. You can leave your underpants and shoes on."

The nurse rattled off the instructions like a computerized recording.

"When you're ready, come on out with the surgical gown on."

Karen followed orders. She found herself fidgeting in the dressing room. The breast cancer had left her a bit squeamish about medical exams and exploratory tests.

"I'm ready," Karen told the nurse.

"Okay, I'll take you into the examination room."

The chilly, dimly lit hallway seemed endless. Karen would have been relieved to know that Johnny was as close as the waiting room, since visitors weren't allowed in the actual imaging room.

She hated using the MRI machine but couldn't deny the value it had in helping to pinpoint her diagnosis. Yet, it didn't give her much ease in going through the process. Her body froze when she looked at the white, tubular, coffinlike apparatus. Being submerged in the confined space gave Karen an eerie feeling of being buried alive.

"Let me hook up the IV."

The table slid Karen inside the tube. There was no physical pain associated with the exam, other than the momentary prick that came from having the IV needle inserted into her arm. She tried to close her eyes and block out the surroundings, to no avail. Her vital signs were too elevated for her to fall asleep. She felt as if the tight space were cutting off her air. Screaming wouldn't help. She had to endure the next sixty minutes any way she could.

It was bad enough having the MRI done on her breasts. Having her head done was worse. The procedure required whatever part of the body being examined to be placed in the center of the machine. That meant her head had to go completely inside the tube. Once inside the machine, Karen couldn't move, but it didn't stop her from weeping.

"God, please be with me."

Tears rolled down her face and wet her ear.

"Help me to get through this." The table slid in a bit farther. "Why do I have to go through this alone?"

A sudden burst of calmness consumed Karen. Her mind was clear. The hour passed and not even Johnny dominated her thoughts.

Karen was happy to have the exam over. Driving home, she was feeling better than she had in the past few days. The headache had subsided to a faint discomfort. Saturday was rapidly approaching. She was ready to start preparing for the party. She made a mental note to stop by the caterer and finalize the menu. She also needed to order champagne and get balloons. *Oh, my goodness,* she thought. There was so much to do.

She pulled out a small piece of notepad paper from her purse and commenced to jot down a long list of to-do items. Planning and organizing. She was beginning to feel a little like her old self. It was a lifestyle she'd come to enjoy.

Karen pulled into the circular drive and wheeled around to the three-car garage after a full morning of running around. She was humming and singing a few tunes from her contemporary gospel CD. The day out had done her good. It was as if the weight had fallen away, giving her a brief reprieve. She pushed the automatic garage-door opener. While the door was opening, she began gathering her items together. Like a ton of bricks, it hit her.

"What am I doing?"

Her marriage was struggling dangerously near separation. She didn't know where they were headed. Where did an anniversary party fit into all of that? She shook her head in dismay and went inside the house.

She looked around the oversize kitchen as though the answer were magically written on the wall. She picked up the note left on the counter and immediately recognized it as Johnny's handwriting. She was eager to read it, knowing that they hadn't spoken since the dispute yesterday afternoon. Karen was expecting to see him when she arrived home from Connie's last night, but Johnny hadn't gotten in before her. She felt him crawl into bed sometime in the wee hours of the morning, and he was up and gone before she woke up.

Perhaps it was a note of apology. She quickly read it in hopes that it was.

Karen,

I have a major production problem in Tennessee. I'm heading back down there this afternoon. I expect to be gone several days. I'll give you a call when I get to the plant.

Johnny

"What! That's it?"

Karen was filled with anger and slammed the note onto the countertop.

"That's all he has to say. I can't believe he's leaving again."

Karen grabbed the phone and dialed Johnny's cell phone number with her heart pounding. She didn't know what she was going to say, but that didn't stop her.

The voice on the line said, "Welcome to the voice-mail system. . . ."

She hung up and dialed his office when the voice mail system answered.

"Good afternoon, Mr. Clark's office. How may I help you?"

"Hi, Sonja. This is Karen. I'm trying to catch up with Johnny."

"Oh, his flight left about ten minutes ago. I know he was heading home before he left," Sonja said with a tinge of confusion.

"I barely missed him," Karen quickly suggested, to eliminate any perception that she didn't know where her husband was at all times. "I was out running errands this morning. When I got back, I got his note."

Karen ended the call, determined not to let on to Sonja how angry she was at Johnny's abrupt departure. "Oh, well, I guess I missed my hubby. I'll just have to wait for him to give me a call from the plane."

CHAPTER 16

The succulent smell of hazelnut and vanilla engulfed the kitchen. Karen stirred a teaspoon of honey into her cup of hot tea. She had longed for a relaxing moment after the hectic morning of errands and the MRI. She slid onto the chaise longue in the family room, careful not to spill a drop of tea. Party plans were under way and the tests were done. The day was looking up. Johnny was the only element that was driving her blood pressure up.

When the phone rang, Karen was ready to give Johnny a piece of her mind.

"This is Dr. Costas's office. The doctor would like to see you."

"Could you tell me what she wants to see me for, please?" Karen was worried. She knew that every time the doctor had asked her to come into the office after a series of tests, it wasn't good news.

"To go over your MRI results."

"When?"

"This afternoon, let's say around two-thirty?"

Karen looked at her watch.

"It's almost two o'clock now."

"I know this is pretty short notice, but I know she would like to see you today. Her schedule is pretty full the rest of the week."

"Fine," Karen conceded. "I'm on my way."

Ten minutes wouldn't make a difference. Karen decided to clutch this rare bit of peace before facing the doctor. She sipped the tea and savored the warm feeling that it gave her insides. She took her time, got dressed, and headed out to get whatever news there was.

Dr. Costas kept pretty close to her schedule. It was no surprise for Karen when the nurse took her into the doctor's office right away. Karen made herself as comfortable as she could while waiting.

She couldn't help but notice the brightly colored poster that said, *Prescreening can save your life—how much do you really know about cancer?* Karen went on to read the bold highlights.

- Over 95 percent of individuals diagnosed with breast cancer in the earliest stage live beyond five years
- 70 percent of lumps found in breasts are benign
- More white women get breast cancer, but more black women die from late diagnosis
- Men and women are subject to both breast and colon cancer
- Nine out of ten incidents of colon cancer could be prevented if polyps are detected and removed in the early stage
- Ovarian cancer is not easily detected
- Cervical cancer of the uterus is detectable through a routine Pap smear
- Twice as many black men die from prostate cancer than white men
- Lung cancer now kills more women each year than breast cancer
- One-third of all cancers could be eliminated with modifications in lifestyle and diet, not even counting smoking

Karen realized how much she didn't know about the other forms of cancer. She made a mental note to talk to Johnny about getting prescreened for colon and prostate cancers. She didn't consider telling him to check for breast cancer, knowing that he was too macho even to consider the thought of getting a "woman's disease." It would be hard enough to talk him into getting his prostate and colon checked, seeing that it had to be done through the rectum.

The physician entered the room dressed in a white lab coat.

"Doctor! I didn't expect to hear from you this fast."

"I wanted to get back with you as soon as possible, so I put a rush on the tests."

Karen was both reluctant and, at the same time, eager to get the results. Once and for all she wanted to put her fears to rest. A clean bill of health was what she hoped for. "Remember Tina?"

"Of course. How is she doing?"

"She's fine. We were together last night for dinner."

"Wonderful. We were fortunate with her case."

"That's what I want. The same results that she's had."

"That's what I'd like for you too, Karen. About your test . . . I've looked at the results from the MRI. It looks like you still have the same small tumor lodged near your brain."

"Tumor!"

"Karen, calm down. Did you hear what I said?"

"What?"

"I said that it's still small. As a matter of fact, it doesn't appear to have grown or moved any. That's good news. So long as it hasn't changed, it's best for us to leave it alone."

Dr. Costas's diagnosis didn't comfort Karen. Connie's struggle heightened Karen's fear about tumors. Doing nothing left Karen concerned. She already felt horrible about not identifying her breast cancer earlier with self-exams. The concept of early detection and treatment was ingrained in her mind after battling the cancer for four years. She didn't see the tumor as an exception.

"So what does that mean for my headaches?"

"It means I need to do some other tests."

"More tests. Why? What else can we test?"

"Karen, the MRI results are good news. However, the blood tests didn't come back as well as I would have liked."

"What do you mean?"

"Your white counts are definitely up."

Karen slumped in her chair and braced herself for whatever Dr. Costas was about to say.

"I'm concerned that your cancer might be back."

Karen didn't say a word. She let Dr. Costas's words saturate her inner soul. Her body was numb. Getting the bad news wasn't an unfamiliar pill for Karen but was no easier to swallow this time around. She knew how often breast cancer recurred in women. Her prayer was not to be one of those patients who yo-yoed in and out of remission.

"Karen, are you okay?"

"Um-hmmm."

She couldn't speak. It required too much energy and would be just the impetus needed to convert the lump in her throat to streaming tears. Crying wasn't something she wanted to do with Dr. Costas in the room.

The doctor rolled the stool over to Karen and took her hand. "I know this is difficult."

Karen remained quiet. She was still in shock.

Dr. Costas could tell Karen was struggling with the news. She wanted to encourage her as best she could under the circumstances.

"Karen, we need to jump on this right away. We have been successful with your treatment in the past. Timing is key."

"What do I have to do?"

"I have made arrangements for you to be admitted to Wayne State University this afternoon."

"That soon!"

"We can't waste any time in getting a clear diagnosis. You will feel better when some of the uncertainty is addressed. If it turns out that we're dealing with the cancer again, I want to know. You know that our best weapon against this cancer is early detection and stiff treatment."

Karen was fidgeting in her seat. She jumped up and paced the room.

"Hospital! I can't go to the hospital today. What about my children? I need to make arrangements for them."

She was becoming more frantic.

"I don't have anyone to take care of them. Johnny's out of town. I have to find out when he's coming back."

"All right, Karen, but we can't wait too long to get the additional tests done. It may come back negative, but with your history, well, I . . ."

"What?"

"Like I said, I prefer to get a jump on the rest of the tests and treatment, if necessary."

"I have to take care of some things at home first."

"When can you check in to the hospital?"

Karen wrung her sweaty palms together and rubbed them on her paper-covered knees. "Tomorrow. I promise to go tomorrow."

"Good. I will make the necessary arrangements. I'll also update your general practitioner on what's happening."

"How long will I have to stay in the hospital?"

"I can't say for sure, but prepare to be there at least several nights."

The ride home was long and slow. The route that Karen had taken so many times to get home from the doctor's office seemed foreign today. A million thoughts and fears flooded her mind. It was a place she had hoped to never visit again. God hadn't been at the forefront of her most recent thoughts, but it looked like that would be changing.

CHAPTER 17

Johnny hadn't gotten the production problem at the plant under control, but his little trip away from home was turning out to be the space he needed to collect his thoughts.

He wasn't sure what was going on with him and Karen. One issue was certain: he was fed up with the bickering. What would it be like to leave Karen? When he had mentioned separation the other day she hadn't responded. Johnny leaned back in his seat and tried to find a relaxing position. In his gut, he didn't see her leaving regardless of how bad it got between them. It didn't surprise him. She enjoyed the accolades that came with being the Clarks, the jet-setting couple living in a big house situated on a couple of acres, with three adorable children to boot.

He hated how difficult it was for her to make tough decisions. Make a decision and deal with the consequences was his philosophy. Her uncertainty was expected. On this rare occasion, Johnny wasn't sure what he wanted. Separation seemed like an option; then again, was it? Maybe it was time to make a move. Leaving the kids would be hard. Abandoning his children was the act of a coward. He would still provide for them. But taking care of the finances for two households would require planning. There was so much that would have to be worked out. Perhaps staying was easier. He wondered if it was possible to hang in there at least until Elizabeth went to college. Before he got too far down that road, he revisited his immediate needs. Karen hadn't given any indication that she wanted to stay in the marriage, but she wasn't doing what it took to keep it together. He was tired of waiting around. If she didn't want him in her bed, there were others who did.

The thought of Ms. Jones brought a smile to his face. The time they had spent together had been memorable, both positively and negatively for him. It had been entirely painful for everyone else, especially for Karen and the kids. Curiosity, a couple shots of Hennessy, and an empty bed got the best of him. He dialed directory assistance. Tyrone's advice was tossed aside. Johnny barreled into dangerous territory.

"Directory assistance for what city and state?"

Johnny responded to the automated voice system, "Rockford, Illinois."

"Thank you, what listing?"

"Isabelle Jones on Avon."

"Please hold for the operator to give you that number. Thank you."

Johnny scribbled the number down. After taking the initiative to get it, he didn't know exactly what to do with it. He went back and forth on what to do. He picked up the receiver and attempted to dial the number three times, never completing the call. The fourth time around he let it go through.

The phone began to ring and all of a sudden it dawned on Johnny that he didn't know what to say. He searched for words but none came. It had been a long time since he and Isabelle had spoken. The phone rang four times and went into a voice message.

"Hi," spoke the soft and sultry voice, "leave a message. Thank you."

Johnny hadn't been sure that she was still in Rockford after all these years. Hearing the voice on the message left no doubt.

"Um . . ." He paused, searching for a suitable message to leave. "Hi, um." It was difficult pulling out words. Perhaps if she'd answered in person, it would have been easier. Tipsy or not, Johnny knew that Ms. Jones was not a situation to be toyed with. Making one call could start an avalanche of events that he might not be able to handle. With the exception of a few grunts, he hung up without saying anything and wondered if Isabelle had caller ID.

He pulled out his cell phone without hesitation. It was still early in the evening. There was a good chance that Annette was already home from work. He closed his eyes and pressed his thumb against his forehead. He was involved with Annette for one purpose. Calling her on a business trip could send the wrong message. It would be better to call her when he got back to Detroit. Perhaps he could visit with her on his way home. That would be the plan.

CHAPTER 18

"Mommy," Chelle whispered, wanting to wake Karen but not startle her.

"Hmmm," responded her semiawakened mom. Karen recognized the voices of her little ones, regardless of how groggy she was.

"We're getting ready to go to school."

Karen prided herself on being a mother. Lately she had been distracted and had left the girls to be more self-reliant than usual. Thank goodness Chelle was able to help out and give her mother a little time to deal with her dilemmas.

"Did you eat something for breakfast?"

"Yes," Chelle responded.

Elizabeth wasn't going to be left out of whatever conversation was going on with her mom. She loved the doses of attention that Karen dished out. She spoke up before Chelle could finish: "We ate cereal again."

Elizabeth jumped on Johnny's side of the bed to get a closer connection with her mom. Whenever her daddy was gone, she saw it as a license to fill the empty spot.

"Chelle wouldn't let me have any more juice."

"You had two glasses. That's enough for one morning," Chelle firmly instructed.

Elizabeth was hoping Karen might override the older sister's restrictions.

"Two whole glasses?" Karen affectionately tickled Elizabeth's tummy and her daughter let out a giggle. "You're going to float away. Don't you think two glasses is probably enough, Bethy?"

The child continued to giggle. "Okay, okay, yes."

"Elizabeth, let's go. Let Mommy sleep."

"But I didn't see you after dinner last night," Elizabeth reminded her mom.

"I know, sweetie. Mommy was tired."

"Oh, yeah, Mommy, Daddy called."

"When?"

"Right after you fell asleep. He told me not to wake you up."

"Convenient," Karen said under her breath.

"What did you say, Mom?"

"Nothing."

She sat up and opened her arms for both kids to embrace her. Elizabeth didn't hesitate for a minute.

"I'm driving you to school today."

"Yeaaaaah," Elizabeth screamed.

"Mom, you don't have to," Chelle said.

"I want to, honey. I need to talk to you both." She paused to get herself together and to hide her fear.

"I'm not feeling well."

"You want me to stay home with you today?" Chelle offered.

"Me too?" Elizabeth jumped in. Nothing was happening without her.

"No, no, my sweethearts. I have to go to the hospital."

"Oh, Mommy, not the hospital." Chelle was saddened in remembrance of how afraid she was four years ago when her mother went to the hospital.

Elizabeth was unusually quiet.

Karen pulled her daughters tight to her chest and squeezed them unrelentingly. She kissed the girls on their foreheads and whispered, "Shhhhh. It's going to be okay, babies."

"How long do you have to be there?" Chelle wanted to know.

"I'll only be gone a few days for some tests. Nothing major."

"Can I come and see you this time? I'm old enough now," Elizabeth said.

She hadn't understood the severity of her mother's illness four years ago. She was barely four years old at the time. All Elizabeth knew was that she couldn't visit her mom in the hospital like Erick and Chelle. Everyone said she was too little. She remembered how much she missed her mom.

Karen tried to console her worried daughters but wasn't able to abate their tears.

"When do you have to go?"

"Today."

Karen wanted to shield the girls from as much as possible. At the same time, she was pleased with how responsible and mature Chelle was. Karen opted to be honest and trust her daughter with difficult news.

"I'm going right after I take you two to school. Don't worry. Daddy's coming home." Karen feathered Chelle's hair back from her face. "He'll probably pick you up and let you come visit me this evening. Would that be okay?"

Chelle nodded with tears slowly rolling down her cheeks.

"Okay, let's get ready to go, young ladies."

Karen tried to get up from the bed. Neither girl would let her move.

"Sweethearts, it's going to be all right."

Karen cupped her hands around Chelle's face and looked her in the eye.

"I love you, Chelle, baby."

Elizabeth wrapped her arms around Karen's waist, not quite able to reach all the way around. The three stayed huddled together for several more moments before making a move.

Karen finally managed to tear herself away from the girls long enough to get dressed and get them to school. Normally only one of the girls would sit in the front seat, but today was different. Both slid into the long front seat and gave Karen minimal breathing space. Each of the girls savored every inch of the ride to school with their mom.

The car eventually pulled up to the private school. Karen put the car in park and turned to look at her daughters. Her eyes were watery but her voice was clear. Karen knew the girls needed to sense that she wasn't afraid and that everything really was going to be all right. She embraced the two girls, with Elizabeth getting securely squished in the middle.

"Aunt Tina will probably pick you up after school."

"Are we going to stay with her while you're in the hospital?" Elizabeth asked.

"No, baby. Daddy should be home this evening. In case he can't get back right away, you might have to stay overnight with Aunt Tina. We'll see. Either way, I will call the school office and let them know who's going to be picking you up. Okay, sweethearts?" She kissed both girls on the cheek. "I'll be back home before you know it. Now go on. Don't be late for class."

"Mommy, I'll walk Elizabeth to the lower school before I go up to mine."

"Thanks, sweetie. You two are beautiful, wonderful young ladies. I am so proud of you both."

Karen knew she couldn't hold the tears back much longer. She hurried the girls out of the car and on their way. "Let's go, girls. I'll talk to you this evening."

"Bye, Mommy. I love you," Elizabeth blurted.

"I love you too, Mom," Chelle softly echoed, and closed the door.

Karen watched the girls walk toward the school. Leaving them was painful. Thank goodness she only had to say good-bye once. She drove two blocks from the school and had to pull over. The tears were clouding her vision.

After she got herself together, Karen pulled away. There were quite a few things she needed to do before heading to the hospital. She needed to get groceries, a few toiletries, and most important, get the girls' care squared away. She would have liked to do a couple loads of laundry but knew there wasn't going to be time. The girls would have to handle that alone this week.

She was at least going to cook a decent meal for the family before leaving. She made enough for several days, figuring that the leftovers would last until she got back home.

The time quickly ticked away as Karen completed her errands and packed a bag for the hospital. The only item left was to cancel the anniversary party and to touch base with Johnny. She needed to make sure that he could come home for the girls. Karen had paged him several times during the day. According to the secretary, his schedule included a closed-door session for the entire morning. There was no way for her to get through.

Karen glanced at the time on the kitchen clock. "I should get out of here by one."

She set the pot of turkey meatballs in the refrigerator. The phone rang just as she was tossing the salad. She wiped the residual dressing from her fingers and hurried to the phone.

"Hello?"

"Hi, Karen."

"Johnny, thank goodness you called."

"I got all of your pages. There's a big problem I'm handling down here. We've been in a meeting all morning."

"I know. Sonja told me."

There was a brief moment of silence. The two still weren't on an even keel.

"Karen, I called you last night, but you were asleep."

"I know. Chelle told me."

Johnny was unprepared for Karen's calm voice. He expected her to be ranting and raving about his going out of town without any prior notice. It was usually a no-win situation. When he neglected to forewarn her about quick trips, she would make a fuss about it. When he did tell her, she still made a fuss. It was an argument either way. He waited for her to get started.

"Johnny . . ." She paused and took a deep breath. "Dr. Costas wants me to check into the hospital this afternoon, and I need you to come home for the girls."

"The hospital! For what?"

"For one, to see what's causing my headaches. And there's also the chance that the cancer might be back. She wants to run more tests."

"Back again! Is that possible, even though your breasts are already gone?"

"I don't know. I guess."

"How do you feel?"

"How do you think I feel? I'm scared to death. I can't go through it all over again. I don't know if I can take it."

Johnny wouldn't say it, but he felt the exact same way. The thought of replaying the cancer treatment all over again was a devastating blow.

Karen felt emotionally vulnerable but refused to break down on the phone with Johnny. His lack of compassion was a pill she didn't feel like swallowing.

"Do you know how long you'll be in the hospital?"

"Not really. Maybe a couple of days, depending on the test results."

Johnny sighed.

"When can you come home, Johnny? The girls need you."

"I'll have to wind things up here and come back tonight."

"Will you be finished with whatever you're working on down there?"

"I don't know."

"What are you going to do if you're not finished?"

"It's not an option, Karen. I'll just have to come back. Somebody has to be there with the girls. I'll do what I have to do."

"Thank you, Johnny. I feel so much better knowing you will be here. They were upset this morning when I took them to school."

"Karen, you don't have to thank me for taking care of my kids. You make it seem like I'm doing you a favor. I'm not. Those are my children too, and regardless of what happens with us, I will always love them and take care of them."

"I'm not worried about that, Johnny. I've always said that you are a good father. I can't deny that."

"Anyway, I won't get in until late tonight. Is there any way that Connie could get the kids and keep them until I get home?"

"I don't think so. You know she isn't driving anymore."

"Nah, I didn't know, but all right. I would ask Tyrone to pick the girls up, but I know he's downtown today. There's no way he'll get back out to the burbs in time to pick them up." Johnny seemed to be at a loss for options.

"I'll call Tina. She's picked them up before."

"Tina!" He didn't elaborate on his thoughts.

"She'll keep them until you get home." Karen knew Johnny wasn't thrilled with the arrangement, but what else could she do?

"I'll pick them up when I get in," he conceded. "Just make sure she doesn't have a lot of mouth when I go get the girls. I won't be in any mood to hear it." Johnny felt that he already had enough on his mind to keep his own blood pressure up without any help from Tina. "I don't need to hear what that hypocritical witch has to say."

"Well, I'm just glad she's able to get the girls for us. She'll probably bring them to the hospital after school."

"I'd rather pick them up there, but"—he paused—"there's no guarantee that I'll be back before visiting time is over."

"I'm sure you'll work it out with Tina."

Karen was tired of being the go-between for Johnny and Tina's spats. She wasn't going to waste her energy trying to smooth the tension between the two. She decided to let it be their problem and no longer hers. She had plenty of her own issues to handle.

"Yeah, right."

"Oh, I'm not expecting Erick to call, since he called last week. But if he does, don't tell him what's going on with me. I'd rather go in and get back out of the hospital before telling him anything."

"I guess you're right. We shouldn't get him all worried before we find out more. He can't do anything from Europe anyway," he said.

"I agree." She checked her watch. The time was ticking away. "I'd better get ready to go. I should be checking in before two."

"Well, I'll let you know when I get into town tonight."

It wasn't the best of times for the couple. Karen was not comfortable going into the hospital on such shaky ground with Johnny.

"I love you."

"You take care of yourself, and I'll see you soon," was all Johnny could muster.

Karen felt rejection from Johnny's response, but not bewilderment.

"Fine. I'll see you soon."

CHAPTER 19

Karen had survived both the boatload of paperwork and the relentless poking and prodding associated with her preadmission process. She dreaded her stays in the hospital. It hadn't become old hat.

"All done, Mrs. Clark. Let me find out your room number and order a wheelchair. We'll have you on your way in a few minutes."

The nurse was full of pleasantries. It wasn't adequate to convert the grim look on Karen's face. Her established routine was to come into the hospital, get the treatment over with, and get back home. She felt strange this time.

Maybe the rest will do me some good, she thought. Johnny would have to keep up with his job, the house, and the girls. It would be good for him. It was something Karen had done for years with little to no appreciation from her husband.

"Am I going to the cancer wing?"

The nurse flipped through the chart looking for some indication of where the doctor wanted Karen.

"You know, I'm not sure. It looks like Dr. Costas has you here for some tests. Looks like you're going to the fourth-floor B wing."

Karen squinted her eyes. Her frequent visits to the hospital made her intimately familiar with the cancer sections. B wing wasn't one of her usual stops.

"Fourth-floor B wing? Why am I going there? That's not the cancer wing."

"I know, Mrs. Clark. The hospital is full, and we won't have any rooms available on the A wing for a few days. You'll probably be on the B wing first, and more than likely you'll get moved to another room in a few days."

"So what's going to happen with me in the meantime?"

"Judging from the paperwork, it looks like your doctor wants the tests done first."

"Which tests am I having?"

The nurse was careful not to exceed her authority and give Karen answers that conflicted with the doctor.

"Did you have a biopsy or a CAT scan already?"

"No."

"I imagine that's what the doctor will order up first, but I'm not sure. You'll have to confirm that yourself."

The nurse perused the chart one more time before sending Karen on her way with the orderly.

Karen sat limp and quiet on the wheelchair-powered ride. It was bad enough struggling with the cancer she knew about. Now there was the added threat of more unknowns. *What more?* she pondered.

The orderly wheeled in and out of elevators, up and down corridors, making his way to the fourth floor B wing. He pulled up to a room across from the nurse's station and stopped. He double-checked the chart to make sure it was the right room.

"Yep, this is it, room four-oh-seven."

He wheeled the chair into the room. The curtain was partially drawn, making it difficult to see the other patient.

"This isn't the right room. I'm supposed to be in a single."

The confused orderly looked at the chart again.

"No, this is the room they have down for you."

"Can't be. I asked for a single."

"I don't know what to say. This is what they have down."

The happy-go-lucky orderly didn't know what to do. "They probably put you in here because all of the single rooms are filled. Matter of fact, this whole wing is full. This is the only bed left."

The orderly sensed Karen's discontent.

"If you want, I can check with admissions to see what they can do."

"No, that's all right."

"Karen Clark, what are you doing here?" a voice echoed from the other side of the hospital room.

She stretched her neck from the wheelchair seat to see who could possibly know her in such an inopportune place.

"Reverend Lane! What a surprise! What are you doing here?"

He glanced over at the patient in the hospital bed. The curtain was blocking Karen's view.

"I'm visiting with Mother Walker."

"Ms. Emma Walker from church?"

"Pull the curtain back so I'ze can see ya," a strong voice piped up.

The orderly honored the old lady's request.

"Now, that's a heap better." The older woman adjusted the pearl-colored glasses on her nose. "Karen Clark, is that you, chile?"

"Yes, ma'am. It's me."

"Well, I'ze glad and I'ze ain't so glad to see ya." She chuckled at her own humor. "I'm um glad to see ya, but ain't glad to see ya in this here hospital."

"Yes, Ms. Walker. Likewise."

"Now, chile, ya know better'n to call me Ms. Walker. Big Mama, Mother Walker, or even Ms. Emma do fine by me."

"Okay, Ms. Emma." The lighthearted dialogue brought a smile to Karen's face.

"Excuse me, Mrs. Clark, I need to get back downstairs. Is there anything you need before I leave?" the young orderly asked.

"No, I'm all set. Thanks."

"You're welcome. Push the nurse's call button if you need anything."

Karen sat on the side of her bed facing Mother Walker.

"How you doing, Ms. Emma?"

"I'ze fine as can be. I'm going home in a few days."

"Good for you."

"We're happy to have her going home," Reverend Lane added.

Mother Walker was known in the church as a mighty prayer warrior. She didn't have much in the way of formal education. Her wisdom came from seventy years of living. After her husband died, she dedicated her life to serving the Lord and helping his people. It was often said that she had a hot line that rang directly to God. She was able to give support without judgment, and it drew individuals to her. Mother Walker was the one called on day and night whenever there was someone in the church who had problems and needed prayer.

Karen wasn't expecting help in the form of Ms. Emma, but there she was.

CHAPTER 20

Tina wanted to ensure that Connie was aware of Karen's trip to the hospital. The three had supported one another through physical battles. They had their differences, but when the situation got serious, pettiness got pushed aside.

Tyrone had recently bought Connie a telephone headset so that she wouldn't have to rush around trying to get the phone. Connie answered the ringing phone to find Tina on the other end.

"Hey, girl."

"Hi, Tina. I'm surprised to hear from you so early in the afternoon. Aren't you working today?"

"Yes, I am. I'm calling to see if you talked to Karen today."

"No, not today. Why?"

"Well, she called me a little while ago and asked if I could pick the girls up from school. She has to go back into the hospital."

"The hospital! For what?"

"Her cancer might be out of remission."

"Oh, no. When is she going to the hospital?"

"I think she left a little while ago."

"I wonder why she didn't call me?"

Tina had her speculations about why Karen hadn't told Connie. She knew Karen shielded Connie from bad news in case she was too emotionally fragile to handle it. Tina didn't share the same sentiment. She believed that Karen and Tyrone were doing Connie a disservice by constantly protecting her from certain situations. Tina felt that they were enabling her to continuously live in denial, even about her own medical condition.

"She probably didn't want you to make yourself sicker by worrying about her."

"Me! She's always worrying about me. I keep telling her that all I have is a few bad headaches from time to time. It's not like I'm an invalid or anything."

Tina shook her head. Why Connie's denial bothered her so much was unclear, but it was evident she had no intentions of being an enabler like Tyrone and Karen.

"I can see how she'd be worried about you. You've had those little headaches for quite a while—quite a long while."

Connie didn't respond to what Tina was trying to insinuate. She was able to block out the negativity that so often came from Tina without it impacting their friendship.

"That girl, why would she be thinking about me at a time like this? She needs to be focusing on herself right now and getting better."

"Humph." Tina was in full agreement. "You know that's how she is. Worrying about everybody and everything except herself."

"Well, if there's any way I can help you with the girls, let me know."

"Thanks, but I should be fine. They're only going to be with me for a few hours until their lying and cheating daddy gets back from Tennessee tonight."

"Tina, why do you have to say all of that?"

"Why not? It's the truth. He's no good, and I don't know why Karen puts up with him. Do you know that I caught him leaving the club with some woman last Friday night? What nerve! I'm sure he lied his way right out of it."

"I don't know what to say. I really hope they're able to work it out. They've been through enough, and I do believe they love each other."

"Love! You have got to be kidding. Nobody who's cheating on you loves you. The only person Johnny Clark loves is Johnny Clark. Karen might tell us a lot, but you'd best believe that she's not telling us everything," Tina said.

"I'm sure there's more to it than we know. We just have to be supportive."

"Yeah, right. You go right ahead. I'm being real about it. Johnny doesn't deserve any support from me. All he deserves is a kick to the curb, and that's all I have to say. I'm through with it."

"Okay. Well, like I said, let me know if there's anything—anything at all—that we can do. Tyrone and I will be available."

Connie was sad. She knew that Tina wouldn't have any appreciation for a long-term relationship until she dealt with her anger and feelings of rejection. Connie picked up the frame that sat next to the sofa. It held a picture of her and Tyrone embracing in front of a sidewalk café in Rome. She kissed her fingers and touched the framed picture. The conversation with Tina reminded her of how grateful and secure she was in her marriage. She decided to call and let Tyrone know how much he was adored. She could also tell him the news about Karen.

"Hi, honey. How's your day going?"

"It's wonderful now that I'm talking to you," Tyrone complimented. "Are you all right? Is something wrong?" Tyrone spent most of his time away from Connie worrying about her.

"I'm fine, honey. I'm calling about Karen."

"Why, what's up with her?"

"She's back in the hospital."

"Oh, no. When?"

"Apparently she just went this afternoon."

"I wonder if it's serious?"

"Tina told me that the cancer might be out of remission."

Tyrone sighed and slumped in his chair. Even though Karen wasn't his wife, he couldn't help but feel compassion for his best friend, Johnny. He had felt that moment of despair so many times with Connie's illness. The worst time was hearing that there had been a setback. Those words had a way of penetrating his flesh and drilling right down to the inner core of his heart and painfully severing all circulation to key organs in his body. That fleeting, lifeless moment had felt like an eternity to Tyrone. He was sure it would have no less impact on Johnny.

"Boy, this is tough. I'm going to check in with Johnny."

"Tina said that he's coming back from Tennessee this evening."

"I'll catch up with him this evening then."

"You are such a good friend, darling. Johnny is blessed to have you and so am I."

"No, baby, I'm the fortunate one, and I count my blessings every day." Tyrone seized every opportunity to flatter his wife. "I'm off to a meeting, if everything else is okay with you."

"Sure, honey, go on. I'll see you when you get home."

"I'll call you before I leave the office."

"Love you."

"I love you too."

Tyrone hung up with a smile on his face. Connie was an inspiration to him. She didn't wait around for a better day. She focused on making each day the best, as though it was her last. He saw her as someone who did more living while sick than most able-bodied people. Every day she found a reason to smile, and that made him happy. He would often say, "If she can find a reason to be happy every day, in spite of her pain and suffering, then who am I to feel down in the dumps?" Being around her had taught him that regardless of how bad the situation was, there was always somebody going through much worse. This was one of the happiest times in his life, even with Connie's illness. For the first time in his life, he knew what it meant to love unconditionally, to love so unprotectedly, and it felt good.

Halfway out of the office, he turned around, went back to the phone, and placed a call.

"You have reached the voice mailbox of John Clark. . . ."

Tyrone waited for the automated voice to spill out the rest of the greeting so that he could leave a message.

"Hey, Johnny, it's Tyrone. Hey, look here, partner; Connie told me about Karen going back into the hospital." He paused for a moment, twirling the minipack of Post-it notes on his desk. "Look, call me if you want to talk. I just want you to know that I'm here for you, partner. I'll catch you later."

CHAPTER 21

Johnny was exhausted from a long day of nonstop meetings and pressing issues at the manufacturing plant. He slung the hanging bag and his sports jacket into the backseat of the car and headed out of the airport parking lot. He slid his hand down his face. Last night it had seemed like a good idea to call Annette when he got to town and stop over for a quick visit. After fourteen hours of work and travel, it was no longer a consideration. Getting home and kicking off his shoes was the ticket.

He pressed the accelerator and made tracks down the Southfield Expressway. The faster he got to Tina's, the quicker his nightmare would be over. He dreaded having to pick the kids up from her. He rolled onto the street where she lived and was glad to see an empty spot. Since she rented the first floor of a duplex, he was able to see his car from her front door. He left it running as a reminder that he needed to get the kids quickly and get back on his way. He knocked on the door, hoping that Chelle would be the one to answer it.

Tina pulled back the corner of the curtain, saw Johnny, and cracked the door open.

"Where are the girls?"

"They're here."

"Tell them I said let's go."

Tina turned toward the living room and said in a soft voice, "Girls, your dad's here." She turned back to Johnny with a smirk. "So you're baby-sitting tonight, huh? Too bad. I know that it's probably going to mess up your little plans. Looks like the only play you'll be getting tonight is playing daddy."

"I'm not in the mood, Tina."

"Don't get all snippity and mad at me because you were cold-busted at the club last week."

"Stay out of my business. I'm not going to tell you again."

"Oh, and what are you going to do, make me? All that barking doesn't scare me. I'm not your wife."

"Oh, that's right. You're nobody's wife."

"You're pathetic."

"And you're a joke. I can't believe that I'm standing here wasting my time arguing with you." Johnny stuck his head in the crack and yelled for the girls to come on.

Chelle shouted toward the door that they were coming as soon as Elizabeth got out of the bathroom. Johnny and Tina continued their tiff in the meantime.

"The only person wasting time is Karen. She should have kicked you out a long time ago. Eventually she's going to get tired of you."

"Yeah, you'd like that, wouldn't you?"

"Um-hmmm."

"That's what I thought. Spoken just like the jealous woman that you are."

"Jealous about what?"

"Because I've never looked your way."

"Looked my way? You must be out of your mind. I can't stand being around you."

"That's what you say. But the truth is that I could chase women all week long and you can rest assured that I will never so much as glance your way. And you can't stand that, can you?"

"You have some nerve, you lying, cheating, no-'count dog. I'd rather be alone than to put up with some trifling excuse of a man who chases every skirt that comes his way."

"Whatever kind of a man I am, the fact remains that I don't want you. Then again, you're used to men not wanting you. What was your husband's name again? You know, the brother who got up and out of here like a squealing pig who'd been stuck under a fence?"

The girls were ready to go, and Tina widened the door opening to let them out. Johnny headed them toward the car. He was two steps behind.

"You good-for-nothing," she yelled, and slammed the door, not wanting the girls to overhear any of her vulgarity.

Johnny chuckled. "Have a nice day," he said, walking away, relishing the victory he had gotten over Tina with the remark about her husband.

CHAPTER 22

Light crept into the cold hospital room. Karen slept with the covers clutched tightly under her chin, clinging to the futile warmth. She chose not to ask for more blankets. A little discomfort was the reminder she needed that this was not home.

The nurse's stethoscope clicked against the electronic thermometer that she had jammed into her pocket.

The noise startled Karen, and her eyes opened slowly. She looked around the room in confusion, not able to figure out where she was.

"Good morning, Mrs. Clark," the nurse greeted, while reading over Karen's chart and pulling back the curtain that separated her side of the room from the other patient.

Karen gradually got her bearings and relaxed a bit.

The nurse placed her cold hand on Karen's pulse. Karen didn't flinch. The nurse read the temperature on the thermometer and jotted notes onto the chart.

"Your breakfast should be here in a few minutes."

The small talk didn't generate a response from Karen. She was silent while the nurse went through the motions.

"When is my doctor coming in?"

"I don't know. Let's see here, who is your doctor?"

She leafed through the clipboard of papers. Karen could have jumped in with the doctor's name and saved the nurse some searching, but she was quite despondent.

"Dr. Costas. She hasn't come through yet. I'm not sure what time she gets to the hospital. I'm sure she'll be in sometime soon."

The nurse slid the dividing curtain back.

"Good morning, Ms. Walker."

"Morning. How ya feeling this fine morning?"

"Why, I'm just fine. But I should be asking you how you're feeling. You're the patient."

"I'ze might be the patient, but I'ze ain't claiming no sickness. I'ze feel good even when I'ze don't feel too good. It's all in whatcha believe."

The nurse smiled.

"That's a good attitude, Ms. Walker. I'll be back with your medicine."

Karen elevated her head with the bed's remote.

"Good morning, Ms. Emma."

"Morning, chile. Didn't seem like ya rested too well. I heared ya tossing and turning in ya sleep last night."

"Nah, Ms. Emma. I didn't sleep too well."

"What's on ya mind, chile? What's worrying ya?"

Karen knew Ms. Emma from her role as a teacher in the church. Many respected her wisdom and consistently supportive attitude. So Karen felt comfortable sharing some of her heart's grief.

"I have so much on my mind." She sighed. "I miss my kids."

That wasn't all Karen was thinking about. She was in distress about her marriage, but didn't feel comfortable enough revealing that tidbit with Ms. Emma.

"Umm. I know how it is to miss ya chile. My grandbaby, Rachel, lives in Chicago. Sometimes I sho' miss her, but it don't cause me to toss and turn all night."

Ms. Emma had seen and done a lot of things in her lifetime. God had given her compassion for others that seemed to go deeper than surface chitchat. She had a way of making a person comfortable enough to lower their guard and open up.

"Ya sho' it ain't something else on ya mind, chile? What is it that's worrying ya?"

"Yes, there is something on my mind." Karen chose her words carefully. "It's my cancer. It might be back, and I'm scared."

Karen was choked up and the words didn't glide out. She was upset and out of sorts.

Yet nothing seemed to excite Ms. Emma. Her tone remained calm and rational.

"Cancer."

Karen was expecting some superficial words of encouragement, which was what she expected to hear once a person knew she had the big C. Not so with Ms. Emma.

"What ya scared about, chile?"

It was not a question Karen was accustomed to hearing. The answer seemed obvious.

"I'm scared of getting sicker and maybe even dying. I'm afraid my kids will be left without a mother." She sobbed softly. "I feel bad."

"'Bout being sick?"

"No, about getting sick."

"Why ya feel bad 'bout that? Ain't nothing you could do 'bout that."

Ms. Emma couldn't see it, but Karen was wiping the tears away.

"I feel like I've let my children down. This cancer is my fault."

"How ya see it being ya fault?"

"Because" was all she could utter past the lump in her throat. It took a few moments before she could get more words through. "I could have prevented this." She began to babble. "I didn't think much about breast cancer—no reason to. My family didn't have a history of cancer. My mother didn't have breast cancer, and neither of my grandmothers had it before they died either. I didn't do self-exams and didn't get a mammogram. I was too young to even think about it. I was planning to get one when I turned forty. I never got the chance. I ended up getting cancer at thirty-five." Karen got choked up. "If only I'd been more in tune with my body."

"Ya feel like ya shoulda done mo'?"

"Yes, I do. I could have done self-exams. If I had checked my breasts monthly, like they recommend, I wouldn't be going through this again and again, and now again. When will it stop?"

"Karen, ya can't give up on the Lord. I knows ya ain't feeling good 'bout the ways thangs is going right now, but don't let that make ya waiver in ya faith."

Karen continued to sob softly. She heard Big Mama's words of encouragement but was in no emotional condition to truly receive them.

"Ms. Emma, I'm tired. I'm just tired of suffering through this cancer. Every time I think I've licked it, it comes back. I don't think I can take any more of this. I'm worn out."

"Baby, ya can't lose hope. Ya have to speak life into ya bones. Proverbs seventeen and twenty-two says that a merry heart doeth good like a medicine, but a broken spirit drieth the bones." Big Mama was known for pulling a scripture out of the Bible at just the right time to help someone through a hard situation.

"Ms. Emma, I've prayed about it for a long time. Sometimes it seems like God has given me all that he's going to."

"Nonsense. As much as He loves ya, chile, He ain't never gon' get tired of ya needing Him and asking Him for help. I'm an old woman, close to going on to glory, but I knows what I'm talkin' 'bout."

"I don't even know what to ask Him for anymore, Mother. I've asked for healing in my body, in my marriage, and in my heart. None of them are fixed. Looks like they keep getting worse."

"Everybody's got a cross to bear. We each got some dark times in our lives. We gon' have some hurt and some pain, but praise be to God that after the darkness comes the light."

"I've had my fair share of darkness. Why do I have to keep getting cancer over and over? Why me?"

"I suspect that's what Job asked God. God probably answered ol' Job and said, why not you? We don't always know the ways of the Lord, but we knows from the Word that He has a plan for us and all things work together for good."

"What's good about dealing with an illness that I can't seem to beat?"

"He don't put no mo' on ya than ya can bear."

"Well, I don't even know what else I can do."

"Oh, glory," the old woman belted out with joy. "Chile, Apostle Paul said in Ephesians that when ya done all that ya know how to do, then ya need to just stand still." Big Mama spoke with confidence and passion. "Stand and believe that God is going to move on ya behalf. Nothing is too hard for God."

"I don't know how much farther I can go living like this."

"Ya know, it ain't always about ya. Sometimes he choose ya to fill shoes that no one else can fill."

"I don't feel like filling shoes for anybody."

"That's how ya feel right now. But what if God heals ya from this cancer? What if ya go on to be a witness to many, many mo' women who might not know about having hope in Jesus?"

"I don't know." Karen respected Big Mama's words of wisdom. Yet nothing she said seemed to penetrate her wall of sorrow. "I feel so far from the Lord. I got so caught up in my home life and my marriage and the kids. You name it. It's funny that years ago, when we had nothing, I loved the Lord and centered my life on Him. It seemed like the more money we made, the less I talked to God. Maybe this is my punishment."

"Oh, no. I can't letcha believe that. No, no. God is a father who loves His children. It ain't His desire to cause ya hurt and pain. In the book of John, it says that He wants to give ya life, and mo' abundantly."

"The only abundant thing I have is fear and guilt."

"Chile, you need a heavy dose of God's peace and joy."

"How can I feel peace, let alone joy, in the middle of all of this?"

"Cuz his peace and ya circumstance ain't got nothing to do with each other. It ain't like ya gots to have one or the other. You can have 'em both at the same time."

Karen's struggle with her spirituality left her unsure as to whether or not the joy and peace Mother Walker was speaking about was achievable.

"I can't even imagine feeling good right now. I don't think that it's humanly possible."

"Oh, let me tell ya 'bout having peace and unspeakable joy in the midst of the storm. That's my testimony, to count it all joy. No matter what ya going through, God's mercy and grace is enough to make ya wanna leap up for joy way down inside yaself."

"Maybe it's just my time, Ms. Emma."

"Whatcha mean, ya time?"

"My time to let go. Why keep going around and around in circles like a dog chasing his tail?"

"Karen, now I know ya know better'n that. Not every sickness is unto death. Chile, ya done lost ya hope. The Word says that through the comfort of the scripture, ya might have hope. God done set the choice of life and death before ya. Ya the only one who can choose whicha way to go. Think about those precious babies of yourn. They needs their mama."

A knock on the door interrupted the women.

A woman entered the room with a tall, slim-figured man close behind. The two looked surprised to see another patient in the room. They said hello as they passed Karen's bed.

"Hi, Mama," greeted the young lady once she walked up to Ms. Emma's bed and gave her a hug.

"Whatcha doing out here so early?" Ms. Emma asked the two.

"We wanted to see you," the tall gentleman answered.

"Rachel, this is one of the women from my church. Karen, this my grandbaby, and that handsome young man is just like my grandchild too."

Karen smiled at the couple.

"Rachel? Ah, Ms. Emma has told me about her granddaughter in Chicago. Nice to meet you."

"How are you feeling today?" Rachel asked Karen.

"I'm getting by."

"Now, what I tell ya? Ya ain't just getting by. Ya delivered. Ya got to speak with authority and life."

Rachel jumped in, "Speak it like you mean it."

Rachel and the man chuckled.

"You know your grandmother, huh?"

Rachel leaned over and laid her head next to Big Mama. "Yes, ma'am, I know my grandmama. Don't I, Big Mama?"

"Umm-hmmm."

"Big Mama, we're going back to Chicago today, since you're doing so much better. Neal needs to get back, and I probably should too."

"I told you to go on home. God here with me. Ain't no need in ya worrying yaself. I'm just fine. Ya either, Neal. Ya go on back home now, ya hear? I know ya gots a lot of work to do with that big job of yourn."

"Big Mama, the most important thing in the world to me right now is being here with you and Rachel."

"That's so nice to see how much you care about your grandmother. Boy, you don't see that much anymore," Karen said.

"I love my Big Mama," Rachel said.

"She ain't so hot on ol' Grandma when I gives advice about her menfolk."

"Big Mama, let's not go there."

"Are the two of you a couple?" Karen looked slightly confused.

Neal smiled.

"People often think that"—Rachel glanced at Neal—"but we're not. We're close friends."

"We're connected at the hip, right, Rach?"

Big Mama didn't wait for Rachel to answer. She cut in. "That's sho' right."

Rachel had heard that song and dance a thousand times. She pushed on to another subject.

"I'll be back next weekend, Big Mama."

"Ain't no need for ya to be running up and down that road to look after me. I done told y'all I'm going to be just fine. Ya need to get home and look after yaself now. Y'all might as well go on and get on the road. Don't wait for the dark to catcha up here."

"You know Rachel isn't going to leave until she's spoken to every doctor and nurse in the hospital about you, Big Mama."

"Ain't no doctor can tell me different once God done told me it's all right."

"Okay, Big Mama, but Neal's right. I'm not leaving this hospital until I know for sure that you're doing as well as you say you are."

Big Mama squeezed Rachel's hand.

"I knows ya care, chile, but ya don't need be doing all that worrying now. You gonna have to take good care of yaself now, ya hear me? Stop all that worrying. Don't help matters no way."

Big Mama looked over at Neal, who was sitting on a chair near the foot of her bed.

"I'm looking to ya to help take care of my chile once ya get back to Chicago, 'cause I knows how hardheaded she can be."

Neal chuckled. "You know that I will."

Rachel smiled and shook her head. It was amusing for her to hear Neal and Big Mama reference her safety as if she weren't in the room. She didn't bother to comment. It would do no good. Rachel appreciated that these were two people who always had her best interest at heart.

So too was it with Big Mama. She was determined to see after Karen whether she approved or not.

CHAPTER 23

The early part of the day had been packed with tests on Karen's breast area. She was left feeling worn out for the afternoon. She tried to shut down and feel sorry for herself, but Big Mama wouldn't allow it. She continued to encourage Karen and to boost her spirit.

"Ms. Emma, I'm sorry to see you go home. It's been such a blessing to have someone to talk to."

"I'ze glad I'ze was here with ya. Don't think ya gots put in this here room by accident."

Karen smiled, remembering how much she had complained about not having a private room when she first arrived. Thank goodness she ended up with Big Mama.

"God made a way for ya to be put in here with me. Now I'ze going home, but I'ze be back to see ya, chile. Reckon I'll get some of the folks from church to come back out here with me."

Big Mama slowly walked over to Karen's bed and patted her hand. "I'ze sho' gon' come see ya, and I'ze gon' keep ya in my prayers."

"Thank you, Ms. Emma. I definitely appreciate that." Karen admired Big Mama's spiritual walk. "You think you could say a word of prayer for me before you go?"

"Yes, ma'am. I'ze don't turn down a chance to go before God on account of somebody."

Karen wasn't feeling too good about praying, but found herself embracing the words of Big Mama.

Time served in the hospital was slow and boring to Karen, especially with Big Mama gone. She drifted in and out of sleep the rest of the afternoon and into the evening, allowing time for a few bites of food.

She wasn't expecting to see her family this afternoon. It was a special treat to wake up and see the girls coming through the door with their daddy close behind.

"Mommy," Elizabeth shouted, and anxiously ran up to Karen's bed.

Karen placed her index finger to her mouth and said, "Shhhhh."

Elizabeth had waited several days to see her mom. She had finally arrived. Karen could get Elizabeth to pipe down, but the ear-to-ear smile was staying.

"Hi, Mom," Chelle greeted with a calmer and more controlled expression.

Karen spread her arms wide in a gesture for the girls to give her a hug. They responded without a spoken word and fell into their mother's loving arms. Having them close to her heart gave Karen comfort. It was the best medicine she'd gotten all day.

"How are you feeling?" Johnny asked. He found a chair in the corner of the room.

Karen nodded.

"What does that mean?"

"It means I'm doing okay. I'm a little tired, but I'm feeling much better with my family being here." Karen brushed Elizabeth's hair back and gave her a smile.

It was an awkward visit for the couple, since they hadn't been on the best of terms when Johnny had left for the business trip a few days ago. Neither had they been able to make any kind of amends before Karen got sick and went into the hospital. Now they were stuck making small talk for the benefit of the girls.

"How are you making out at home?" Karen asked the girls.

Chelle was able to get a word in before Elizabeth. "We're doing okay."

"I've been helping out with everything too," Elizabeth echoed.

Chelle helped her pull a chair close to the bed.

"When are you coming home?"

Johnny, who was flipping through the *Wall Street Journal,* stopped long enough to hear her response.

"I don't know, sweetie. The doctor hasn't told me that yet. I hope it's soon."

Nearly an hour passed before Karen and Johnny directed any conversation toward each other.

"We got the equity loan approved but it's less than we need."

"What are you going to do?" Karen asked.

"I'm not sure, but I have to do something to keep us above water."

Karen sighed and slid the palm of her hand up her forehead with her eyes closed.

"It's getting late and we need to get on home," Johnny reminded the girls.

"No, we haven't been here that long."

"It's time to go, Elizabeth," Johnny strongly reinforced. "You have school tomorrow."

Elizabeth recognized her father's tone. It meant business. She shed a few tears, but did not speak another word in opposition to his order.

It bothered Karen to see the girls so sad about her hospital stay. "I want both of you girls to know how sorry I am."

"Sorry about what, Mommy?" Chelle wanted to know.

Karen was emotionally choked up trying to get the words out.

"I'm sorry that I got sick again on you girls." She was talking to the girls but also, periodically, directed her eyes and comments toward Johnny. "I know that I've let all of you down."

Johnny was at a loss for words, but Chelle wasn't. She was quick to comfort her mother.

"Mommy, it's not your fault that you got sick."

Elizabeth handed Karen a tissue and grabbed another for herself.

"I should have taken better care of myself. I really messed up."

"No, you didn't mess up, Mom. I love you."

"Me too, Mommy," Elizabeth threw in.

Johnny remained silent. He wanted to reach out to Karen but didn't have a read on how receptive she would be. Most of the time he was not sure what she wanted from him. Asking him for one thing and then judging him on something else was the norm. For the time being he elected to keep quiet.

The girls pulled themselves together long enough to walk out with their father.

Chelle stopped at the doorway, turned to her mom, and said, "I almost forgot; happy anniversary, Mom. I know that it's not until tomorrow, but I just wanted to say it anyway."

"Yeah, Mommy, happy anniversary. See you tomorrow."

Johnny had forgotten about their anniversary. If it hadn't been for Chelle's prompting, it would have passed without his acknowledgment.

"Thank you, my sweeties." She looked past Johnny, expecting him to say something, but he didn't. "Oh, yeah, Chelle, thank you for sending out the cards to cancel the party."

"You're welcome."

"I helped too. I put on the stamps."

"Thank you, baby." Karen blew Elizabeth a kiss.

Johnny hadn't planned to come out to the hospital until tomorrow. He was glad that he had come before their anniversary. He'd forgotten about it but had no intention of publicizing it. His oversight was one less thing he needed Karen needling him about in the future.

"We'll see you tomorrow," he told Karen.

Karen wept openly when they left. It felt like her heart had been ripped out, because she knew how much fear her illness was causing the girls. She knew that the emotional roller-coaster ride was hard to deal with at their age.

She fretted that it was too much for them. One year she was well and everything was great. The next year she was sick and the girls were scared. She couldn't keep putting them through this. She closed her eyes to push out the remaining tears. Maybe they were better off without her. Karen felt she was in a no-win situation. She either wanted to be alive or dead. There was nothing as bad as living in the middle. If she got better, the kids would have to deal with the uncertainty of not knowing how long it would last. If she didn't get better, the children would have to deal with her death. Her thoughts were scrambled. After much agonizing and unrest, she fell asleep.

CHAPTER 24

The morning rushed in, not that it made any difference to Karen. The emotional drain of going in and out of remission, added to the pressures at home, was taking its toll. She was slowly slipping into depression.

A conflicting effect of the depression was that all she wanted to do was sleep away the problem and wake up with it resolved. Yet she couldn't find enough peace to get any sleep. The very thing she needed was exactly what she wasn't able to get.

"Here's your breakfast tray, Mrs. Clark."

Karen, who was balled up in the fetal position, pulled the cover tightly around her neck.

The dietician pushed the cart closer to the bed.

Karen ate a few bites of the toast and a couple spoonfuls of oatmeal. Between the poor taste of the food and her loss of appetite, the tray remained virtually untouched.

The morning dragged on. Karen watched a few game shows and soap operas intermixed with short naps.

Her doctor walked in. Karen was in the middle of a nap but heard someone enter the room and immediately woke up.

"Dr. Costas."

Karen was a bit groggy, but she was eager to get the test results about the breast cancer. She wasted no time in getting to the point.

"Has it spread?"

Karen's candid question caught Dr. Costas off guard. She wanted to check Karen's emotional stability before breaking the news. The nurses had noted signs of depression in the chart. Dr. Costas wasn't surprised but was nonetheless concerned.

"Is your husband planning to come out here today? I was hoping to talk with the two of you together."

"Doctor, what did the results show?" This time her voice was stronger and louder.

Dr. Costas set the chart on the edge of Karen's bed and put both hands in her white lab coat pockets. "I did get the results." She spoke softly. "They didn't come back the way I would have liked."

Karen was speaking in a near hysterical tone. "So you're saying the results came back positive."

The doctor nodded in agreement. She knew that any dialogue would only engage Karen in a more dramatic reaction.

"Oh, God, it is back." She hung her head and wept. "Why me?" she screamed so loudly that the nurse came running in from the hallway.

"Is anything wrong?" the nurse asked the doctor.

"We're fine."

"You're fine!" Karen bellowed. "I'm not!"

"Karen, I'm going to need you to calm down. You're just going to wear yourself out. Please, Karen, take a deep breath. I'm going to order something to help you relax. Nurse, I'm putting Valium on her chart. Could you please rush it along?"

"Yes, Doctor. I'll get it right away."

"Karen, I know this is a tough time for you."

Karen remained quiet. She avoided pressure-filled situations and usually settled for less than what she wanted or needed. It wasn't like her to have outbursts like the one she was currently having. A part of her was embarrassed.

"I know it isn't the best time to talk about our next steps. I want you to get some rest first." The doctor clasped her hands together and drew them up to her lips like she was contemplating more to say.

"Karen, there is no easy way to say this."

"What else could there be?"

"The tumor—"

Karen cut Dr. Costas off before she could finish the statement.

"You told me the tumor hadn't grown any more. That's what you said."

"That's true, but now that the cancer is back that changes our position a little bit."

"How?"

"I need to do a biopsy on your tumor to ensure that it is not cancerous."

"What would make you think that it is?"

"I can't say for sure without the biopsy. I'm still optimistic from the MRI results. I really don't think the tumor is an issue, but I still need to check it just to be sure."

"Can't we work on the breast cancer first and then deal with the tumor?"

"Ideally, it would be nice to segregate the illnesses in your body and deal with them one at a time. However, we don't have that luxury. Do you recall when we talked about radiation therapy?"

"Yes."

"Well, in order to set ourselves up for the best possibility of success, we need to hit the breast cancer hard. That requires a substantial dose of radiation. That means I'll need to make sure that there is no other cancer in your body before we begin the treatment."

"What difference does it make?"

"Each human body can safely be exposed to a certain amount of radiation in a lifetime. We will be approaching that level with your new breast cancer treatments. So you see, I need to make sure there is no other known area of cancer in your body. If there is, it will affect the amount of radiation and the treatment options that I plan to use for the breast cancer."

"What you're saying is that I will basically be using my lifetime allocation in one shot."

"That's one way of putting it." Dr. Costas hesitated before sharing any more information with Karen. She had known Karen long enough to anticipate her response.

"Karen"—Dr. Costas spoke gently—"most likely we will need to follow up with chemo."

"Chemo! Oh, God, no." Karen dreaded the thought of going through the sickening process again. The nausea and exhaustion had been unbearable for her the last two times around.

"Chemo makes me too sick. I definitely don't want to do that. I don't know which makes me feel worse, the chemo or the cancer." Karen sighed in disgust at her options. "What about the radiation? If I take the treatment now, what would happen if I got cancer again down the road? What treatment options would I have left?" Karen had her suspicions about the answer.

Dr. Costas avoided giving any confirmation. She was aware of the new drugs that had recently been approved by the FDA as well as some other experimental ones out there. She felt uncertain about using them without more research on their results. She preferred treating Karen with options that she was familiar with, like surgery, chemo, and radiation treatments.

"Let's not worry about such a hypothetical scenario." She patted Karen's blanket-covered legs. "Right now, I want you to put all of your energy into fighting this round of cancer. You need to be as optimistic as you can. A positive attitude couldn't hurt on your road to recovery. Okay?"

"Thanks for being honest with me, Dr. Costas."

"The nurse will be in with something to help you relax. We'll talk tomorrow about the treatment. In the meantime I will be ordering up the biopsy."

"Will I have to get my head shaved?"

Dr. Costas knew how traumatized Karen had been the first time she lost her hair from the cancer treatment. It was less traumatic the second time around with the help of wigs and appealing short hairstyles.

"Because of the location, they will only need to shave a small part off the back. You won't have to lose all of your hair this time."

"What about the radiation?"

"Well, that I can't say. Twenty percent of patients don't lose their hair. Let's hope you're in that group."

"Humph. Hope."

"Don't worry about the hair. You look great with the short haircut."

"Yeah, but short and bald are two different things."

Karen embraced her femininity. To have no breasts and to be bald at the same time didn't make her feel good about her womanhood. She didn't think it would make Johnny too happy either. She had heard him say time and time again that her appearance didn't bother him. She hadn't believed him. How could it not bother him? It bothered her.

CHAPTER 25

Dr. Costas called Johnny to give him the update on Karen's condition.

"Johnny, this is Dr. Costas. I'd like to talk to you about Karen."

"Why, what's wrong?"

"Well, Mr. Clark, to be honest, Karen isn't doing too well. She's not handling the news about the cancer very well."

"I guess not. She—no, we—thought you had gotten it all. Her breasts are already gone. How could she still have breast cancer? I don't understand it."

Dr. Costas sighed.

"Breast cancer is a tough cookie. You never really know if you've gotten it all. Sometimes it takes years to resurface in the other breast or in the lymph nodes found in the armpits. It can also spread to a number of other areas. Unfortunately, it's very common."

Johnny still couldn't understand how this could happen after all of the treatment and confirmations that the cancer was in remission. "Her breasts are already gone. How can she still have cancer? I thought the whole objective of removing her breasts was to eliminate any place for the cancer to grow?"

"Yes, to some degree, you are correct. The problem is that Karen's cancer has metastasized. That's when the cancer spreads beyond the initial area. The biopsy confirms that it has spread across her chest area and even into her shoulder areas. We're hoping that it hasn't spread to any of her vital organs."

"How will you know if it has?"

"Well, I am waiting on the pathology report. That should shed some light on what we're working with."

Johnny's silence was an indication that he was struggling with the diagnosis.

Dr. Costas continued trying to enlighten Johnny with as much information as she could about Karen's condition. "Johnny, like I said, breast cancer is tough. The size of a breast doesn't increase or minimize one's chance of getting cancer. I know that she wasn't predisposed to cancer through her family history. Often there is no rhyme or reason for why some people get cancer and others don't. All we can do is treat it to the best of our ability."

Delivering the bad news to the couple touched Dr. Costas deeply. She had developed some level of emotional connection with the Clarks, having treated Karen for over four years.

"I'm disappointed too, but what Karen needs right now is a tremendous amount of support."

"I always give my wife support," Johnny said in a tone that sounded like he was offended.

"Oh, I know, Johnny. I apologize. I didn't mean to imply that you don't."

Johnny felt a bit embarrassed for rushing to a defensive position at Dr. Costas's comment. It made him look guilty.

"I apologize for my snappy comment."

"There is no need for apology. This is going to be an emotional time for both you and Karen, which is really the essence of my call. Karen is not handling this well."

"What do you mean?"

"She is quite depressed, and that's not good for us. She has to be strong to fight this disease. I think she's giving up hope of recovering."

"What are her chances of recovering?"

Dr. Costas wanted to be as completely honest with Johnny and reveal the severity of the prognosis, while not being too pessimistic.

"I really don't know, Johnny. I want to believe that we have a shot at Karen's full recovery."

"She's already had the lumpectomy and chemotherapy. That didn't work. Then she went back into the hospital to have both of her breasts removed with the mastectomy. That didn't work. The radiation and chemo combination didn't work. What else is there?"

"Well, we have her scheduled for treatment. She hasn't exceeded her lifetime intake of radiation. I recommend that we use an intense radiation treatment immediately followed with chemo. Let's hit it hard. I think it's the best shot we have."

"Did you tell her about the chemo?" Johnny knew it was something Karen hated having to go through.

"Yes, I did."

"I know that didn't go over too well."

"No, it didn't. She was so upset about the chemo that I wasn't able to tell her the rest of the news."

Johnny couldn't imagine what else could be left. "What's that?" he asked, although he wasn't eager to hear the answer.

"Karen has been given a significant amount of chemo and radiation."

"And . . . ?"

Dr. Costas knew how much the couple had already endured. She felt awful about pouring more salt in their wound.

"Well, the good news is that the treatments work to kill off the cancer cells. The side effect is that in the process, it also kills the bone marrow and red blood cells. It might also break down the immune system."

"What are you saying, Dr. Costas? Are you telling me that the treatment is worse than the disease? Which one is going to kill her first?"

"I know that it doesn't sound very good, Johnny. But I feel obligated to share all of the scenarios with you. It's only fair that you know what we're dealing with. The fact is that after we get past the cancer, there is a possibility that we might have to deal with leukemia if her bone marrow is depleted to a significant level."

"Good grief! Does it ever end?"

"All we can do is stay hopeful and take one step at a time. We just have to constantly evaluate our options as we go."

Johnny was filled with gloom.

"Let me know if you need me to sign anything for the treatment."

"Thank you, although that shouldn't be necessary. Karen is still fully coherent. She has to make the final decision. However, I think it would help if you could confer with her about it. Like I said, having you and the children around her might give Karen the extra motivation she needs to fight. It's going to be key. We need her strong going into this treatment. It is quite intense and will take a great deal out of her."

"I'll see what I can do. I'll talk with her about it today."

"Good."

"Will she be able to come home during the treatment?"

"The treatment could be done on an outpatient basis, but with her history of cancer, I recommend that she stay in the hospital. We would be better able to handle any unforeseen complications."

"Thank you, Doctor, for calling. I appreciate it."

"There's no need to thank me, Johnny. I would say that I'm just doing my job, but it goes beyond that. Karen has been such a likable patient the entire time that I've known her. She has a great deal of life in her. I'd like to see her continue to enjoy it. I honestly would."

When Johnny got off the phone, he couldn't find enough willpower to move from his seat.

Where is all this headed? he wondered. He felt helpless. What could he do? Should he tell the kids or should he wait? Johnny stood up scratching his head. Being indecisive was not a position he often found himself in. He was the one in charge and calling the shots. He handled the tough decisions that others dreaded without so much as a flinch. Nothing was out of his control, except for Karen's cancer. He was at a loss.

He sat on the bedroom sofa with his head back and staring at the ceiling. He leaned over and grabbed the family's personal phone book off the end table. He thumbed through it and found Erick's number in Europe. He dialed 011 and hung up. Maybe he shouldn't call. It would probably scare Erick. He couldn't help her way over there anyway. Johnny shook his head. He was uncomfortable being in such an awkward situation. Was it better to tell Erick later, after they had more information? Johnny grew tired of going back and forth on whether or not to alert Erick to his mother's condition. If it were him, he'd want to know. Johnny decided that Erick was old enough to handle tough situations.

Johnny dialed the number. There was no guarantee that Erick would be around. He was taking full advantage of the Stanford exchange program. The first thing he had done in Europe was to get a

EuroRail train pass. He would often call his parents after spending a weekend travelling the countryside via train.

"Morning, Stanford University. Might I help you?" the British accent echoed.

"Yes, my name is John Clark. My son, John Erick Clark, is in the exchange program from the U.S. I need him to give me a call at home."

"Very well, sir. I will inform him that you telephoned straightaway."

"Thank you."

"Good day, sir."

It was already eleven o'clock at night in London. Johnny suspected that Erick would be calling back tomorrow morning.

The girls had an after-school program at church. Johnny decided to use the short break to take a nap before picking them up and heading to the hospital. He kicked back and got comfortable on the sofa for a quick snooze.

Johnny wasn't expecting any calls. He was slow to answer the ringing phone. He didn't feel like talking to anyone, but felt obligated to answer it with Karen being in the hospital.

"Hello," Johnny greeted with minimal emotion.

"I have a collect call from Erick. Will you accept the charges?" the automated voice asked. "Press or say one now."

"One."

"Thank you."

After a few moments and oceans of static, there was a human voice on the other end of Johnny's line.

"Hey, Big Dad."

"Boy, what you doing calling collect?"

"The dorm monitor gave me a message to call home. I figured it must be important. So I called."

"This is going to cost me an arm and a leg. What's wrong with your calling card?"

"I already used up my minutes for the month."

"We're barely through half of the month. How did you use up six hours?"

"I talked to Mom a couple of times this month."

"You sure didn't talk to her no six hours' worth."

"Some of it, and the rest of the time I used to talk to my friends that are at the main campus."

"Boy, I am not spending all of this money for you to keep in touch with your buddies in California. That's what a summer job is for. You are thousands of miles away. You could have any kind of emergency. You'd better start doing a better job at spreading that card across the month."

Johnny needed to conserve on all spending. The home equity loan was netting twenty thousand dollars less than he'd hoped to get. According to his calculations, the extra cash would have provided a financial cushion. Instead, he had to tighten his financial belt.

"Look, I didn't call to get into your irresponsibility. I wanted to tell you that your mom's back in the hospital."

"For what?"

"Her cancer is back."

"How'd that happen?"

"I really couldn't tell you. We're all shocked."

Erick hadn't forgotten the first time he saw his mother so unhappy. He was eleven when he overheard her telling Aunt Connie about that woman, Isabelle. She cried and cried. He didn't understand what was wrong at the time, but figured it out later. It made him cry to see her so sad. Many times when his parents would go into their bedroom and close the door, he would sit at the top of the front staircase and doodle in his sketchpad. Muddled voices escalated to shouting and screaming, finishing off with silence sprinkled with sobs, over and over, night after night. It was easy to catch her crying after that. It wasn't long before she got the cancer. Then she really cried, kind of like she did when that Isabelle woman was around.

Erick had it rough during his teenage years. His mother was in and out of the hospital. His father was always working. There was no time to give him advice about girls or school. He was expected to be a man and take care of his sisters without any guidance. His mom would have been around to help him through the teen years, had it not been for his father. She was always there for Erick. It was his father's fault. He couldn't wait to get as far away from home as he could and be able to grow up on his own without bearing a shoulder of responsibility for the family.

"What did you do to her?"

"What do you mean, what did I do to her?" Johnny was outraged, and his tone of voice left no room for speculation. "What the heck do you mean?"

Johnny tolerated no disrespect from his kids. How old or independent they were didn't make a difference.

"I've been reading up on cancer in my hum-bio class. Lifestyles, stress, pressure, and even suppressed emotions like grief, hurt, guilt, and anger may be contributing factors in getting cancer and relapses by weakening the immune system."

"So what! I don't care two nickels about what you read."

"It's obvious that you don't care about Mom. If you did, you wouldn't be seeing other women right under her nose. I wonder if that has anything to do with her getting sick?"

"Who do you think you're talking to? Let me tell you something, young man, don't you ever disrespect me again. You'd better remember that Karen is my wife, not yours. Don't you ever tell me how to act with my wife. That is not your place. You have some nerve, boy. Don't get so high and mighty that you take leave of your senses. Don't forget that I'm the one footing your bills. You're not so much of a man that you're able to take care of yourself without my help." Johnny was furious and held nothing back. "Look, I have to go. Here's the number to the hospital and my calling-card number. Call her. I know she wants to hear from you."

Erick was a perfect blend of Johnny's and Karen's personalities. The passive and compassionate side of him wanted to apologize to his father for stirring the waters into such a heated discussion. The other side didn't want to apologize for saying what he honestly felt to be the truth.

As it turned out, he didn't have to make a decision. Johnny hung up before he had a chance to say anything.

Erick grunted, holding the receiver. He slammed the phone onto the hook. "Some things just don't change." He walked back to his room feeling the weight of the world on his undeveloped shoulders.

Johnny was furious with Erick, partly because he was afraid there might be some truth in what he was saying. He couldn't get the words out of his head, no matter how he tried to shake them.

Could that be right? Could her cancer be from suppressed hurt and anger?

Johnny didn't want to believe it, but if it was true, he had a great deal to think about. It was only twenty-four hours ago that he was contemplating getting back on the roller-coaster ride with Isabelle or Annette.

"I wonder if . . ." he questioned himself. "Nah, couldn't be."

Johnny knew how traumatized Karen had been during the exposed affair with Isabelle and the subsequent pregnancy. Karen had gone through a sizable depression but decided to stay in the marriage. He knew that staying didn't negate her hurt. All of these years, he pondered. He shook his head in disbelief at how the storybook relationship had gone so sour. He stayed because taking care of Karen and the kids was the right thing to do. They had a better life with him around. He questioned whether staying was still best for the family. The couple had survived, but things had never been quite the same since. Every time the couple got into a major disagreement, Karen threw Isabelle up in Johnny's face. He tried to ease her mind, with no success. She hadn't shown any indication that the trust was being restored. Who had really benefited from his staying? Karen ended up with cancer. He was miserable in the marriage and so was she. He didn't get along with his son. Johnny twirled the pen between his fingers. His reflections were making his head pound. He could only hope that the affair with Isabelle hadn't contributed to Karen's illness. He couldn't handle the idea of being a factor in her getting cancer. The guilt pricked at his peace. He felt sick.

In all of his getting and acquiring the finer aspects of life, Johnny felt that he was losing the most important piece—his family. He couldn't help but feel that all of his hard work had been for naught.

His pager vibrated on top of the end table. Johnny picked it up and read the coded digits on the illuminated screen. It was Annette. The few females who were fortunate enough to have his pager number were given a special code to use. It minimized the chance that Karen would find the phone number for another woman on his pager. Johnny deleted the number and set the pager back on the table. Sex was the last thing on his mind.

CHAPTER 26

A room had opened up on the cancer wing two days after Big Mama left the hospital. That was almost a month ago. She had been an inspiration to Karen. Now that Big Mama had been gone for almost a month, there was no one around to encourage Karen.

She was tired of being poked and zapped. What had it all been for? She initially came into the hospital to have some additional tests done in hopes that the cancer wasn't back. Since then she had added a brain tumor biopsy and the need for intense radiation therapy.

At least the biopsy had gone well. There was no malignancy or growth in the tumor. It provided no threat to her life.

The dietician wheeled in the lunch cart.

"Lunchtime, Mrs. Clark."

Karen barely lifted an eye toward the lady.

She rolled the tray up to the bed.

"Umm. Let's see what we have here? Turkey, green beans, and vegetable broth. Looks good."

The doctor left strict orders with the staff that Karen had to eat. She was showing advanced signs of depression. She wasn't eating or sleeping. She picked at her food, taking only a few bites every meal. She had lost close to eighteen pounds in the last month.

Dr. Costas knew that Karen's malnutrition and dehydration were direct results of her insufficient intake of food and liquids. As much as Karen disliked the constant nag of a needle sticking into her arm, Dr. Costas had no other choice but to administer the necessary fluids and meds through an IV.

Karen's counselor came in behind the dietician.

Dr. Costas was concerned about Karen's increasing anxiety and decided that it was best to get a counselor involved before her patient sank deeper into the pit of depression.

"Why don't you try to eat some of it, Karen?"

"I'm not hungry," she responded in a groggy voice.

"Come on, you have to eat. Dr. Costas left specific instructions. You need to eat so that you can get your strength back."

"I'm strong enough."

"Not strong enough to bounce back from the therapy."

The counselor elevated the bed slightly. She wanted to make Karen comfortable and get her positioned to eat.

"I don't even know if the therapy worked."

"Well, I personally hope that the radiation has completely eliminated the cancer."

"I've already been through all kinds of surgeries, treatments, and medications. What did all of that do for me? Nothing! I'm right back here, sick again."

The counselor wanted to lift Karen's spirits. She knew that the sense of hopelessness wasn't good for her long-term outlook.

Once Karen got into the downward spiral of depression, it seemed nearly impossible to break her out of it. Neither the children, Johnny, nor the church members could shake her.

"You have to keep hanging in there, Karen."

"Why?"

The question was unexpected by the counselor.

"Because we want you to live a long, happy, healthy life with your family."

The children did generate some kind of a positive reaction from Karen.

"Well, I'm tired. I'm sick of being sick."

"Karen! You can't give up so easily. There is a very good chance that all of the cancer is gone with the radiation."

Karen didn't have a response. She was determined to believe information was being kept from her.

"I don't feel like going through more treatment, only to end up back here a year from now. I'd rather get it over now and be done with it."

"How can you say that? What about your children?"

Tears formed in her eyes. The thought of leaving them hurt, but not even they could overcome Karen's depression.

"What good am I to my children lying here? I think they'll be better off without me. I know Johnny will."

"How can you say something like that? Children always need their mother. I'm sure they miss you and are hoping that you'll be coming home soon."

"They do need a mother, one who is home and able to take care of them." Karen blew her nose and wiped her eyes. "That's not me. I've let them down by letting myself get sick again. I'm sure that Johnny has a replacement in mind. They don't need me."

Karen should have been strong enough to go home by now, but she wasn't. Dr. Costas was struggling with her diagnosis. From all medical accounts, the treatment was successful, yet Karen wasn't showing any improvement. There was no physical explanation for why Karen seemed to be getting sicker. Dr. Costas could only speculate that it was psychological. Even so, Karen had vehemently refused to take any drugs for her depression and anxiety. It appeared to Dr. Costas that Karen didn't want to get better. Regardless of how much encouragement came through the door, none of it remained. Dr. Costas was concerned about her longtime patient. She knew that no medicine in the world could restore someone's broken will to live.

CHAPTER 27

Colorful cards and balloons lined the windowsill. It was Sunday afternoon and the room was crowded with well-wishers from the church. They were squeezed into the room like sardines. As the weeks passed, Karen's group of visitors got smaller and smaller. The first couple of days, her room was packed. The longer Karen was hospitalized, the less people carved time out of their schedules for a visit. The crisis in Karen's life warranted support, but wasn't catastrophic enough for people to alter their ongoing day-to-day activities. Giving a few hours and a greeting card every so often was as good as it got for most of her visitors.

Most of her adult life Karen had spent putting on a smiley face for others. She tried to act upbeat, but the effort was too great. Struggling to maintain an elite lifestyle was one thing. Hiding depression required much more resilience.

"How you feeling, Karen?" one visitor asked. Most didn't know what to say to her. They searched for words to break the ice.

"I'm a little tired." She managed to squeak out a grin, something far short of her radiant smile. How many times had she been asked that question for which there was no answer? It was more like a substitute for "hello," seeing that no one wanted to really hear about how sick she was.

Karen mostly kept quiet and dozed off. Occasionally she responded to something a visitor said.

"Karen, we had a guest speaker at church today. The message was truly anointed."

"Umm, sure was," one of the older women affirmed.

"The speaker is going to be at church this evening too. I don't usually go back in the evening, but I am tonight."

"He was just that good, Karen," one sister stated.

"It wasn't just him. It was the whole atmosphere," Elder Jones clarified.

"Yessss."

"God is sho' good."

"All the time," three people synchronously chimed in.

During her confinement, Karen hadn't been able to keep up on current events or other happenings on the outside. It left a limited number of discussion topics for visitors.

"So, the weather has been nice. After that little bit of rain last week, it warmed up nicely," spouted one of the visitors.

"Yeah, they say March winds, April showers bring May flowers," someone said.

Elder Jones shook his head. "Spring already! The year is almost half gone. Time is just flying by. Seem like it was just Christmas."

Karen listened, but didn't join in.

"It'll be Mother's Day before we know it."

"I hope we have you home by then."

Karen gave a weak grin. None of the conversation was really directed toward her, except for a few pointed statements here and there.

Reverend Lane and Big Mama cut through the crowd with Mrs. Pierce. Big Mama's walk in righteousness commanded a certain level of respect from those in the church. The group made way for her as she made her way to the bed, like God parting the Red Sea for Moses. Unlike the other visitors, Big Mama had a specific purpose. Every time she came across a sick person, her objective was first to find out if they knew the Lord. Then she commenced to praying for their physical and spiritual healing.

"Hi, Karen."

"Hi, Ms. Emma. Thank you for coming."

"Now ya knows I'ze gon' get here sooner or later this here day." She patted Karen's hand. She looked around the room to see many of the elders and sisters congregated in the room. "I'ze see we have some powerful saints gathered here."

Some people were starting to look at their watches, suggesting that it was time to tactfully announce their departure. Big Mama's entrance was going to be a nice, easy out for some.

"Oh, look at the time. Three-thirty. I'd better get going," a sister noted. "It'll be time for the evening service before I know it."

"Yeah, I'd better head out too. Mother Walker, here, you can have my chair," Elder Jones offered.

Big Mama moved at her own pace, appearing to be in no hurry. Her philosophy was, "pace yaself, chile. When ya rush through life ya just hurrying to death. Ya gotta live one moment at a time."

"Before y'all get to getting, I'ze want to pray for this chile. The Good Book says that where there's two or three gathered together, God is in the midst."

Not a word of defiance was uttered. The crowd, both old and young, gathered around Karen's bed without hesitation.

Big Mama pulled out her small bottle of anointing oil and rubbed it on Karen's forehead.

"Lord, ya know ya chile. Ya knew her before she was born. Ya knew that she'd be lying in this here bed this day before she even got here. Now we ask ya to pour out your healing blood on her. Ya may not come when we wantcha to, but ya always on time."

"Yes, Lord," Elder Jones interjected.

The circle of prayer continued for nearly a half hour, with each person speaking a word. Big Mama believed in tarrying, or, as she would say, "taking as much time as ya need to do God's business."

Johnny and the girls walked in near the end of the prayer. He wasn't eager to join in the circle, so he opted to stand near the doorway and not interrupt. He was content to wait for them to finish until he saw Big Mama rub some oil onto Karen's forehead. It wasn't unfamiliar to him. On several occasions he had heard Karen refer to it as anointed oil.

Shortly after Karen joined the church years ago, she had brought home a small bottle of the oil. Johnny forbade it. The oil bought no favoritism with him, even though she tried to explain that it was used in conjunction with prayer. It seemed like evil voodoo to him, and he refused to have it done in the house or anywhere around him.

As a result, Karen used the oil, but only on isolated occasions. He'd seen it on those times when he'd gone to church with her. He didn't have any control over what was spoken and done at church, but this hospital room was well within his dominion. He burst through the crowd with the girls in tow.

"Excuse me," he interrupted with a voice of authority. "I don't mind if you want to pray for Karen, but I prefer that you not use that oil stuff."

Those praying were stunned at Johnny's outburst and didn't know how to react. Everyone remained quiet. Subtle attitudes and uneasiness clogged the room.

Karen was embarrassed, but too upset to cry.

Elizabeth worked her way to her mother's bed.

Reverend Lane, being one of the leaders in room, wanted to bring peace to the situation. "We apologize for upsetting you, Johnny. Maybe we'll leave now and let you and your family have some quiet time with Karen."

Big Mama slowly walked to Johnny and stood in front of him. Deep down, he didn't want to set this old lady straight, but he was poised for anything.

She asked him, "Is ya getting enough to eat?"

"What?" Johnny grunted in surprise at the peculiar, seemingly out-of-left-field question.

"If ya ain't, some of us womenfolk at the church can fix ya some meals and bring them over to the house for ya."

Her generosity caught him unprepared. The only response he could give was, "Uh, no, I'm, uh, okay right now."

Big Mama knew exactly what she was doing. She had enough wisdom not to throw fuel on a fire. Where some saw a strong man in Johnny, Big Mama saw a frightened man lashing out like a cornered bull.

Her natural reaction would be to pray for someone in his condition, but she sensed that the last thing he wanted was more prayer. Big Mama wasn't one to force religion. She knew that Johnny would find his way to God without her pushing.

"Well, I'ze gon' keep ya whole family in my prayers every day till God show what He's gon' do for ya." Not a word of animosity came across her lips. Unlike some of the other churchgoers, Big Mama had learned a long time ago to accept people for where they were with the Lord. She knew that Johnny wasn't a very religious man based on the little bit Karen had shared with her when they had shared a hospital room. Silent prayer was the only way to reach a hard-hitting man like Johnny.

"Karen, I'ze sho' glad to see ya. God bless ya." Big Mama led the way out of the room.

"Thank you for coming by, Ms. Emma. Thank you for the prayer."

The room emptied as each said their good-byes.

Karen had not been up for a lot of company, but was glad that so many people from the church had taken time out to visit. She was outraged at Johnny for being so rude. His thoughtless, selfish, controlling attitude was one thing she didn't miss about home.

"Hi, Mom." The way was clear for Elizabeth, who pulled a chair close to the bed.

"Hi, baby." Karen was glad to see the girls, but she wasn't as enthusiastic with them as she usually was. She was battling exhaustion on every front. She felt tired of being sick, tired of Johnny's domination and unfaithfulness, tired of being emotional, tired of being away from the kids, tired of hoping for a better day, and just tired of being tired.

She mustered enough might to give Johnny a look of frustration in her weakened condition.

There was nothing more for him to say. He'd already said too much. At the time, he was quite comfortable with his actions. Seeing the piercing look from Karen, he wasn't feeling as easy about it. He kept quiet.

"Did you have to stop them from praying for me?" Her words were slow and lethargic. It took the sharp bite off and made them easier for Johnny to swallow. "It's not like you're praying in their place."

Johnny didn't respond. He knew she was upset and didn't want to agitate her any further. He searched for a neutral topic. "Erick called."

Karen was curt. "I know. He called me right after he talked with you."

Johnny was hoping that Erick hadn't told her the details of their heated confrontation. Talking about other women wouldn't be a winning discussion.

Karen rolled her eyes from his direction and returned to her conversation with the girls.

He realized that the discussion was over. It was becoming clear to him that the hospital was her domain, where she was the one calling the shots, not him. Johnny planted his feet on the floor, dug his body into the wing-back chair, and tilted his head back with eyes closed. He folded his hands and tried to catch a nap until it was either time to go or Karen was ready to talk to him. Whichever came first.

CHAPTER 28

The nightstand was awkwardly placed behind Karen's head, next to the bed. She strained to reach backward for the phone. She pressed multiple numbers, having to start over repeatedly. Finally, she was able to get through to the church.

"Reverend Lane, this is Karen Clark."

"Yes, Karen." He sat up straight in his chair, bracing for the worst. "Is something wrong?"

"Nothing new." She paused. "I'm calling to apologize to you and the other saints. I am truly sorry for the way my husband acted yesterday."

"Karen, there is no reason to apologize. You and your family are going through a very trying time. We understand the impact this kind of trial can cause. Rest assured, Karen, there are no hard feelings."

"I just wanted to let you know how I felt."

"Why, thank you, but don't you worry another moment about apologizing to us. You put all of that energy toward getting yourself better."

"Thank you for being so understanding. Could you please extend my apology to the others?"

"I will do just that."

"Can you especially apologize to Ms. Emma for me?"

"Like I said, Karen, it is not necessary, but I will do as you ask. Is there anything else you need me to do for you?"

"No, that's it."

Completing the one call was the only item Karen had on her to-do list for the day. Good thing, because the small task seemed to zap all of her energy. Now that it was done, she recoiled back into her depressive shell and fell asleep. Hours later she woke up to see Big Mama sitting in the chair reading the Bible. Karen focused her eyes to make sure she wasn't merely seeing things.

"Ms. Emma, is that you?"

"It sho' is."

"How long have you been here?"

"Ooh, I'ze say about two hours."

"That long!" Karen thought she'd only been asleep a few minutes. Looking at the clock, she realized that it must have been more like four hours. She wasn't expecting Big Mama, but Karen was glad to see her. Being able to apologize in person was better than having Pastor Lane pass the message along.

"I didn't know you were coming out here today, especially after Johnny acted the way he did yesterday. I'm so sorry."

"Ya don't owe me no apology for ya husband. He only doing the best he know to do with ya being sick and all. I didn't pay him no mind."

"But you did stop praying when he busted in."

"Why, sho' I did. I meant to show him respect. Praying for his wife when he didn't want me to wasn't going to be help for nobody. There would be a nasty spirit in the midst. Besides, I'ze still praying for ya. Ya don't have to pray out loud to seek the Lord for somebody. When I'ze was speaking to ya husband I'ze was praying. Ya got to pray at all times, without ceasing. Karen, he needs just as much prayer as ya do. He's a strong-headed man. He's hurting and don't have nowhere or nobody to turn to. He needs the Lord, and I'ze aim to pray till he finds him."

"I appreciate you praying for my family. They'll need somebody to pray for them if I'm gone."

Big Mama sensed the melancholy in Karen's spirit.

"Prayer can sho' fix a heap of trouble."

"Not for me, Ms. Emma. I'm tired of dragging my family through this agony."

"Whatcha mean, chile?"

"I have caused my children so much pain. They don't say it, but I see it in their eyes. Hurt isn't difficult to see if you love somebody. I've been thinking about what's better for the girls—for me to be around sick all of the time or for me to go on and let them get on with building a new, more stable life. It'll be easy for Johnny to get a new wife." She wanted to say that he'd already found a bed partner, but decided not to bring it up with Big Mama. She would keep it inside.

"Karen, sugar, it ain't ya decision to make. How long ya live, that belongs to God and God all by Hisself. Don't ya be in such a hurry to die. We's all going in our due time."

"How do you know this isn't my time?"

"Well, do ya feel like that's what God's telling ya in ya spirit?"

"I don't know what I feel right now."

"Well, if ya don't know, then ya need to wait on the Lord until ya do know. In the meantime, ya got to hold fast to ya confession of faith. That means believe for the best no matter what things look like. After ya done everything ya know to do, then the Word tells ya to stand. Just stand still and wait till ya hear from the Lord."

"I've gotten tired of waiting, Ms. Emma. This is the third time around with my breast cancer. I don't have any hope left."

"Then tell God ya need him to give ya some hope. He will give ya whatever ya need."

"Is he going to heal me once and for all? Will I get up and walk out of here, never having to come back again? Will I go home to a husband who loves me?"

"I don't know what God has in store for ya. It's all according to what His will is."

"See, that's what bothers me. We talk about prayer and faith. It's easy to preach about faith when all is well. How many times have I told someone to just have faith when they were going through a tough time, never realizing how hard it is to believe when you're the one in the situation?"

"Ya only human, Karen. Ya gon' get weak. That's why God says in second Corinthians that he is strong when we are weak."

"Why me?"

"I ain't able to tell ya why God allows some to get sick and not others."

"I know that God isn't to blame for all of the bad things that happen to people. I have done enough in my past to bring on my own cancer. I have enough guilt to last a lifetime. Maybe I brought this all on myself. This could be my punishment."

"Don't ya ever believe that God let ya get sick to punish ya. He loves ya. We all have sinned and made mistakes and fallen short of the glory of God. We ain't got all of the answers about ya sickness. We ain't got to know all the answers. We ain't God. All ya can do is pray and believe for your healing."

"I pray and I believe in God. So why aren't I healed completely?"

"I'ze don't know, chile. No matter how close I'ze get to the Lord, no matter how much I'ze wants to seek His face, I'ze ain't gon' never know all His ways."

"Maybe I'm doing something wrong. Maybe I should have just fasted and prayed and believed for a healing, instead of going through all of this medical stuff."

"I'ze can't tell ya how or when He gon' heal ya. He can move through a miracle, or He might touch ya through the medicines and the doctors. I'ze don't know what He has for ya. Just don't ya put Him in a box."

"What do you mean by putting Him in a box, Ms. Emma?"

"What I'ze mean is that He can touch ya in more ways than ya knows how. So you don't want to tie His hands."

"Do you think that I was always supposed to get cancer, or was it something that I did to deserve it?"

"No one deserves cancer, just like no one deserves trouble with they heart or trouble in they marriage or being po'. The truth is that some things we don't have no control over. What I can tell ya is that there is a plan for everyone's life and only God knows what that is. He promised to never leave ya or to forsake ya. God didn't promise that everything would be easy and that ya wouldn't have some suffering. But He's able to work it out."

"I could have done without suffering with this cancer."

"Talking about suffering." Big Mama grinned. "What about the Lord? Now there was a man who loved God, did a whole heap of good things, and yet bad things still happened to him. It would make ya cry to hear everything that happened to him, but lo and behold you find out in the Word that all of it was part of a bigger plan. Yes, indeed. All that suffering the Lord had to do could only have been done by him. That was his calling, the purpose of his whole life. He had to die before we could live. He didn't even see forty years on this earth. But he went when it was his time, after he'd done what he was supposed to do. But he didn't stay dead. On the third day, he got up from that ol' grave on Easter Sunday with all power in his hands."

Big Mama shook her fist in the air. "Oh, glory.

"Ah, you know the story. No matter how much suffering he did in that ol' body of his, it couldn't hold down his spirit. Nah, nah, that's what kept him hooked into his father. Oh, glory. Thank ya." Just the thought of the Lord being crucified on a cross and then having God raise him from the dead made Big Mama shout hallelujah wherever she was. "It just brings tears to my eyes to know that one man's life, through his suffering, brought hope to so many after him." Big Mama bent over to pull a tissue from her purse.

"Are you all right, Ms. Emma?"

"Yes, chile, I'ze fine. I'ze just full with the holy spirit."

"I wish that I knew God like you do and was able to have more faith. But for right now, I don't see my way getting any brighter."

"Everybody's got a cross to bear. Maybe that's why some folks get sick and some don't. Could be that the cancer is the cross ya gots to bear, and that ol' heart attack might have been mine. Ya cancer could be a little piece of the whole puzzle God done planned for ya life. I don't righly know. What I'ze know for sho' is how much He love me, and that's done been good enough for me."

"Perhaps I don't want to carry this cross far enough to see the rest of the puzzle."

Big Mama generally had enough compassion and words of comfort to bring a person around to the side of hope, but Karen didn't seem to be budging off her seat of depression and hopelessness.

This chile is in a sho' heap of pain, Big Mama discerned. "Why ya feel that way?"

"Because I'm mad. I'm hurt. I feel guilty, and most of all, I'm tired."

"Whatcha mad 'bout?"

Karen was speaking her mind, no holds barred. However, she hadn't taken complete leave of her senses.

"I'm mad at Johnny for putting me through so much crap. I'm mad at myself for not checking my breasts. And"—she chose her words carefully—"I'm mad at God." She waited for a reaction from Big Mama but got none. "Did you hear me, Ms. Emma? I'm mad at God too."

“Yes, chile, I hear every word.”

“Isn’t that terrible? You think maybe that’s why I’m not getting healed because I am so mad?”

“Well, let’s see. Do ya love ya parents?”

“My parents died a long time ago, but I love them. They were very good to me, and I miss them.”

“Did ya ever get mad at them ’bout something even if it turned out not to be their fault?”

“Yes . . .” Karen reluctantly answered, not knowing where Big Mama was headed with the question.

“And ya still love ’em, huh?”

Karen nodded in affirmation.

“Why, there ya go. Love saw ya right past all that mad.”

“I wish it was all that easy. All of this guilt and anger is eating me up inside. I can’t seem to let it go.”

“Ya have to let it go. In order for ya to live, ya gon’ have to let some of that junk in ya die. If’n it don’t kill ya body, it will sho’ kill ya spirit, and that ain’t no way to live.”

“You’re right; this isn’t any way to live.” Karen wouldn’t voice any more of her inner feelings to Big Mama but continued to contemplate her situation. She didn’t want to be mad any more than she wanted to keep enduring a struggling marriage. What could she do? Getting well and rushing home wasn’t the supercure. All she had to look forward to at home was more of the same. Staying on the endlessly running merry-go-round was a sobering image.

CHAPTER 29

Karen had been in the hospital a month, and Johnny was feeling the pressure. Chelle was quite the little trouper, cleaning, cooking, and getting Elizabeth off to school every day. Chelle wanted to carry the housekeeping load but she was only fifteen years old. She still had her own schoolwork and teenage livelihood.

Johnny sat in the home office located near the front foyer. The junk mail and bills were scattered across the desk. He was much more organized in his personal affairs when Karen was around. He hadn't realized before that she routinely went through the mail and separated out the junk from the substance. He had to do all of it on his own without her assistance.

Chelle walked into the office doorway, not quick to interrupt. Johnny saw her standing there and signaled for her to come in.

"Daddy, the water faucet is leaking in Elizabeth's bathroom. What should we do?"

Johnny sighed from being overwhelmed.

"Did you turn the water off?"

"Yes."

"I'll take a look at it then."

"Last year mine did the same thing and Mommy had the plumber come out and fix it. It had something to do with a washer or something like that."

Johnny hadn't known anything about it. He was amazed to know Karen handled various problems around the house without his input. He shook his head. She wasn't home to handle the day-to-day activities and it was all falling in his lap.

Chelle was headed back out of the room when she remembered something.

"Oh, yeah, Daddy, I need some money to pay for our field trip."

"Field trip? I didn't know that sophomores still took field trips."

She smiled, happy to see her father in an easygoing mood.

"We've already had three trips this year. Mommy went on two of them with me."

"I didn't know that. Your Mommy seems to do a lot, doesn't she?"

Chelle nodded her head in agreement. The comment about her mother brought a smile to her face.

Johnny couldn't figure out how Karen used to do it all, work, take care of the house, and keep up with children.

"Daddy, don't forget that lower school is off tomorrow for teacher-parent conferences."

Johnny didn't try to pretend that he had any clue what that meant for him. He was quickly realizing how out of touch he was with the children's schooling. Karen took care of all that business.

"Chelle, what do I have to do?"

"You have to go meet with Ms. Bartel, Elizabeth's teacher. You should have a note with the time on it. She gave it to you last week."

Johnny aimlessly flipped through the papers on the desk. He scouted through the mound of bills, which included the mortgage on the summer home, the boat maintenance and slip fee, an invoice from the fur storage company, a notice from the landscaper that he'd be out to do the annual spring cleaning, the boating membership fee, the monthly tuition bill for the girls, and the supplemental insurance for Karen, in addition to the basic utilities, phone, cable, mortgage, credit cards, car notes, and a variety of insurance. He retrieved the Stanford letter while searching through the pile. It read, *Spring Quarter—Tuition, Room & Board, Miscellaneous Fees—Total: $10,000.* He tucked it in the top drawer. It would have to wait for the equity loan check. Johnny was expecting it any day and checked the mailbox as soon as he got home each evening.

"It's a purple envelope," Chelle eased in to help bring structure to his futile search.

That little bit of information was all he needed to hone in on the document. He ripped open the envelope and glanced over it. The time read two-thirty.

"I have a meeting at two-thirty tomorrow." He rubbed his chin. The stress was kicking in, and the day hadn't really begun.

"We're not off in upper school tomorrow, so I won't be able to stay at home with her."

"Where does she usually go on days off?"

"She stays at home with Mommy. When Mommy was working, she just took off for the day."

The answer wasn't as simple to Johnny as it seemed for Chelle. He didn't shy away from his obligations as a father. He needed a job to provide for his kids, but without a family the job was insignificant. Which came first? He never had to wonder when Karen was home. Her role as a mother and wife had freed him to live without having to set priorities between the family and his career. Without her picking up the slack, he was feeling the full weight of his responsibilities. He had blindly believed that it was all his efforts that had gotten him to advance on the job. Never had it been so apparent to him that Karen's support and efforts within the home helped him to thrive outside of the home. He was starting to appreciate Karen's worth in the relationship, whereas he used to think she was home all day, sitting around carefree and eating bonbons. One month of overwhelming reality had erased that notion.

"We're heading out to school, Daddy. We'll see you tonight."

Johnny waved the girls off, gulped down a swig of orange juice and headed off to work later than normal and with more worries than he cared to sift through.

Even the peace that he expected at work didn't come. The day was hectic. It hadn't been necessary before for him to bring personal matters to the office. Today Johnny was doing the best he could to balance work and home.

"Sonja, can you please get Ms. Bartel on the phone at my daughter's school?" He handed her a business card with the phone number. "See if I can reschedule the parent-teacher conference for sometime tomorrow evening."

"What if she doesn't have any evening slots?"

"Anything except two-thirty. I have that meeting tomorrow with the production crew from Tennessee."

"That's right. I'll see what I can do."

Sonja made the call and went to Johnny's office to relay the information. Even though the door was open, she still knocked.

"Excuse me, sir. I was able to speak with Ms. Bartel. Tomorrow evening is not going to work. I had to set you up for nine o'clock tomorrow morning. That was the only time she had that wasn't in conflict with your meeting."

"Thank you, Sonja."

The appointment meant that he would have to miss part of the morning at work. Johnny wasn't thrilled with the time, but there was nothing he could do about it. He had to figure out what to do with Elizabeth for the day. It hadn't been a problem when Karen had gotten sick the other times. He had paid for a live-in nanny and she took care of the kids. Funds were flowing back then. He could afford the gourmet option for child care. Times had changed, and he was looking for more of a sack-lunch kind of solution.

Off and on he contemplated what to do with Elizabeth. Before he had only had to concern himself with the big issues. It was turning out that all of the little things Karen handled daily added up to be just as significant and time-consuming as his obligations. He was developing a greater appreciation for Karen as a wife and mother now that he was on the front line at home. By the time Johnny got home, he was worn out. The idea of spending a couple of hours doing bills before bed wasn't a thrilling scene. It was getting tighter and tighter without Karen's financial input. Johnny thought about getting rid of the Porsche and saving the seven-hundred-and-fifty-dollar monthly payment. His insurance would go down as well. He didn't want to let his toy go, but the financial options were limited. A roof over their heads, food in their stomachs, working utilities, and an education were necessities. Luxuries were expendable.

Chelle helped with dinner, but there was still more that had to be done around the house, like cleaning. The girls did the laundry and washed the dishes regularly, but that was pretty much all they could handle. The house was not nearly as clean as the way Karen kept it. Johnny couldn't afford a service. Several women from the church had offered to come by and clean, but he didn't want strangers rooting around the house. At least that was how he had felt a month ago, when the place was still clean. Times had changed, and so had Johnny's attitude about receiving help.

After much pondering, he gave up on getting someone to take care of Elizabeth for tomorrow. Connie had doctor appointments and Tyrone was going with her. The baby-sitter was unavailable. He even let Chelle call Tina to see if she could help out. Unfortunately for the girls, Tina couldn't take off work for the entire day, since a couple of the other secretaries had already requested the day off. Johnny had run out of choices.

Chelle and Elizabeth were doing their homework at the table.

"Chelle, you're going to have to stay at home with Elizabeth tomorrow."

"Daddy, no. I have preps for my midterms."

Johnny felt bad about putting his daughter in such an awkward situation, but he didn't feel that there were any other alternatives.

"I have to go to school tomorrow," Chelle reiterated with tears in her eyes.

Johnny sighed and rubbed his forehead. The stress was mounting. Chelle was his last resort, and that wasn't panning out.

"What now?"

Elizabeth was quiet. She felt like Johnny and Chelle were both upset because of her. She began to cry.

"Why are you crying, Elizabeth?" her father asked.

"Because you and Chelle are mad at me."

Instinctively, Chelle jumped to her sister's defense. "No, Elizabeth, I'm not mad at you. You didn't do anything wrong. Don't cry. Finish your homework."

"Yeah, Elizabeth, don't cry," Johnny consoled from afar.

Chelle felt bad about making her sister cry.

"Daddy, I'll stay home with her."

Johnny felt worse.

"No, Chelle, you go to school. I will take her to work with me."

Elizabeth's eyes got big. Her father's job was always made out to be a big deal in the family. For a little girl like Elizabeth, going to work with her father was like going to the White House to meet the president. It was an honor. She dried her eyes and perked up.

Johnny didn't know how he was going to do it, but he had to do whatever it was he had to do. Taking care of the kids wasn't easy without Karen. He was doing the best he could without the help of his partner.

The three were able to get through the evening without any fanfare. Early the next morning Johnny dropped Elizabeth off at the office. Sonja had agreed to watch the little girl.

Johnny headed to the school to meet with Ms. Bartel. He had never been to a parent-teacher conference for any of the kids. Karen had faithfully gone to each conference and reported the findings back to him. He didn't know what to expect. His kids were intelligent, well mannered, and quite exceptional in school. He assumed the teacher would go over Elizabeth's grades, attendance, and conduct, and at the end, hand him a few of her completed assignments. He planned to be in and out in fifteen minutes or less.

"I don't know that we've ever met, Mr. Clark. I have always dealt with your wife. Anyway, thank you for coming today. I would have called you sooner, but I knew the conferences were coming up."

"Called me sooner about what?"

Ms. Bartel placed a scoring chart in front of Johnny. She took a pencil and drew attention to several numbers.

"As you can see, Elizabeth's grades have dropped dramatically over the past month."

The numbers were clear, but Johnny had a hard time processing them.

"She is quite an active and talkative student. Recently she has been withdrawn and very emotional."

Johnny sat back in the chair. He didn't know what to say. Everything was falling apart. It was hitting him on every side. Nothing seemed like status quo.

"Elizabeth has been an excellent student all year. This change is totally unexpected."

"Huh." Johnny sighed. "Unexpected for you? What about for me?"

"I can imagine, Mr. Clark. I didn't feel alarmed until I began to see the change in her behavior. Do you have any idea what could be causing this change?"

"Yes," Johnny eked out. "We are dealing with a major issue at home."

The teacher let Johnny take his time and get out the words.

"My wife is back in the hospital with cancer."

"I didn't know that." The school had a policy that suggested parents inform the school of any significant events in the student's life that might have an impact on their school performance. She flipped through her file to see if there was a note somewhere that she'd overlooked. She found none.

Outside of Karen, Chelle was Johnny's eyes and ears about school business. He was unaware of the policy and had not informed anyone about Karen's condition. If Chelle hadn't informed the school, then it hadn't been done.

Johnny felt so out of control. Unknowingly, he was letting so many important items fall through the cracks. Johnny felt he was letting his children down. They needed to be able to depend on him, now more than ever.

"Elizabeth is very close to her mom. I guess she's having a hard time with her illness." Johnny was disturbed. "I guess we're all having a rough time."

"I'm sorry to hear about Mrs. Clark. My prayers are with her and your entire family."

"Thank you."

"Now, about Elizabeth. I would like to immediately get her set up with the school psychologist. She may need an outlet to discuss her feelings. We need to get on top of this," Ms. Bartel firmly suggested to the distraught father.

Johnny nodded in agreement.

"All I need is your signed consent."

"You got it. Whatever I need to do for my little girl, I'll do it."

He felt guilty and embarrassed about not being more in tune with his daughter. It bothered him that he hadn't noticed. He was so stretched between paying the bills, running the house, working, keeping the girls alive, and visiting Karen at the hospital, there was no room for anything else. He hadn't stepped foot in Floods in over a month and couldn't remember the last time he'd responded to Annette's pages. Only the important areas of his life were getting attention. There wasn't room for extras.

Johnny couldn't imagine being a single parent. He couldn't raise the kids without Karen.

CHAPTER 30

The consistent routine entailed checking Karen's vital signs every six to eight hours. Her breathing was shallow, her temperature hovering around a hundred and four, and her pulse was weak.

"Doctor, what is going on with Karen?" Johnny didn't like the way she looked. "Is she getting any better? Why is she sleeping so much?"

"Johnny, I can't explain what's happening with Karen. Her vital signs are weak, and I don't know why. She's in a light coma, but at least she's still breathing on her own."

"Is it from the cancer?"

"No, I don't think so."

"What do you mean, you don't think so? If you don't know, then who does?"

"What I mean is that the cancer should not be causing this much deterioration on her body. We completed the treatments. Her body should be much stronger than what we're seeing. I know that she was suffering from malnutrition and dehydration a week or so ago. However, I am confident that we talked her into letting us administer the IV fluids in plenty of time to ward off any related setbacks."

"So why is she in a coma?"

Dr. Costas shrugged her shoulders, at a loss for words.

"I'm sorry, Johnny, but I just don't have an answer for you. For some unknown reason, Karen is getting sicker. There's no medical explanation for it."

Johnny scratched his head in utter frustration.

"If you don't know what's wrong with her, then how can you treat her?"

"We're doing the best we can. We'll keep her on the fluids, meds, and oxygen until we see some kind of change." Dr. Costas seemed a little uneasy. "Johnny, there is something else we need to discuss."

"What?"

"In the event Karen isn't able to continue breathing on her own, do you . . ."—she hesitated before giving the final blow—"want to have her put on life support?"

It felt like a trick question to Johnny. He and Karen had never discussed a living will, even though they'd been through her life-threatening illnesses in the past. There was no good answer. If Karen couldn't breathe on her own and needed the machine, that wasn't going to be good. If she couldn't breathe on her own and he chose not to put her on a respiratory machine, that wasn't going to be good either. It was a no-win dilemma, one that Johnny wasn't eager to rush into.

He always had options and never ran away from making a tough call. Johnny prided himself on being able to get the job done under the most adverse conditions. He sat in the chair, rubbing his palms together. He didn't have the answer for this problem.

"I don't know what to tell you." He felt like sticking his head in the sand and letting the matter pass.

"Johnny, Karen isn't doing well right now. Before her condition gets worse, I'm going to need an answer."

"You'll have to give me some time to make a decision."

Dr. Costas needed an answer, but felt it was inappropriate to apply any more pressure on Johnny than she already had.

The doctor left and Johnny found himself alone and confused. He didn't know what to do. He eased back in the chair and let the sound of calm usher him into a light sleep. Johnny wasn't tired, but the sleep felt good. It gave him a few moments of desperate escape from this bad dream. He wanted to sleep away the problem and wake up with it all behind him. He wasn't going to admit it, but he was experiencing common symptoms of depression.

He was awakened by the nurse's routine check. He slowly opened his eyes. The short, two-hour nap was the most uninterrupted sleep he'd gotten in weeks. Once he was able to get his eyes focused, Tyrone and Connie came into view.

"Hey, chief."

"Hi, Johnny," Connie softly greeted him. She rolled her wheelchair around the bed to get closer to Johnny, careful not to bump Karen's bed. She gently took his hand and said, "How's she doing?"

Johnny was visibly struggling with Karen's being comatose. His words didn't flow as freely.

"Not good, Connie. The doctor came in earlier and asked me if I wanted to put her on a life support system if it comes to that."

Johnny wasn't crying, but he was choked up. Connie sensed his pain and tried to console him by rubbing his hand.

"Hang in there, Johnny, no matter what it looks like. You have to keep the faith."

"I'm trying, Connie. It's a lot easier said than done."

Tyrone stood behind Connie's chair and placed his hands on her shoulders in support. He knew that she was hurt also by Karen's condition, since they were such good friends. She patted Tyrone's hand.

"Honey, can you roll me back some? I don't want to hit the bed."

"My goodness, it looks like a party up in here."

Everyone in the room turned around to see Tina standing in the doorway.

"Hi, Tina. I didn't know you were coming out here today," Connie said.

Johnny didn't have the same smiley face for Tina that Connie had. She was the last person he wanted to see at a stressful time like this.

Tina didn't see Johnny roll his eyes at her. Tyrone did. He knew that Johnny probably needed some air.

"Hey, Johnny, why don't we go grab a cup of coffee?"

"I don't know, man. I should probably be around, just in case something—I don't know what—happens."

"Come on, man. You could use a break."

"Yeah, go on, Johnny. I'll be here with Karen. Go on with Tyrone. You need some time," Connie said.

Johnny conceded and took the couple up on their offer.

The two men headed to the cafeteria in virtual silence. Tyrone knew Johnny didn't need advice. A shoulder to lean on and a listening ear would suffice.

The two women left in the room weren't nearly as quiet.

Tina took a chair between the bed and Connie's wheelchair. "How long have you been here?" Tina asked.

"Not long before you came in." Connie lowered her voice. There was the possibility that Karen could hear the conversations going on around her while she was unconscious. Connie wheeled her chair toward the door, expecting Tina to follow her cue.

Once the women had relocated into the hallway, Tina asked Connie, "Any news?"

"Apparently the doctor hasn't seen any improvement. They're hoping she can continue breathing on her own, without life support. Johnny is pretty upset. I feel so sorry for him."

"Humph. I don't feel sorry for him. Some of it's probably his fault anyway. He's done enough dirt to drive anybody to the grave."

Neither woman saw the men coming around the corner until they were well within range to hear the conversation.

"Tina! How can you say something like that? This is not the time or place for you to be talking about Johnny like that. We need to be supportive."

"Supportive! Please. How supportive has he been to her? Karen might have to pretend that he's the ideal husband, but not me. I don't have to live with him. I can say exactly how I feel about the jerk."

"Jerk." Johnny chuckled. The humor in his voice didn't last long. "Girl, you got some nerve bringing all that negativity up in here. I guess it's not enough for you to be miserable at home alone; you feel it necessary to come over here and try to make everybody else miserable too." Johnny was getting louder and angrier with each word. "You need to get up out of here. My wife is sick and you show up with this crap. Get out of here."

"Calm down, partner," Tyrone said. "Take it easy."

"Yes, Johnny, try to calm down. All of this aggravation can't be good for you," Connie insisted.

"You're right. I don't know how I let this witch get to me."

"Witch! No, you didn't call me a witch, especially when you're the one with the bag of tricks."

"Please stop, you two." Connie was determined to maintain some peace and quiet in the hallway. She knew how irritating excessive noise could be for people who were sick. "We are here to give Karen support. This is not about any differences the two of you might have. If anything, the two of you need to be in prayer together."

"Prayer? Girl, please. There you go. You're always trying to shove prayer down somebody's throat. It doesn't work for everybody," Tina said.

"Yes, it does work—for anybody," Connie replied.

"Why hasn't it worked for you?" Tina questioned.

Tyrone had been quiet while everyone else talked back and forth until Tina crossed the line. He didn't tolerate anyone saying anything about Connie in his presence.

"Whoa, wait a minute, Tina. You need to contain yourself. You're letting your mouth get way out of line."

Tyrone was sensitive to how people interpreted the demeanor of his wife. She was passive, and some saw it as an opportunity to push her around. He was quick to protect her whenever necessary.

"That's okay, honey." She sat on the edge of her wheelchair. This time she chose to speak up for herself. "Listen, Tina, let me tell you something."

Both Tyrone and Johnny were shocked to see Connie stand up to Tina. Even Tina found herself curiously listening.

"I know that you are angry and bitter because your husband left you once you got sick. I'm sorry about that. I can only imagine how you feel. I've told you time and time again that it wasn't your fault that you got cancer, but it's not our fault either."

"Cancer? Connie, you of all people shouldn't be talking about cancer. You don't even acknowledge your own condition. How can you possibly understand how I feel?"

"Tina, that's . . ." Tyrone jumped in. He had heard enough.

Connie patted Tyrone's hand, letting him know that she was fine with Tina's outburst. Connie smiled with her lips tight, seeming unfazed.

"Tina, I do know what you went through with the cancer. I could be angry and bitter, just like you. I choose not to be. I have decided to focus on the good in my life and block out the negativity. It's what keeps me alive. Because I don't walk around with my head hanging down and acting mad with the world, you think that I'm living with my head in the sand about the brain tumor."

Tina wanted to respond, but Connie left no room for interruption.

"I know exactly what the doctors have said about the tumor. I just choose not to claim it as my tumor. I know they don't expect me to live, but that doesn't stop me from living and believing. Every day that I'm alive is a good day for me, no matter how bad I feel. I am too grateful to waste my time with a bunch of negativity."

Tina was speechless.

"Now don't get me wrong; I am appreciative of the doctors for their help. But they don't determine how long I live or even how I'm going to die. I can choose life or death. Some people in my situation spend so much precious time focusing on just staying alive that they don't do any kind of living. I don't have the luxury of worrying about tomorrow. Every day has to count for me, because I don't want to die knowing that I spent all of my time just trying to stay alive."

Tears streamed down Tina's face from a combination of shame, guilt, and hurt. Connie was the friend she had so often viewed as the weak duckling who needed protecting. Through her teary vision, Tina saw a strong, soft-spoken woman who let her actions speak for her. Tina admired few people and saw most as hypocritical. She respected the fact that Connie didn't just talk about living right. She actually practiced it. Tina felt odd. It was as if the armor surrounding her heart had been penetrated and the hurt was exposed.

"With my faith in God, I choose to live every day that I am alive as though it is my last, and I'm okay with that."

Tyrone hugged Connie as she eased back in her chair. Her hope was that things would start to look up for both of her friends.

CHAPTER 31

Johnny walked into the kitchen carrying bags of groceries. He set them down on the counter and pulled out the honey-roasted chickens, plastic containers stuffed with corn, rice pilaf, and green beans. The girls were light eaters, but Johnny got two chickens anyway, since they were small.

"You girls hungry?"

The kitchen had become Chelle and Elizabeth's nightly study area. "A little," Chelle answered without disrupting her schoolwork.

He proceeded to pull the paper plates from the cabinet. Johnny had never realized the benefit of using disposable eating utensils. Convenience had never been an issue when Karen was home running the household. She handled the vast majority of the work. Johnny and the rest of the family had taken their meals and the daily cleaning for granted.

"Anybody feed the dog yet?"

The girls froze, knowing the outrage that could follow this question. Karen wasn't there to rescue them. They knew blaming the other for not getting the chore done was not going to help this time. Without a word of denial, both girls dropped their pencils and hopped to their feet.

"Wait, wait," Johnny told the girls in a strong voice.

Both girls stood still with bewildered looks on their faces.

"Don't worry about the dog. I'll feed him from now on. Since Mommy's gone, we all have extra work to do around here. And the two of you have enough to do between the chores that you're already doing and your schoolwork. Sit back down and do your work. I'll go out and feed Mindy."

The girls sat back down and went right back to their homework. After Johnny went outside, Chelle told Elizabeth, "I'm glad we don't have to feed that dog anymore."

Elizabeth said, "Me too," and went back to doing her math homework.

Erick fumbled with his keys outside the front door. He hadn't been home since Christmas. The thought of being thousands of miles away with his mom in the hospital was too much to bear. He had used the remaining balance on his credit card to get a ticket. Coming home took a great deal of courage. He wasn't looking forward to facing his father, based on the last conversation they had had.

Erick finally got the door opened and carted his duffel bag and backpack inside the foyer. There wasn't any activity in the front room. He headed for the kitchen and family room area. The chatter got louder as he approached the room. His steps got faster. He felt a special bond with his younger sisters and had missed them.

When he hit the doorway, Elizabeth caught the first glimpse. For a moment she wasn't sure if it was him, but quickly concluded that it was. "Erick," she screamed, and leaped from the chair, running toward him.

The screeching yell startled Chelle. It took a second for her to get her bearings. Once she did, she too rushed over to him.

They all hugged one another in unison.

Johnny heard the scream and came rushing in the back door to see what was going on. He was shocked to see John Erick standing in the kitchen. The sight of him didn't draw the same excitement from Johnny as it had from the girls. He loved his son, but his stubborn side often diluted his outward display of affection. Johnny was still feeling the sting from the comments Erick had made in their last conversation.

"Hey, Dad."

Erick tore himself from the girls and humbly walked over to his father. He knew his father's staunch commanding side. He knew that if there was going to be reconciliation, it had to be initiated by him. Erick did have a streak of his father's stubbornness. It was tempered with his mother's willingness to concede. The main reason he came home was to be with his family and offer support to his mom. He was determined that nothing was going to interfere with that, especially not an ongoing fight with his dad.

"I apologize for how I talked to you on the phone."

Erick didn't take back what he had told his dad on the phone. He apologized for how and when he had said it. Afterward he extended his hand for his father to shake. Erick wasn't sure where his father's head was. He didn't know whether he'd accept the apology or not.

Johnny looked at his young son and processed his apology. For a moment he did nothing. Then he reached out and grabbed his son, with tears filling his eyes.

"I'm glad you're home, son." Johnny patted Erick on his back. Johnny had been trying to hold it all together around the house. With Chelle's help, he'd gotten by. But too much was falling through the cracks, like Elizabeth's emotional welfare.

John Erick had no idea how much his father admired him. Perhaps it was because Erick was one of the few people in Johnny's circle who would stand up to him. Johnny's outpouring seemed to be a confirmation of the happiness that he was feeling to have his son home at this critical time. He wasn't able to verbalize his feelings.

The hug was sufficient for Erick. It was more than he'd ever gotten in the past and more than he could ever have hoped for.

"I'm glad you came home too, Erick. I miss you a lot when you're gone. Are you going to stay here?" Elizabeth's little eyes beamed.

Johnny was glad to see her smile. Of the two girls, Elizabeth was having the most difficulty with her mother's illness. Her grades were slowly climbing back up, primarily resulting from the school counseling.

"I can use your help around here," Johnny told his son.

The girls adored their big brother. He was protective, while at the same time affectionate with them. Johnny took care of them, but there was nothing like the extra dose of doting that they got when Karen was around. Erick was a welcome sight.

CHAPTER 32

The hypothetical scenarios had become an agonizing reality. Johnny didn't hesitate to put her on the life-support machine when Karen had actually stopped breathing last week. He wanted her to stay alive any way possible, even if it was by assisted means.

The rising and falling of the breathing machine created a rhythmic hum. *Tzzzzzt, tzzzzzt* blended with *beep beep*.

Weeks ago, the unfamiliar setting and nagging noises would have made it impossible for Johnny to get any sleep in Karen's hospital room. His tolerance and the frequency of lengthy days and overnight stays had increased as her condition worsened. His trench coat barely shielded his upper body from the cold draft. He clutched the garment like a toasty wool blanket.

Beep, beep, the IV alarmed. Within a few minutes the nurse came in to change the bottle. She tried to be quiet, seeing the large man crunched into the high-backed chair pushed into the corner. It didn't matter. Johnny had been catnapping most of the evening. He couldn't get comfortable, no matter how he shifted his weight around in the chair.

Johnny grunted during his stretch.

"Oh, Mr. Clark, I didn't mean to wake you up."

"You didn't wake me up. I haven't really slept in days." In the middle of his sentence, Johnny covered his mouth. He got a whiff of the foul breath seeping across his lips. His shirt was wrinkled, his mouth dry, and his feet sweaty. He could only hope that the nurse didn't smell his less-than-desirable aroma. He immediately jerked his arms down and pinned them to his sides.

"Perhaps you should go home and get some rest. We'll call you if anything changes. You won't do Mrs. Clark any good if you let yourself get run-down."

Karen's condition was slowly deteriorating. As long as Karen was unstable, the nights seemed endless for Johnny and her medical team.

Johnny didn't know what to do. He hadn't always come through for Karen, but this time he wanted to be there for her, whichever way her condition went. If she woke up, he wanted to be the first face she laid eyes on. If she didn't wake up, he knew that the anguish of not being at her bedside would eat him alive.

"I'll wait to see if someone else shows up before I run home. How are her vital signs? Any improvement?"

The nurse shook her head in disappointment.

"There has been no change. She's weak, but she's still holding on."

Johnny couldn't have pictured this scenario several months ago. Wrinkled shirt, tart breath, hair stubbles, funky feet, and a drooled chin were a far cry from the clean-shaven, impeccably dressed, handsome man standing at the entrance of Floods.

"On second thought, I will run home for a few hours." He wanted to go home, get cleaned up, and come right back to the hospital and stay for the night. The nurses paid close attention to Karen, watching for any dramatic change in her condition that might warrant contacting the doctor.

It was eleven-thirty on a Thursday night, and Dr. Costas still happened to be awake when her pager vibrated on top of the desk before falling to the floor. This was her month to be on call, so she picked up the pager.

It was the hospital. She dialed the number back.

"Intensive Care Unit."

"This is Dr. Costas. I got a page."

"Oh, yes, Doctor. We wanted to let you know that Karen Clark's vital signs have deteriorated dramatically. Her pulse and blood pressure are both low. Her fever is also spiking."

"Is she still on the fluids?"

"Yes, she is. We also put her on an ice pad to help get the fever down. It topped off at a hundred and five over an hour ago. It was at one-oh-four-point-eight when we checked fifteen minutes ago."

"Doesn't sound too good."

"I thought you'd want to know."

"Do I need to come out to the hospital?"

"No, I don't think so, Doctor. We've done everything that we can do."

"I guess we just have to wait and hope that she makes it through the night. Is anyone from her family there?"

"No, Mr. Clark left several hours ago. I think he's coming back, though. He's been staying here through the night. If you want me to, I can call him. I just thought it would be best to call you first."

"You were right to call me first," Dr. Costas conceded. "I will give Mr. Clark a call. I was hoping that it wouldn't come to this, but here we are. Can you give me the emergency number in her file? It should be their home number."

"Sure thing, Doctor. Hold on while I get that number."

Dr. Costas tried not to cross any ethical lines. However, she and Karen did connect on more than a purely patient-doctor level. Dr. Costas was grieved to know that Karen could very well be approaching the final phase of her battle with the breast cancer. Karen's warm personality chiseled a hopeful smile on Dr. Costas's face.

"I have that number for you."

Dr. Costas scribbled the number onto a notepad. "Keep me posted on her condition."

The doctor stood in her office, slow to make the unavoidable call.

Johnny had taken a hot shower when he got in from the hospital around ten P.M. Exhausted, he had stretched out across the bed to catch some of the Pistons and Sixers game, intending to eat the sandwich Chelle had made for him.

The ringing cordless phone lying next to Johnny's head sounded like an alarm clock. He woke up with the television playing and the sandwich untouched. He unconsciously grabbed the phone just to stop the testy noise.

"Hello," he answered with an edge in his tone.

"Johnny, hi. This is Dr. Costas."

Johnny popped up in the bed.

"Is something wrong?" His heart was pounding. He had asked the question, but wasn't ready for the answer.

"I got a call from the hospital. Karen has a fever near a hundred and five, and her other vital signs aren't looking too good."

"What does it all mean?"

"Johnny, it means that Karen has taken a turn for the worse. She's in critical condition. I'm not looking for her to make it through the night."

"What else can you do? There has to be something you haven't tried."

"We have done everything that we can medically do to turn her prognosis around. Nothing that we've tried has gotten the results that I was hoping for. I'm sorry, Johnny. I feel bad having to give you this news. I was hopeful that she would overcome this last bout. Really, I am truly sorry."

"I'm going to the hospital. Will you be there?"

"I won't go unless her condition takes the final turn for the worse," Dr. Costas answered. "At that time, we will need to make some decisions."

"Like what?"

"Remember when we talked several weeks ago about whether or not you want to terminate the life support and let her expire naturally?"

"I'm not ready to make that decision."

"I realize how difficult this is for you."

"I need more time to think about it. I can't give up on her. I don't care what it looks like." Johnny's voice was building momentum.

"You need to try to keep yourself calm. You're going to need to be as rational as possible in the upcoming hours."

"I'm going to do the best that I can."

"I wish that we could do more. If you need to get in touch with me, have the hospital page me, no matter what time of night."

Johnny clicked off the cordless phone. He slid over to the side of the bed and planted both feet on the floor. His head hung down, with his eyes tightly shut. Drops fell onto the floor. There weren't any boo-hooing wails coming from his room, just a continuous stream of tears. He didn't know what to do first. He thought about informing the kids, then decided against it. The thought of telling the children that their mother was dying tore him apart. The tears intensified. Johnny felt grave turmoil. He tried to get himself together. He wiped away the tears and dug deep inside to find enough strength to get off of the bed and make some necessary decisions. He allowed himself a brief moment to grieve and think. Finally he was able to make it to his feet.

This was one of the few times that he felt lonely from being an only child with both parents deceased. It was a similarity that he and Karen shared. Despite their limited extended-family circle, the Clarks hadn't felt an overwhelming void in the past. Tonight was different. The first person who came to mind was Tyrone. He had been a longtime friend who had proven himself to be dependable. That was exactly what Johnny felt that he needed.

Tyrone and Connie were already in bed. When the phone rang, Tyrone rolled over to grab it. Instead, he knocked it onto the floor.

"Hello," Johnny said.

Tyrone fumbled for the phone with one hand, searching for the tabletop lamp switch with the other.

"Hello?" Johnny reiterated in a deeper tone.

"Hey, fella." Tyrone finally got himself together. He squinted his eyes to bring the digital clock into focus. Midnight. Tyrone knew this was important. He sat up in the bed, braced to hear whatever news Johnny was about to lay on him.

Connie woke up upon hearing all of Tyrone's noise.

"Is that Johnny?" she whispered.

Tyrone nodded in affirmation. She sat up in the bed too.

"What's up, buddy?"

Johnny had decided before calling Tyrone that he would hold it together. It was the manly thing to do. At least that was what his rational mind had said, but his heart wasn't in agreement. He struggled to find the words. They wouldn't roll off of his tongue.

Tyrone knew Johnny was struggling with something, so he tried to help out.

"Is there a change with Karen?"

"Yes," he solemnly admitted, as though he were releasing the weight of a heavy secret. "Her doctor called me a few minutes ago and told me she wasn't doing so good." Every word he spoke was slow and life draining. "They don't expect her to make it through the night."

"Oh, no, Johnny. Man, I don't know what to say."

"What, what?" Connie asked, tugging on his arm.

"Karen's not doing well."

"Is there anything we can do?" Connie asked Tyrone loudly enough for Johnny to hear.

"Yeah, what can we do to help you?"

"I'm going to the hospital. I was wondering if you could meet me there? I don't feel up to going out there by myself."

"Don't say another word. Consider it done. I'm on my way right now. I'll see you there."

"Tyrone . . ." Johnny paused to find the words that would adequately convey his appreciation. "Uh, thanks, partner. You're all right with me." The lump in Johnny's throat moved up and squashed his vocal cords. He couldn't get any other words through.

"Don't say any more. I know what you're trying to say. I'll see you in a few minutes." Tyrone hung up the phone and sprang to his feet. "Connie, I'm going to meet Johnny at the hospital. It doesn't look good for Karen. I can tell he's taking it hard. I want to be there for him. Honey, do you mind if I go?"

"Do I mind if you go? I expect you to go." Connie kissed Tyrone on the cheek to seal her approval. "But I'm going too."

"Sweetheart, do you think that you should? What about getting your rest? You need to conserve your energy." He rubbed her head and kissed her forehead.

"You know Karen would be there for me. I'm going and that's that, Mr. Sims."

Tyrone adored his wife. When she firmly spoke her mind, he was not one to try to change it.

"Let's throw something on and get on out of here, young lady."

Tyrone's support gave Johnny enough boost to get off the bed and begin to make his way toward the hospital. The severity of the moment was plain. He was glad to have Tyrone meeting him at the hospital, but felt he needed something more. He was trying to rally every ounce of hope from any willing source.

I should tell the pastor. He picked up the phone and then thought twice about it. *Nah, it's too late to call.* Johnny remembered the pastor telling him to call anytime. *Maybe I should.* He went back and forth on what to do. He didn't feel close enough to the pastor to make a middle-of-the-night call. *What if something happens to Karen? I need somebody who can be there to pray.*

He was trying to sort mixed feelings. One part of him wanted to believe that Karen would defy the doctor's prognosis and live. The other part of him felt he should have someone there who could pray for her one last time, if necessary.

Whichever way it went, prayer couldn't hurt. He needed all of the spiritual strength he could muster. He tucked pride in his back pocket and proceeded to dial the pastor's phone number.

"Reverend Lane."

"Yes, Johnny." The pastor was gifted with a sharp ability to recognize voices with ease.

"You asked me to call you if there were any changes with Karen."

"Yes."

"Well, she's taken a turn for the worse. The doctors don't expect her to live through the night."

"Are you at the hospital?"

"Not yet, but I'm on my way," Johnny confirmed.

"Would you mind if I met you out there?"

"No, I wouldn't mind at all." Johnny was happy that the pastor had offered without having to be asked.

"Is there anything else I can do to help?"

"I was also wondering if there was any possible way that old lady could come with you."

"Which old lady?"

"The one who came out to the hospital to pray for Karen. I can't remember her name."

"You mean Mother Walker?"

"Yes, her." Johnny hadn't been too comfortable with all of that praying mumbo jumbo that she was doing in the hospital. But there was no doubt that she knew God in some fashion. Anyone who could offer a prayer was going to be a welcome sight in ICU room number three.

Johnny carefully made his way to the stairway, trying to avoid turning on the lights. It was late, and he didn't want to wake the kids.

"Dad," came Erick's raspy voice as he stood in the frame of the doorway. "Are you heading out?"

"Yes, I am, son. I'm going to check on your mom."

Johnny wasn't expecting any of the children to be up. He wasn't prepared to share the latest news with them, not just yet. If there was any possible hope that Karen would get better, he was going to cling to it.

"Do you want me to go with you?" Erick had no idea how dire his mother's condition was. Since Big Dad frequently spent nights at the hospital, this late-night run didn't seem abnormal. It was not an indication that anything was wrong.

"No, Erick. If you could, I need you to stay here with the girls."

"You got it, Big Dad." Erick wiped his sleepy eyes and watched his father descend down the stairs and out of sight.

CHAPTER 33

Johnny got to the hospital first. The intensive-care unit was hushed except for the minor movement around the nurses' station. Karen's condition had weakened. Johnny didn't know what to expect. He entered the room gingerly. The room was dark, barring the light above the head of her bed.

Tzzzzzt, tzzzzzt blended with *beep, beep* saturated the ICU room.

Remembering how full of life Karen was, Johnny found it difficult to look at the lifeless body lying still with a machine breathing for her. Recent years had been peppered with countless ups and downs in the marriage. Johnny hadn't foreseen the relationship ending like this. He had contemplated when and how to leave Karen numerous times, wanting to escape the clutches of her dependency. But never had her dying been an option.

Salisbury steak, mashed potatoes, and apple sauce was the lunch Johnny remembered being served the day he met Karen, standing in the high school cafeteria line. He was captivated by her beauty the first moment that he laid eyes on her. Her wit sealed his interest.

With time came changes. The financial pressures eased and Johnny's career took off, and so too did the animal magnetism that they had for one another. The couple grew apart with his focus on the business end and hers on the religious side. With both squared off in their corners, finding common ground became difficult.

"Karen"—Johnny gently took her hand—"I don't know if you can hear me. If you can, I want you to know that I love you. I am so sorry about Isabelle and the other women. I'm through with all of that. Believe me when I say that I never meant to hurt you. I just got caught up. Please forgive me. I want us to work things out. I didn't realize how much you mean to me." He forced the words out with his voice cracking at times. "You can't leave me, Karen. I need you. Please help us, God." He laid his head on her leg and allowed his mind to drift away to an easier place.

Johnny was out of his comfort zone. He couldn't order up a team to fix the problem, demand results from an assistant, or simply write a check to cover the damage. The closest he could get to a SWAT team was the group of friends and family that he was able to conjure up for support and prayer. He wiped the tears from his eyes and continued holding his wife's hand. He would have given anything to be able to slip into a restful sleep, far away from this moment. He tried but grief wouldn't let him taste a pinch of peace.

A few minutes later, Tyrone wheeled Connie in.

Johnny was glad to see the couple. All three knew the purpose for being there, and no small talk needed to be uttered.

Connie immediately rolled over to Johnny and patted his shoulder.

"How you holding up?"

"I . . ." he began, and then went silent. He covered his mouth with his hand. Not another word could find its way out. He broke down and wept openly.

Tyrone was taken aback. He had never seen Johnny so torn apart and vulnerable. It wasn't like him. Johnny was someone who tried not to show signs of weakness, let alone emotional hurt.

Tears swelled in Connie's eyes to see Johnny so broken.

"It's going to be all right, Johnny. We'll be here with you for as long as you need us."

"Thank you," he choked out, "for being here." His lips quivered. His wailing moans cast a somber feeling in the room.

Reverend Lane, Big Mama, her friend Mrs. Pierce, and two other people entered the grief-riddled room. They were the ones who provided emergency prayer for situations such as this.

Big Mama wasted no time adjusting the tone in the room.

"Good morning."

Hellos were quietly returned from the bunch in the group. Johnny still felt a bit awkward about the last run-in with Big Mama. He avoided direct eye contact with her.

"Johnny, I wants to thank ya for letting me come out here. It's sho' a blessing to me."

It was just like Big Mama to make a person feel comfortable around her, even if he had mistreated her in the past. Living without regrets and bottled hostility was her motto.

"No, Ms. Walker, I want to thank you for coming." He gave a deep sigh, which was the residual lump from his earlier crying episode. He felt bad enough for losing control in front of Tyrone and Connie and much worse for doing it in front of strangers. Johnny wasn't able to suppress his emotions. His moans continued.

"We're gonna believe God for healing."

He used to say, "I'm not into that touchy-feely crap. Leave that religious stuff for the poor slobs who don't have anything else going for them. I prefer to put my faith in my hard work and a few lucky breaks." Now that Karen was nearing the end of the line, Johnny was receptive to prayer, since his professional success, financial stature, and social prestige weren't helping Karen.

"I don't know why this happened to Karen. She is such a good person. It's not fair. There's a whole lot of mean people out there who don't have a sick day in their entire lives."

"I can't say why one gets sick and another don't. All I know is that thangs don't always look a certain way, but all thangs work together for good, the Word of God says." Big Mama wanted to give him a ray of hope without giving him a false sense that every question could be answered.

"It just doesn't seem right to me. She goes to church all the time. She believes in God, and it hasn't done any good."

"Johnny, it might not look like it, but believing in God has done Karen a world of good. I know," Connie added passionately.

He was careful about the words he chose for Connie. He considered her situation to be fragile. He was hurting. But the last thing he wanted to do was to say something that would hurt Connie and Tyrone.

"I'm sorry, but I just don't see how you can say that. I don't think I could keep up as much hope as you do if I had to go through what you've gone through. I honestly don't know how you do it. It's been hard enough for me with Karen's cancer. How do you do it?"

"Johnny, I made up my mind a long time ago that I wouldn't go up and down with my emotions. I am at peace with my circumstances." She grabbed Tyrone's hand, knowing that it wasn't quite as settling for him.

"How can you be at peace? I mean, what if you don't get better?"

"Whichever way it goes, I'm all right with it."

"You sound like it doesn't matter whether you live or die."

"It does matter, but not in the way you think."

Johnny looked puzzled.

"All that matters to me is that God's will be done in my life."

"So why would it be God's will for you to die? I thought Ms. Walker said that everything God did was supposed to be good."

Connie chuckled. She was amazed at the number of times that God had used her condition as a tool to share his message of hope.

"When you look at me, what do you see? And be honest."

Johnny was reluctant to be brutally honest, despite Connie's disclaimer.

"Please be honest. I'm tougher than you think."

Johnny looked at Tyrone as if to ask, "What do I say?"

Tyrone shrugged his shoulders slightly, giving Johnny the go-ahead to answer Connie openly.

"Okay, I see a nice young woman who is crippled from a brain tumor."

"That's right. You see me from the outside, like most people. But God sees me here." She spread her hand across her heart. "He knows the inner me, the real Connie."

"With all that faith, why hasn't He made you well?"

"How do you know that He hasn't?"

"Because you're still sick."

"That's how you see it. You know how I get my peace?"

"No," Johnny admitted, but he was curious to know the answer. A bit of peace was exactly what he was hoping to get.

"I have peace because I see myself the way God sees me, healthy in my spirit, in my heart, and in my soul. I am full of life, enjoying every day He gives me, not with pity or sadness." She sat up straight in her chair with strength and conviction. "I am truly blessed just as I am. I don't mean any harm when I say this, but people like you throw away challenging days looking for the easy ones. It's like you're digging through a table of clearance clothes, picking out the few good pieces, and throwing most of them away because they're not to your taste. To someone with no clothes, they're all good. So it is with life. I don't know what tomorrow is going to bring. That's why every day that I'm alive is a good day, no matter how I feel and no matter what happens in it."

It was hard for Johnny to debate such a heartfelt expression whether he accepted her religious convictions or not. He did maintain his belief that there was a tinge of denial in Connie.

"I just don't get it, Connie; I'm sorry. How can you feel blessed when you can't even walk on your own?"

"I'm not walking on my own, Johnny, but I'm still breathing." She affectionately rubbed Tyrone's hand. "God could have let me die years ago, but He didn't. I'm still alive. So every moment that I'm alive is a blessing. Every moment that I can spend with Tyrone and my loved ones is a blessing. It eases whatever pain I suffer."

Connie's passionate words brought tears to Tyrone's eyes. No one in the room could say a word. One of the sickest people in the room had brought in the most light.

"All right, all right with all of this mushy stuff. Hey, chief, how about a cup of coffee?"

"Nah, I'd better hang around here."

"Johnny, go on and get some coffee. You just told Ms. Walker how tired you were. Go on. We'll be here with Karen."

Reluctantly, Johnny gave in. "I could use a little break. Thanks."

Big Mama wasted no time humming one of her favorite gospel songs, "God Is," while Connie prayed softly with the other warriors.

The men aimlessly found their way to the hospital cafeteria.

"How you holding up, partner?"

"I'm hanging in there, man, but to be honest, I don't know how. Honest to goodness, I really don't know how."

"I know it gets rough, but brother, that's all you can do is hang in there."

"Tyrone, you know, it's kind of funny. I've spent the last four years trying to figure out how to get rid of this woman." He sighed and then chuckled. "Now just the thought of her leaving me"—he paused—"is too much."

"Don't even think like that. Have faith, man. You have to go all the way. How do you think I feel when I look at Connie's frail body? I want to scream, but what can I do? All I can do is love her and support her. So that's what I do."

"But it's not at all what I thought it was going to be like."

"What?"

"Me and Karen, with her being sick this way." He shook his head in despair. "I just don't want her to go out like this. I wish there were something else I could do for her." He wiped the tears from his eyes. "I want to save her, man."

Tyrone patted Johnny on his shoulder.

"Don't be so hard on yourself, Johnny. It's no joke watching somebody that you love suffer. The bottom line is that there is only so much that you can do for her. You are only human. You can't be her savior." He smiled, thinking about his wife. "If nothing else, Connie has drilled that into my head, man. All you can do is believe and pray. That's it. The rest is out of your control."

Tyrone fumbled in his pocket for a cigarette. It was a habit he had begun when Connie got sick several years ago. He never smoked around her, which limited his puffing opportunities. He wanted to quit but found himself clinging to it during stressful times. This was one of those times. "Let's take a walk outside."

CHAPTER 34

The prayer team had their hands locked in a semicircle around Karen's bed when Johnny and Tyrone entered the room. Big Mama was leading the prayer while others joined in softly.

"Yes, Lord," came from one.

"Have mercy, Father. Pour out your healing blood," prayed another.

Each person took the lead at some point in the round-robin session.

Not knowing what else to do, Johnny broke the link between Big Mama and Mrs. Pierce to join the circle. Big Mama squeezed his hand in acknowledgment and continued in prayer. The group wound down to a close after an hour had passed.

Big Mama wrapped both her hands around Johnny's and said, "Ya gots to hold on, son. God didn't say that ya wouldn't have some challenges in ya life. It ain't all gon' to be a bed o' roses. But what God did say is that He will never leave you, nor forsake you—that is, if ya let Him." She continually rubbed his hand with gentle compassion. "Hold on to the Lord."

He shook his head. "Ms. Walker, I don't know how." He bit his lip, and his body trembled from holding back the sorrow that was bubbling up inside. He couldn't move forward without some peace from God or somebody. Ten years ago, he hadn't cared whether God existed. Through all of Karen's suffering, it had come to this.

Big Mama knew that Johnny was ready to accept the Lord. He needed the deep, penetrating comfort that only God could give. She thought about all of the years Karen had probably prayed for her husband to accept the Lord as his savior. She marveled at how the cancer, the thing Karen loathed the most, was the element being used to turn Johnny's heart toward God. She never grew tired of seeing how God would take something bad and turn it for good. Her heart was overjoyed, as it always was when someone wanted to know more about God and His love. She would say, "The angels in heaven is sho' singing today, 'cause another one of God's children done found they way home."

The rest of the room was silently praying. They knew this was the moment of truth for Johnny.

"Johnny, the first step to knowing God is to repent. Do ya know what that is?"

"Kind of."

"It means ya have to ask God to forgive ya for ya sins. 'Cause once ya come to the Lord and ask for forgiveness, He don't hold none of that ol' mess ya done over ya head. He lets ya start off fresh and clean. Praise be to God."

It was hard for Johnny to believe that some of his past could be wiped away so easily. He recalled how difficult it had been for Karen to let go of Isabelle. "How can God forgive me so easily when I don't forgive other people all the time?"

"That's the ol' Johnny. The new Johnny gon' know how to repent before God for his mistakes and how to love ya neighbor even when they do ya wrong. Forgiveness ain't always easy, but if God can sho' forgive us, who is we not to be able to forgive somebody else?"

"Yes, ma'am."

"Now, Johnny, I'm gon' walk ya through to salvation."

"Okay."

"Say, 'Father, please forgive me for my sins.'"

Johnny did as directed.

"Now do ya believe that the Lord is the son of God?"

"Yes, I do."

"Do ya believe that the Lord died on the cross for ya sins?"

"Yes." he sniffed.

"Do ya believe that God raised Jesus from the dead and that he lives in heaven with our Father?"

"Yes."

"Do ya understand that ya gon' have to die to ya ol' sinful nature and be reborn into the teachings and live in the ways of the Lord?"

"Yes, I understand."

"Do you accept Jesus Christ as ya personal savior?"

"Yes, I accept Jesus Christ as my personal savior."

"Then if'n ya believe in ya heart and confess with ya mouth that Jesus is Lord, then ya will be saved."

"I do." He sniffed again.

"Then welcome to the Lord's family."

"That's it? That's all I have to do?" Johnny didn't know what he had expected. Fire and brimstone, chariots of angels? He did feel some sort of release. He didn't know if it was guilt, stress, or just an emotional relief. "So I'm different now?"

"The old man ya used to be is dead and now ya reborn into the kingdom of God. Johnny, He wants ya to know that He loves ya with an everlasting love. No matter what ya go through from here on out, He promises to be with ya. Now ya can put ya faith and hope in Him. He won't never let ya down." Big Mama hugged him and the rest of the crowd followed suit.

After a brief moment of praise, the crowd thinned out.

"I guess we're going to head out, Johnny. God bless you, brother."

"I'ze gon' stay here. I'ze want to fast and pray for a while."

"Well, Mother, I'll pick you up later today."

"Why, thank ya, Pastor. If'n it's all the same to ya, I'ze rather call ya when I'ze ready, 'cause I'ze don't know how long it's gon' be. It might be a while."

"You're going to stay here!" Johnny couldn't imagine someone committing so much time to help a virtual stranger. He was practically living at the hospital, but it was expected of him. He was the husband.

"I'ze aim to stay until I'ze hear from the Lord, and some answers only come from fasting and praying. Oh, pardon me, Johnny. I'ze will be here if'n it's all right with ya?"

"Yes, ma'am, it's okay with me. Thank you for being here. I know Karen would want you here."

"No need to thank me, son. This is what I'ze called to do, praise be to the Lord."

"I'm going to stay for a while, too," Connie told Tyrone.

"Honey, don't you think that might be too much? You've been up all night. Don't you think staying might tire you out? We have to think about your health too."

"Tyrone, what good is my health if I can't be here when the people in my life need me? You know how I feel about Karen and Johnny. They're more than friends. They're family. They need me to be here, and I'm going to be here. I'm not going home, baby."

Tyrone wasn't comfortable with Connie's decision but didn't hesitate to respect it. As much as he wanted to shelter her, Connie was determined to live life to the fullest, unhindered by her condition. That was something he'd accepted early on.

"The boss has spoken," Tyrone joked. "That's that." He kissed Connie on the forehead and she smiled.

"Do you all mind if I have a few minutes alone with Karen?" Johnny requested.

No one hesitated to give him the time he requested. They all shuffled into the hallway.

The room emptied out and only Johnny and Karen remained. He stood above the bed looking down at her. His mind could have gone down any number of depressing paths, but he chose to stick with his small flicker of hope. He pulled a chair close to the bed with one hand and grabbed Karen's with the other.

"Karen," he said softly into her ear, "I don't know if you can hear me. I don't even know if you want to hear me, but I'm here with you. I'm even thinking about God. Can you believe that? What a surprise, huh?" He squeezed her hand tighter. "I love you, Karen, and I need you. The kids need you. I want you to pull through this. You can do it. I know that you can. You have to wake up, because I want another chance to work out this marriage. I love you. God, please let her live. I want to be a better husband. Karen, please forgive me."

Johnny realized that there was a long list of items that he needed Karen to forgive. He was hoping that they'd get buried in the past and be unable to jeopardize his optimistic outlook.

Johnny poured out his heart to Karen and then rested his head on her leg. After nearly an hour, he stood to his feet and slowly walked toward the door. Big Mama, Connie, and Tyrone were the remaining warriors left standing in the hallway. Each saw Johnny open the door, but no one rushed in. They wanted to move at his pace.

"You okay, chief?"

"Yes, I am. I feel like it's going to be all right now."

Big Mama nodded her head. "It sho' is."

"You can all go back in the room if you want."

"I'm going to head home, if you don't mind," Tyrone said. "I want to grab a couple hours of sleep before work."

"Hey, no, that's fine, man."

"If you need anything, Johnny—I mean anything—give me a call or let Connie know. She knows how to get in touch with me at all times."

"Thanks, man. I couldn't get through this without you. You're family, man."

The two men clasped hands and each pulled the other into his bosom, patting each other on the back with his other hand.

Big Mama went back in to pray.

Before Connie wheeled in, Tyrone kissed her. "Connie, honey, promise me that you won't overdo it."

"I promise, baby." She hugged him, and he left. As she watched him walk away, Connie thanked God for giving her such a fulfilling life with the man of her dreams. She turned the chair around and faced the door. With each turn of the wheel, she reflected on her blessings.

CHAPTER 35

Johnny had faithfully sat by Karen's bedside through the all-night vigils. The long nights had lingered into the mornings. Just before daybreak, the walls began closing in on him. He had stepped out of the room for a brief moment to take a walk and get some fresh air.

The rays of light shining through the window punctured the darkness in the room. Big Mama was sitting in the corner chair reading Psalms Ninety-one from her Bible. Connie was praying softly.

By the grace of God, Karen was still hanging on.

The nurse entered the room, conscious not to distract those present. She took Karen's pulse and then placed the thermometer censor on her limp finger.

"How's she doing?" Connie asked the nurse.

"Amazingly, her vitals are much stronger. Her fever has dropped from over a hundred and five to a hundred. Her pulse is up to seventy-threee beats a minute, and her blood pressure is stable."

"Praise the Lord." Connie attributed the improvement to God.

"The two of you have been here most of the night, right?"

"Yes, we've been here praying since one o'clock Saturday morning."

"For three days! Boy, that is some sacrifice to stay here all that time. How wonderful of you. Mrs. Clark is very fortunate to have such a supportive circle of friends and family." She pushed a few buttons on the IV machine.

"We's glad to be here. Long as God give us the strength we gon' stay here and pray for our sistah." Big Mama planned to be around for a while.

"Well, whatever it is you're doing, keep it up. The only chance she has at recovering is through by some unforeseen miracle." The nurse completed her examination and left the room.

A few minutes later, Tina stormed into the room.

"What is going on here?" Her voice was condescending and sharp but not loud.

Connie had been mixing her prayers with a few nods for the past couple of hours. Tina's entry startled her.

"Shhhhhh," Connie insisted.

"What is going on, Connie?"

Connie took the lock off her wheelchair and turned it around to face the door. She beckoned for Tina to follow her into the hallway.

"Tina, what is wrong with you, bursting into the room like that?"

"I call the hospital to check on Karen every morning before I go to work. When I called this morning, they told me that Karen's condition had deteriorated Friday night and that her family had been at the hospital all weekend. Everyone, that is, except me. Is that true?"

"Yes, Tina. It is true."

"So how did you find out, and why wasn't I told?"

"Johnny called us around midnight Friday."

"Johnny, humph, of course I'm not surprised that he didn't call me. But Connie, what about you? Why didn't you call me? I was out of town for the weekend, but I checked my messages. Since I didn't hear anything, I thought she was still the same. Had I known what was going on, I could have been here before now."

"Tina, I couldn't call you to come out here."

"Why not? She's my friend too, you know."

"You're right, and yes, I do know that. But the truth is, Tina, Johnny needs our support. The doctors were expecting Karen to die Friday night. There was no way that he was going to feel comfortable having you out here. He had enough pressure on him as it was without getting into it with you. Remember what happened the last time that the two of you were in the room together. He didn't need that this weekend; no one did."

Tina had to concede that what Connie was saying made sense, although it didn't bring much ease to her unrest.

"Still, you could have called me just to let me know."

"You're right, Tina. I apologize for not thinking to call you. All I've had on my mind is Karen."

Tina softened and relaxed the bass in her voice and the confrontational stance in her posture.

"I understand. It's okay. How's she doing, anyway?"

"She's showing signs of progress, thank the Lord."

"How long do you plan to be here?"

"Ms. Walker plans to fast and pray for as long as she needs to. I can't fast right now, but I plan to pray with her for as long as I'm able."

"Well, I can't stay all day with you, but I can be here a few hours."

Connie didn't feel comfortable with Tina being at the hospital. She was expecting Johnny to return at any minute from his run home. The last thing he needed was to have Tina hanging around.

"Tina, I don't feel that it would be good for you to stay here. Johnny will be back here any minute."

"Connie, I came all the way out here to be with Karen. Why should I have to leave?"

"Because this is about Karen. Everybody else, including you and me, has to take a backseat. That man needs to be able to spend this time with his wife in peace. Even if you don't think much of Johnny, you owe at least that much respect to Karen. Don't you agree, Tina?"

Whether or not she liked it, Tina wanted to honor her friendship with Karen by backing off and showing Johnny some respect. She felt bad about not being able to stay with the group. Her sharp tongue had given her power in the past. At this moment, all she felt from it was overwhelming alienation.

"I hope that nothing happens to her. I would feel so terrible for not being here." She hung her head. "Will you call me if her condition changes, good or bad?"

Connie took Tina's hand and gave a half grin.

"I promise to call you."

"Thanks." Tina slung her trench coat over her arm and walked toward the bank of elevators. It was all she could do not to cry.

* * *

Johnny returned shortly to find Big Mama and Connie still faithfully sitting at Karen's side.

"Any change?"

"Her temperature is down to a hundred, and all of the other vital signs are good."

"Thank God. By the way, Connie, I thought I saw Tina pulling out of the parking lot."

"You probably did. She just left."

"She was here, then. I thought that was her."

"Don't worry, Johnny; she thought it best not to stay around. You know how the two of you can get going at times. You don't need that, and she knew it."

"Tina definitely has some issues. I can't deny that. But I know that she does care about Karen. She could have stayed."

Connie's eyebrow arched.

"Trust me, I don't have enough energy to go toe-to-toe with Tina. If you talk with her again, let her know it's no problem."

"Are you sure?"

He nodded in affirmation. "Somebody has to take the first step. Might as well be me."

"You! That's a big surprise. I know that the two of you don't get along too well."

"You're right. We haven't gotten along, and that's the way it's been. That's not the way it has to be."

"Good for you, Johnny. I'm glad to hear it. I know Karen would be happy as well. You're an all-right guy. I'll let Tina know. I'm sure she'll want to come back out here."

Big Mama continued reading Psalm Ninety-one, but heard every word. She was pleased on the inside to know that Johnny was taking his repentance seriously and taking the necessary steps to seek forgiveness from those he'd wronged. It was a huge step toward spiritual development, and it appeared that he was on track.

The morning hours ticked by. The nurse checked Karen's vitals every couple of hours. She continued showing progress, pieces at a time.

Johnny was watching the TV and holding Karen's hand when he felt a tightening. He didn't pay any attention. When the tightening turned into a weak squeeze, his heart jumped. *Could it be?*

"Karen, Karen," he whispered, "can you hear me?"

Her hand squeezed his. Johnny sat up with zeal and concentration. He also had the undivided attention of Big Mama and Connie.

"Is she waking up?" Connie asked Johnny.

"I don't know. I think so. It feels like she's squeezing my hand."

Connie rolled close to the bed and took Karen's other hand. Big Mama turned up the heat on her prayer. The room was instantly converted to a cheering forum.

"Karen, come on, honey, wake up. Come on," Johnny encouraged.

One eye slowly flickered and peeped open. Johnny saw it.

"She's waking up. Come on, Karen; you can do it."

Karen forced her eyes open with all of the energy residing in her body. The light kept them partially closed, but they were wide enough for her to see Johnny and for him to see her.

"You're awake. Thank God." Johnny softly wept. "Welcome back, honey. It's good to see you."

Connie gave a sigh of relief and wiped her eyes. Big Mama praised the Lord.

Karen couldn't talk with the tube in her mouth. Her eyes roamed the room frantically. The weeklong sleep had left her disoriented. All in all, Karen had been out of it for most of the time she'd spent in the hospital.

Johnny rang the nurse's button to inform the staff of her change.

It took only a matter of minutes before several people rushed in from the nurses' station. They had prepared themselves for Karen to pass away in the middle of the night, and were poised to make the appropriate code-blue emergency call.

When the nurses got into the room, they stood in astonishment. Fully prepped to try to revive Karen's stopped heart, they were quite surprised to see her eyes open. The nurses couldn't say anything. All they replayed in their mind was how sick she had been all weekend. Now she was awake and alive.

"She's awake!"

"Yes, she is," Johnny acknowledged with pride.

The nurses checked her vital signs and did a quick examination.

"Boy, this is a miracle. There is no other way to describe this. I'd better get Dr. Costas on the phone."

Karen was pointing to the tube.

"You want that out, don't you?" the nurse asked Karen.

Karen nodded yes.

"Let me call Dr. Costas and find out what she wants to do."

Joy and happiness consumed every nook and cranny of the room. Johnny couldn't express enough how grateful he was to Connie and Big Mama. Several hours after she woke up and began regaining her orientation, Connie and Big Mama left in order to give Johnny and Karen time alone. Their work was done for now, although neither intended to cease praying for the couple.

Johnny stayed put. He watched an entourage of staff members parading in and out of the room throughout the afternoon.

"Well, Mrs. Clark, we haven't gotten approval to remove the tube yet. But we do need to draw some blood and take another look at you."

Johnny stepped into the hallway while the medical staff was working with Karen. He checked his watch. It was after five.

"The kids should be home by now. Let me give them a call." He was eager to share the good news with them. He pulled out his cell phone and anxiously placed the call.

"Erick, I have good news. Your mom has made a turn for the better."

"She has! Oh, yes!" he sang out with glee.

"She woke up late this morning. She's alert and the doctors say she's doing good," Johnny said.

"That's great."

"Yes, thank God."

"Can I talk to her?"

"Not right now. The breathing tube isn't out. She might not be able to talk for a day or two. But she's doing much better."

"Do you want us to come to the hospital?"

"Well, I'm certain that she's anxious to see you kids, but why don't you wait? The doctor said that she'll be tired for a while. I think we should give her a day or so."

"Okay, Dad. Do you want to tell the girls about Mom?"

"You can go ahead and tell them, son."

"You know they're going to ask when they can come out to see her. What should I tell them?"

"Tell them they can come out tomorrow after school. I want to get back into the room with your mom. I'll see you when I get in. It might be a little late, so why don't you grab some money out of the desk drawer and you guys go out and get something to eat?"

"Will do, Big Dad. See you later."

Johnny was preparing to disconnect the call when he remembered something else.

"Erick." He spoke loudly, wanting to catch him.

"Yeah, I'm here."

"Don't let Elizabeth eat too many sweets. She gets a little hyper in the evenings, and I want her to be able to sleep tonight. All right, son?"

"Sure thing, Dad. I gotcha covered."

Johnny broached Karen's room feeling good. Perhaps his dire straits were turning around.

CHAPTER 36

Karen was sleeping peacefully. Johnny had decided to go home and get some rest himself. Being awake most of the past seventy-two hours had left his body fueled from nervous energy.

He eased up the long driveway, giving the garage door time to fully open. One of the other two cars was missing. Johnny figured the kids were still out. He slowly made his way from the car to the back stairs, bypassing any stops along the way. Once he sat down, he knew his body wouldn't have enough strength to get back up. He gingerly climbed the stairs, feeling every aching muscle.

Johnny walked into the bedroom. He immediately peeled off his shirt and tossed it onto the couch with the other heap of unhung clothes. The room was in chaos. Since it was so spacious, he was still able to get around unencumbered. He knew the room needed to be cleaned, but tasks such as that had been low on his priority list for the past couple of months. All he could do was just get by.

"I think I'll get into the whirlpool before I go to sleep." He took his socks off and rubbed his feet. "On second thought, a quick shower will have to do."

Johnny took the shower, brushed his teeth, and put on his pajamas.

He uttered a sigh of relief. The shower had given him a renewed burst of energy. He hadn't eaten all day and contemplated grabbing a snack from downstairs.

There was a knock on his bedroom door.

"Yes, come in."

Erick eased the door open with the girls standing behind him. "You decent?"

"Yeah, son, come on in."

"Hi, Daddy." Elizabeth was glad to see her father. She had clung to the rest of her family during her mother's absence and, in doing so, strengthened their bonds.

"Daddy," Chelle cut into the conversation, "I'm so glad to hear about Mom. Erick told us that she's awake and wants to see us tomorrow."

"She sure does. I know she'll feel even better once she sees you all."

"I can't wait to see her. I'll be glad when tomorrow gets here," Elizabeth added.

"In the meantime, young lady, you need to finish your homework and get ready for bed." He kissed her on the forehead.

Johnny had made great strides with Elizabeth. He had worked on expressing more affection with his children ever since the counselor pointed out the need. It wasn't a gesture that naturally flowed for him. It required conscious effort on his part.

"Don't forget that we have a meeting tomorrow afternoon with your counselor, and you need to be rested. Erick, can you hang back for a minute? I want to talk with you about something."

"No problem, Dad."

The girls left the room skipping. Even though Johnny had shielded them from the true severity of Karen's illness, the part that they did know had been a haul. None of it seemed to matter to them now. Mom was coming home.

Johnny didn't completely understand the source of his newfound peace. He was sensing small changes in himself. He didn't feel the burning desire to dominate every situation or to break someone down emotionally before they got to him. That had been his survival tactic in the past.

After Big Mama had led him to the Lord, Johnny found himself doing self-evaluations. *Life is too short,* he echoed. He uncovered areas that he didn't like and felt a burning desire to tear down some of the walls and defenses that he had crafted into his life. *It might take some time, but I have to get it right,* he promised himself.

"Son, I want to thank you for coming home." Johnny slid his hands into his pockets. It was hard for him to humbly lay it out. He had the desire to freely open up, but a significant part of the old prideful, domineering Johnny was still around. It would take commitment, work, and time before he could make the changes that he wanted in his life.

"It's okay, Dad. I wanted to come home." Being his father's son, Erick slid his hands into his pockets. He shrugged his shoulders, not sure how to respond. Hearing his father express gratitude was not a scenario with which he was familiar. "I needed to come home."

"No, son, I needed you to come home." Johnny removed his hands from his pockets and extended them toward his son.

Erick saw the tears rolling down his father's cheeks. The sight touched him. He hugged his dad. Grown or not, he longed for a hug from his father. He had always admired Johnny just as much as he despised his overbearing ways.

"You helped me get through a difficult time. I couldn't have done it without you." He pushed Erick back to arm's length so that he could talk with eye contact, however watery his were. "I also want to apologize to you for the things I said over the phone." Johnny held his head back to temper the flow of tears.

Erick shook his head out of discomfort. This long-awaited moment with his dad found him unprepared.

"It's all right, Big Dad."

"No, it's not all right. Son, I know that I haven't always done right by you and your mother."

Erick continued to shake his head, not knowing how to receive this emotional outpouring.

"I know that I've made mistakes. I hope you believe me when I tell you that I never meant to hurt you or your mother. I love you all, and I want the chance to prove that to you."

"It's cool, Dad. I know that you love me. And"—Erick looked away—"I want to apologize to you for what I said."

"Nah, son. You don't owe me an apology. I am so proud of you for sticking up for your mom and for your sisters. You are a man, and I respect that. I couldn't be prouder of you, Erick."

"Thanks, that means a lot to me coming from you," Erick told him.

Johnny patted Erick on the back.

"What about school, son? You lost most of the quarter."

"I don't know yet. I can get an extension on a couple of the classes.

I'll probably take calculus over. I'll just have to see. Right now I'm going to hang around here. I know you need me to be here, and I'll stay out of school as long as I have to. This is more important than any school."

"Son, I don't want you to get burdened with trying to take care of us around here. You've already given up enough time. It's time for you to go back to school. That's what your mom and I want for you. So what about the summer? Do you think that you can make any of that work up in summer school?"

"Hmmm. That's a thought. I could do that. Maybe I could go back to Palo Alto early, instead of waiting until September."

"Good, now we're getting somewhere. Think about it, and if you decide to go back early, just say the word."

"Thanks, Big Dad."

"I love you, son, and don't you worry. Everything around here is going to be all right. You can believe that." Johnny draped his arm over Erick's shoulder. "Let's grab a bite to eat."

CHAPTER 37

Four days had passed since Johnny got the news of Karen's impending demise. By some miracle she had gotten past that brush with death. He glided into her room as if on the wings of an eagle. She was out of ICU and back into a normal room for the first time in weeks. She was sitting up in the bed with three pillows propped behind her head when he walked in. It did him good to see her making remarkable strides.

"How you feeling?"

"Tired." She scrunched her face and swallowed slowly. Her throat was still sore from having the breathing tube inserted for the past week. She needed to constantly swallow small sips of water. She saw the bright bouquet of flowers in his hand. Her eyes widened and her eyebrows arched.

Flowers still in hand, he wrapped his arms around her like an extra-large shirt on a small body, careful not to grip too tightly. He didn't want to cause any pain to her rejuvenating limbs.

Karen was limp in his arms. She was slow warming up to his newfound affection.

Johnny sensed her reluctance and pulled back. He set the flowers on her meal tray.

Lilacs and gardenias drew her close. She breathed in the sweet fragrance and soaked in the nectar for a few moments.

Johnny took a seat near her bed.

"Where are the kids?" she asked in a muffled voice.

"Erick's bringing them out after school. I had some errands to run."

"You look tired."

He stretched his arms into the air. "I don't know why. I slept like a baby last night, for the first time in a long time." He stretched out his long legs. "When I woke up, it was almost noon."

"Noon!" Karen knew that was odd for Johnny. Up and out of the house before six was his routine. It ensured his ability to get to the office well before the primary production line started up at seven.

Karen looked at her husband sitting in the chair and wondered who was this strange man showing compassion and warmth without prodding. It couldn't be Johnny. She had left a controlling husband and a load of emotional baggage at home a few months ago. Idiosyncrasies and all, she knew the old Johnny. She didn't know if it was worth getting to know the new one. The entrance of her doctor interrupted her assessment of the man in the chair.

"Dr. Costas."

"Good to see you, Johnny. How's our patient?"

Dr. Costas was elated to see the turnaround in Karen's condition. She couldn't explain why Karen had come out of the coma. It didn't stop the doctor from taking pride in acknowledging her patient's miraculous recovery.

Karen's speech was slow. "Better."

Dr. Costas patted her legs, which had become her standard comforting gesture. She flipped through the chart, pleased to see the vital signs in normal ranges. She placed her thumb on Karen's pulse and heartbeat to verify for herself.

"Nice strong pulse. Strong heartbeat. Any aches?"

Karen sipped her water and shook her head no.

"Any discomforts?"

Again she shook her head no.

"Good." Dr. Costas crammed the stethoscope back into her oversize pocket. "How's your appetite?"

"Umm," Karen muttered, and rocked her hand back and forth, implying that it was so-so.

"That's what I would expect." She gave Karen a comforting smile. "You've been on liquids for months with a nasty tube down your throat for a week. It's going to take some time for you to be able to handle a normal diet with solid food. In the meantime, we will keep you on the liquids."

"For how long?" Karen whispered.

"You're tired of the needles, I bet."

Karen nodded.

"Thought so." Dr. Costas sighed. "Well, to be quite honest, I don't know. We need to leave it in until you regain some strength and an appetite."

Karen frowned. Dr. Costas read Karen's look of dissatisfaction.

"Karen, we are treading in unfamiliar territory here. I can't medically explain why your health deteriorated to a comatose state. I have even less scientific rationale as to why you came out of the coma."

"So are you saying that this was a miracle?" Johnny questioned.

Dr. Costas folded one arm and slowly rubbed her forehead with the other. She was proud of the fact that she'd built her profession on making statistically and medically proven diagnoses. To admit that Karen's recovery was outside of that realm was not something she felt comfortable doing. Yet she had to acknowledge that something other than the medicine and her expertise had brought Karen around.

She threw her hands up and fluttered her lips.

"I can't say that it was a miracle, but I will say that Karen's will to live—or her faith, or belief or whatever it is you want to call it—was a major factor."

Johnny didn't expect the doctor to admit that Karen's recovery was based on their faith and prayers. What she did say was close enough. He chuckled to himself, recognizing that all of that religious talk did mean something after all.

"Dr. Costas, when can I take her home?"

"Depends on how quickly she regains her strength. We'll work on the appetite first. If she gets enough strength to go to the bathroom on her own, then I'll have the catheter removed. I suspect that if all goes well, it could be a week or so."

It wasn't as soon as Johnny would have liked. At least it was a goal to shoot for, which was more than he'd had in weeks.

"I hate to say this, but the coma was our secondary issue. We still have to deal with the primary issue."

"Which is?" Johnny wondered, sitting up in his seat.

"The cancer. After Karen gets settled and back home, we'll need to follow up with some more tests. I'm hoping that we've gotten all of it with this last round of treatment. Once I get the pathology report, I'll know whether or not we'll still have to do the chemo."

"Are you saying that she could still get sick again?"

Dr. Costas didn't want to be the grim reaper in any way. "I'm saying that we aren't out of the woods yet. We will need to monitor the situation and be prepared for anything. I don't want to alarm you, but I also don't want you to become too relaxed with your health and diet. We have to take this one day at a time and go from there. All right?" her elevated voice rang out.

Karen thanked her in a quiet voice. In the not-so-distant past, she would have panicked and within moments spiraled to the depths of depression. The revived Karen received the news with calmness.

It was the first time that both Dr. Costas and Johnny had seen Karen remain calm in light of a less-than-ideal prognosis. Neither of them knew the source of Karen's newfound peace, but both looked pleased to see her with it.

Johnny grabbed Karen's hand.

"Don't worry; we'll be fine. It will work out. I know it will."

"That's good. We can use as much positive energy as possible. Anything that can help us get you to where you need to be, I want to consider. Do you have any other questions for me?"

Johnny looked at Karen, who was shaking her head no.

"I don't think so, Dr. Costas. Not right now."

"Well, I'll be around if you do. Take care of yourself, Karen. I'll see you on my rounds tomorrow."

"Thanks for everything, Dr. Costas," Johnny told her.

Dr. Costas waved on her way out.

Johnny wasn't sure how Karen was really feeling about the not-so-good news. He wanted to find a way to encourage her in spite of it. He sat on the side of the bed so that she wouldn't have to strain her voice.

"Karen, I don't want you to worry about what the doctor said. She's only doing her job, but she doesn't have the final say. Just like you came through the coma, even when the doctors didn't believe that you would, you can get past the cancer."

"Johnny, I heard you praying for me when I was in the coma."

"You did! What else did you hear?" Johnny wondered.

"Nothing else, I don't think. I can't remember anything else."

"Did you hear Ms. Walker or Connie? They stayed in this room and prayed for you for almost three days," Johnny told her.

"Connie too?"

"Can you believe it? She refused to leave until you showed some kind of change. Tyrone talked her into coming home for a few hours each day to eat and take her vitamins."

"I guess that I'm not really surprised. That's how she is. She's just a real friend."

"I don't know how she did it. You can see how weak she is."

Karen sipped from the cup of water and shook her head.

"Connie and Tyrone have been good to us. We owe them a lot." Johnny reflected on the amount of support that the couple had given him. He didn't know how he would have gotten through some of the trying moments without them.

"Ms. Walker too. I have to thank her," Karen noted.

"Don't worry about it. I'll thank her at church on Sunday."

"Church! You! Sunday!" Karen was shocked to hear Johnny talk about church—and it wasn't even a holiday.

"Yes, me. I'm going to church. I can do that, can't I?" he teased.

"Of course you can. It's just that . . . well, you know, church and religion haven't been your thing."

"You're right, but my back was against the wall. I had nowhere to go except to the people from the church. I'm not saying that I'm ready to preach or anything like that," he joked, "but I'm ready to see what God is all about. Ms. Walker helped me with some of that."

"Yeah, it's hard to be around her and not be interested in the Lord. And she was here all that time?"

"Most certainly was. The pastor and some of the other church members came out the first night. There was some serious praying going on in this room. And you didn't hear any of that praying or anything?"

"Nope. All I remember is hearing you." She took a tiny sip of water and let it glide down her throat.

"I had no idea that you could hear me."

"Johnny, you helped me pull through. When I heard you crying and asking the Lord to let me live, it made me want to live. I figured that if you could trust God for my healing, then I could too." She sipped the water.

"I had a choice, Johnny. I could have chosen to live or to die in that coma. It was my free will. I could easily have chosen to go ahead and let go, but I didn't. I didn't because I heard your voice. I heard you say that you love me, that I mattered to you." Her eyes watered a little. "Do you know how long I've wanted to hear that?"

Johnny took his wife into his arms and held on, wanting to protect her from now on. It felt good to be connected and not arguing.

The children entered the room before she could respond. Karen figured what she had to say could wait until later.

"Hi, Mommy," the two girls greeted her. Elizabeth wasted no time in executing her normal routine: she hurried to Karen's bedside and gave her mom a hug.

Karen swallowed hard and opened her arms wide. "Hi, babies."

"Hey, Mom." Erick was able to squeeze into the pileup his sisters had formed around their mom long enough to give her a peck on the forehead. He plopped down on the chair next to his dad and gently removed the designer shades from his face. "Hey, Big Dad."

"Hey, son." Johnny looked around the room. He was content to see his entire family together in one place, well and happy. None of his professional, financial, or social accomplishments could have brought him more fulfillment than this priceless moment. This was what it was all about.

"Mom, did Dad tell you that I'm planning to head back to California for the summer quarter?"

Chewing on a piece of ice, she shook her head to indicate no.

"Yep, I'm going to make up a few classes and maybe even take an extra one."

She smiled with ease. To see the two men in her life bonding was a miracle by itself.

CHAPTER 38

Johnny had attempted to call Isabelle Jones two months ago. The time seemed more like an eternity.

He had left no more than a grunt and a hello on the message service. It was enough for Isabelle to recognize his voice. She'd thought about calling him back for weeks. It was a door she was reluctant to open, but Johnny's magnetism still had some potency. She didn't know what to expect. Curiosity got the best of her. She made the call. She didn't have his number but suspected that he might still be with Tennin Automotive. *He's probably president by now,* she guessed. She grinned, remembering how much he loved his work. They hadn't talked in years. What would they talk about?

She hung up the receiver, only to pick it back up a few seconds later.

"Oh, what the heck. Won't hurt to say hi."

She dialed directory assistance to get the number to Tennin Automotive in Warren, Michigan.

Johnny had been out of the office for over a week. When he walked into the office, Sonja was thrilled to see him. She jumped up and shook his hand.

"Mr. Clark, thank you for the message. I am so glad that your wife is getting better. That must be a tremendous relief. I've been praying for her and for your entire family."

"I appreciate your prayers, Sonja. Prayer is what got us through."

"Oh, I almost forgot." Sonja went around to the other side of her desk and pulled a three-foot card from underneath it. "This is from the team."

Johnny opened the card to see names and good wishes expressed in every space. He was visibly touched and dared not try to verbalize his gratitude.

Sonja read the expression on his face and grabbed his hand with a smile. No words were necessary.

Johnny went into his office, sat down in the big-backed leather chair, and soaked up the moment. He slowly worked through the stack of presorted mail on his desk. His last two cell phone bills were on top of the stack. The envelopes were slit open across the top. That meant Sonja had paid them with the other monthly business expenses. He didn't feel a need to see the itemized detail. He knew the numbers that had been called. He didn't expect the effects of the stress to vanish overnight. It would take some time to bounce back to a normal routine. His world had been turned upside down. That didn't stop any action around Tennin Automotive. Johnny was treated like a valued asset to the company and had shown his gratitude by devoting countless hours and untiring efforts toward his job. He turned back and forth in the seat twirling a pen. This place didn't miss a beat.

"Sonja," he said over the intercom, "what do I need to focus on first?"

"The production manager in Tennessee wants to speak with you as soon as you get a chance."

"Good, let's start there. Can you get me the latest production reports and then get him on the line please? I also need you to set up a meeting with my entire management staff."

"Some are in Tennessee this week."

"Try to get them all on a conference call."

"Will do, sir. I'll get right on it."

Johnny was back in the saddle, but somehow it felt different to him. Work was his comfort zone, and even that was going to take some adjustment. It wasn't so thrilling to be back in control and running the show. The rest away from the office had done him good.

Sonja knocked on Johnny's door.

"Come in."

She opened the door and walked a few steps into the room. "Mr.

Clark, I checked everyone's schedule, and the only time that seems to work for everyone is five-thirty this afternoon. So I'll go ahead and get that confirmed?"

"Um . . ." Johnny contemplated while flipping through his day planner. "Wait. That's going to be too late in the day." He knew it would conflict with the time he had scheduled to meet with Elizabeth's counselor. Erick was still around. Their mom was showing tremendous progress, but Johnny knew the girls needed his assurance and support. He fully intended to do his part.

"Too late!" Sonja responded in surprise. Johnny was a driven boss. There were times when he had conducted meetings after nine o'clock at night. He did whatever it took to get the job done, and expected everyone in his group to have the same dedication.

"Yes, that's too late. Try to get them together this afternoon; otherwise it will have to wait until tomorrow."

"I'll see what I can do, Mr. Clark."

Johnny continued to work through the stack of items Sonja had placed on his desk. Out of the corner of his eye, he saw one of the lines on his phone light up. Then it dawned on him that he'd forgotten to remove the forward from his phone.

"Good morning, Mr. Clark's office. May I help you?" There was silence on the line. "Hello, Mr. Clark's office. Can I help you?" Sonja raised her voice the second time around in case there was a bad connection and the person on the other end was having difficulty hearing her.

"Yes, uh, hi," the soft voice said. "Is Mr. Clark in?"

"Let me check. Please, ma'am, who might I say is calling?"

"Um, tell him it's a friend."

"Can I give him a name, please, ma'am?"

"That's okay. Thank you. 'Bye."

Sonja found the woman's timidity strange. She didn't consider relaying the partial message to Johnny. She had enough real work to worry about now that he was back in the office.

Her intercom beeped and Johnny's voice came across.

"Sonja, I forgot that my phone is still forwarded to yours."

"You're right, Mr. Clark. You just missed a call."

"Anything important?"

"No, I don't think so. They didn't leave a message."

"Good. I have plenty of calls to return as it is, without adding new ones. If you don't mind, Sonja, I'm going to leave the forwarding on while I play catch-up. Otherwise, it might get too hectic for me."

"No problem, Mr. Clark. I will take care of it."

"Oh, Sonja, any calls that come in from the hospital or from my family, I want them put through immediately, please."

"Absolutely, Mr. Clark."

Johnny's stack of backlogged tasks wasn't shrinking. He was determined not to overload himself. He knew that the most important tasks would get done, and the rest would have to be put on the back burner. Killing himself to get the job done didn't seem as appealing as it once had. Watching someone go through a life-threatening illness had opened his eyes to what was important.

CHAPTER 39

The bedcovers were snuggled tightly around Karen's body, as she slept in her own bed for the first time in over two months.

Johnny lay still in the bed next to his wife. He propped himself up, resting on his fist, and looked at Karen while she slept.

He admired her beauty. Only a few stubbles had managed to grow back on her head from the radiation therapy. What a difference a day made, he thought. It had been less than three months ago that he couldn't see much beauty in the marriage, let alone in Karen. Every time he thought about the recent chain of events he became nostalgic. It amazed him to know that the cancer—the very element that had managed to broaden the wedge between them over the past years—was the same tool that God was using to put hope back into their marriage. He marveled at how it all had played out.

Karen began stirring. Her eyes slowly opened. She positioned her hands over them like a visor. The light coming through the blinds was modest, but was too much for her. She looked around the room in a daze, not able to get her bearings. The slight confusion was short-lived once her eyes focused on Johnny.

"Good morning," he greeted her. "Did you sleep well?"

"I think so. What time is it?"

Clocks were conveniently located on both sides of the bed, but he chose to lean over and read the one on her side.

"A few minutes after six."

"Umm." She stretched and moaned. "I've been sleeping for that long?"

Last night had been the first time in several years that the family had all sat down at the table to have dinner together. They laughed, talked, and shed a few tears. Karen tired out around eight o'clock and went to bed. She'd been asleep ever since.

"You were tired, Karen. It's going to take some time to get your strength back." He gently glided his hand down her arm and spoke softly. "Don't rush yourself. There's no hurry."

Karen didn't jerk her arm away from Johnny's touch, but she did tense up. The simple gesture let Johnny know that she didn't want him to rub her arm.

"Does that bother you, my touching you?"

Karen didn't want to start an argument so soon out of the hospital. Johnny had been right. She didn't have that kind of energy. She searched for sugarcoated words that would get him to back off without opening the old floodgates of bickering.

Johnny detected her reluctance to speak truthfully about the situation. So he tried to set the tone whereby she could open up to him. He didn't want to lose out on the opportunity that they had to make the relationship and their communication right.

"Karen, it's okay to tell me how you feel. I know you're thinking about how I normally react. I promise not to fly off the handle."

Karen's lips didn't move, but her eyes said it all.

"Really, Karen. I mean it. I love you, and I want to make this work. We can do this, if it's what you want. You have to want it too, Karen; I can't do it by myself."

She nodded with a one-sided grin. "I don't know what I want."

"You're still not sure about the marriage? Why can't we start over?"

"I don't think it's that easy. There's a lot of water under the bridge." Karen sat up with Johnny's assistance. "Being in the hospital this last time around made me think about my life, my marriage, our kids, and you. I realized how much time has been wasted pretending that we have it all together. That I have it together. I'm through wasting time. I'm not going back to what we had."

Johnny hung his head, dreading what might come out of Karen's mouth next.

"I've apologized to you for the past, Karen, and I am truly sorry about all the things that happened between us. But there's nothing I can do about the past, other than learn from it and not make the same mistakes."

"I know that you have apologized, and I accept it. But that's not all there is to it. Forgiving is easy to do when you love somebody, but putting everything behind us will take some time. You broke my trust, Johnny. The women, the lies—it all hurt. Even when you knew how much damage Isabelle had done. It's like you didn't care."

"What can I say, Karen? I'm sorry about the women. And I do care. I realize that it's no excuse, but I don't know what to do half the time. We keep doing the same thing over and over. I always reach out to you after you get sick. You are fine with me for the first couple of months. Right after the honeymoon period is over, you stop wanting me sexually. But you don't want a divorce. That can't work. We have to decide if we're staying together or not. I want to be with you, but I need you to want me too."

"I'm not saying that it's all your fault. But it's still a lot to get over."

"I don't expect you to forget everything that's happened. Shoot, I can't even forget, as much as I'd like to. No matter how I might want to, Karen, I can't promise that we won't have challenges in the future. That's part of living. What I can promise you is that I will be one hundred percent committed to this marriage and that I will do whatever I have to for it to work. That's my commitment to you. All I ask is that we both let go of the past, so that we can build a future." He put his hand on top of hers and looked directly into her eyes. "What I am saying to you, Karen, is that you either have to forgive me or let me go."

Karen couldn't overlook the sincerity in his tone. The biggest part of her wanted the relationship to work. She was just more apprehensive than Johnny was to jump back into the marriage with both feet first. One thing she did know was that he was right about letting go of the past. If she couldn't remember anything else from her lengthy conversations with Big Mama, she recalled the part about forgiveness. She couldn't recall exactly how many times Big Mama had quoted Psalm 103, but parts of the chapter were embedded in her mind. She thought about the parts where it said that God's mercy and love enabled him to forgive sins, to not stay angry forever, and to not punish people to the extent that their shortcomings deserved. For Karen, Big Mama had been clear that forgiving also meant forgetting.

"I'm not saying that I'm eager to walk out on nineteen years of marriage. Believe it or not, I do still love you. Just give me some time to figure out what I want. Can you do that?"

"That's good enough for me." He gave her a loose hug, afraid to squeeze too tightly. "I want this to work out for us, Karen. I believe it can. If God can get you well with everything that was going on with you in the hospital, then I know there's hope for this marriage. I really feel that we can do this." He kissed her cheek and eased back to his side of the bed.

The mere concept of *God* crossing Johnny's lips was a miracle to Karen. Here was a man who had lived on his own terms, accountable to no one, not even God. It encouraged Karen's heart to know Johnny was making a spiritual change. It had been a major area of contention in the past. It was the one thing that she had held over his head. Reflecting on their marriage, Karen had to admit that she, too, had played an active part in the struggles.

"Johnny," she said humbly, "I can't blame you for all of the bad things that have happened to us, just like I can't take credit for all of the good times. We have both done our fair share of damage. What you did seems more wrong. Truth is, I know that it has taken both of us to tear down this marriage. I used religion to make you feel less than a man. I've judged you and used religion to justify it. That was wrong, and I am sorry. I didn't mean to do it. After a while, it made me feel good to have something that you didn't. I am truly sorry."

Johnny hung his head. "And I used my career to make you feel like you weren't contributing. Neither one was right."

"That's not all. I kept throwing Isabelle in your face. I wanted to remind you over and over about your mistake. I wanted you to feel wrong and to hurt like I was. I wanted to punish you by not having sex with you; at least that's why I did it at first. Then I ended up losing interest for real."

Karen leaned toward Johnny. The two embraced, with both giving emotional sniffles.

"I know that you didn't mean it, and I accept your apology. I love you, Karen, and I want you to forgive me."

"It's been rough, but I do love you, Johnny, no matter what."

Karen wiped her eyes with a tissue that Johnny handed her.

"Where do we go from here?" he asked.

Karen shrugged her shoulders. "I'm not sure, maybe counseling?"

Johnny interrupted and said, "Hey, wait a minute. Counseling, well, uh . . ."

Karen was trying to adjust to the about-face in Johnny. Was it too good to be true? Had God finally answered her prayer for peace at home? To see the compassion and concern in her husband after years of prayers was almost too overwhelming. All she could do was soak it in and enjoy it.

"Would you go to counseling?"

He swung his body around, folded one knee on the bed, and let the other hang over the side. He nestled her hand into his and looked into her eyes.

"I'm willing to go," he said.

Her eyebrows rose. Johnny had consistently opposed counseling and letting someone know his personal business. He didn't have a problem with her going before, if it was going to help her. He hadn't seen the need for himself.

"You can believe me when I tell you that I will do whatever I have to do to make this work. I mean that. I had plenty of time to think about some of the changes that I needed to make while you were in that coma."

Karen basked in the moment.

"Johnny, it's seven-thirty! You're late for work."

He didn't leap to his feet or show any anxiety.

"I'm not late. I don't have any meetings this morning. Besides, I am right where I need to be." He grunted. "When you were in that coma, I thought about a whole lot of things. I decided that I'm not going to let that job kill me. One thing I know is that the job will click on whether I'm there or not. There's more to life than work and money."

Karen squinted. "Johnny Clark"—she chuckled—"what happened to you when I was in that coma? You're like a different man."

"I've felt different ever since I accepted the Lord. Karen, I have to admit that I've never felt better in my life. I was able to take a hard look at my life. I saw some things that I liked and some areas that I am not so proud of. All in all, I feel good. I can't explain it."

"You don't have to. I know how it feels. It's like a peace of mind that you get. I had to look at my life too. I really believed that it would be better to quit everything, life, you, the kids, the cancer, everything. Now I realize that quitting wasn't what I really wanted. I'm glad to be here."

"What I want is a chance to enjoy my life. I'm tired of worrying about what we look like to others. We need to focus on what we look like to each other."

Johnny rubbed her hands. "We can make it."

CHAPTER 40

Tyrone was the man behind the grill. Turkey sausage, burgers, salmon, and ribs lined the double-decker racks. The aroma from the barbecued meats wrapped around the house in a cloud of smoke. It was like an invisible arrow, pointing visitors to the deck.

The summer heat felt good against Connie's skin. It was one of the simple pleasures that she could still appreciate with little physical effort. One by one, the gang poured onto the deck to partake in the Labor Day barbecue.

The Clarks were the first to arrive.

"What's up, buddy?" Tyrone greeted him. "Hey, Karen."

She handed him a bowl of potato salad to add to the table of delicacies.

"Where are the kids? I know Connie was looking forward to seeing them."

"Their youth group from church had a swimming party. Anything to do with water, they're in it." Karen got close to Tyrone and whispered, "How is Connie doing?"

"Not good, Karen. We got the news a couple of days ago. That's why she wanted everyone to come over for this get-together."

"Ah, Tyrone, I'm so sorry." Karen stood silent for a moment, not knowing exactly what to say. "You know that you have our support."

Karen put on a brave face and approached Connie. "Hi, lady, looking all summery with that straw hat. You go, girl."

"This old thing," Connie said with a smile. "I'm glad you could make it. Look at your little Afro. It looks good on you."

Karen smoothed her short hair, acknowledging Connie's compliment. "My stubbles are finally growing out since I'm off the chemo. I'm sticking with the natural look this time around too. I'm giving up on the wigs."

"Well, it looks good on you. You always could pull off the short hairstyles."

"I love it. All I have to do is wash and go," Karen boasted.

"That works for me. Hey, where are my girls?"

"I was telling Tyrone that they went to a swimming party with the church group. You know how those girls are about water. I can't keep them out of the pool. They send their love."

Tina strolled into the fold, wearing a slenderizing linen dress and carrying a bowl of fruit salad. She found a spot to place it on the serving table. Johnny was at the table fixing plates for him and Karen.

"Hey, what's up, Johnny?" Tina took off her shades.

"What's going on, Tina?"

"Not much. I've been meaning to ask you about Karen. Is she really doing as well as she's been telling me?"

"Far as I know, everything is looking good. She's back in remission."

"Good, good. Just wanted to know. You know how she tries to hide what's really going on."

"No, she's really doing well. I've been going to the doctor with her. So it's true."

"Great."

"Let me get this food over to Karen."

"Yeah, I can see that she hasn't missed any meals. Who's cooking at home, you?"

"Ha, ha, ha, funny. You know that Karen's cooking. How else could we eat?"

Tina smiled.

"See you later," Johnny told her, and walked off.

Tina fixed her plate. Karen had told her that changes were happening in their marriage. Tina preferred to make her own evaluation. She hadn't seen Johnny the last couple of times that she had stopped by Floods. And each time she'd spoken to Johnny over the past few months, he'd surprised her with his pleasant demeanor. She'd even been welcomed to their house while he was home. It was a nearly impossible feat, but she was watching a leopard change his spots in plain view. Maybe there was hope for men yet.

The food and company kept the deck filled well into the evening. Slowly the guests trickled out, leaving Tyrone, Connie, and their three closest friends.

"Why don't we go inside before the mosquitos flare up out here?" Tyrone suggested.

The gang moved the party from the deck to the sunroom. Tyrone made sure Connie was comfortable. Laughter filled the air. It brought a smile to Connie's face to actually see Tina and Johnny in the same room, let alone civilly participating in the same conversation.

Tyrone got everyone's attention on Connie's behalf.

"Okay, everyone, listen up. Connie has something she wants to say."

"What's up, Connie?" Tina was learning to exercise more tact but was still not a diplomat.

"I'm dying, Tina."

"Yeah, right, Connie," Tina interjected, not knowing that Connie meant the comment literally. "Everybody's dying."

"I mean that I'm expected to die soon." At times, her words slurred.

Tina gasped and quickly shifted to a serious mode. She restated the word as if it would somehow make more sense if she heard it again. "Dying! Don't talk like that. What happened to your faith, Connie? You have to believe that you're going to get better, just like Karen and I did. You can do it too."

"No, Tina. This is my time."

"How can you say that? How do you know?"

"Tina, I know because the pain is too much to bear."

"Can't you get back on the medication? That will take away the pain."

"No, it's not that easy. I got tired of taking medicine a long time ago. How would you like to take pills all day long, and the best you can hope for is a few good hours in a week? Life is not worth dragging on like this. No, Tina, this is the kind of pain that only death can ease. I feel it in all my bones."

"You can't give up like this."

"I'm not giving up; I'm resting in the peace that God has given me. I want you to know that when I first got diagnosed, I prayed to God for strength and understanding on what I should do. I prayed for healing for the first year or so. Then, all of a sudden, one day I knew in my spirit that my time was near. I knew that my body would not recover from this tumor. God has given me two years to prepare for this. It's my time, and I'm at peace with it."

"I thought you believed in healing."

"I do, but getting healed in my physical body isn't for me, not this time."

"Forgive me, Connie, but it's not as easy for me. It hurts to see you this way. You're too young to be in this condition."

"No, I'm not, Tina. Everybody has to die. And I know the Lord. I know that my spirit will live through eternity."

"I know everyone has to die, but why does it have to be like this?"

"Because I'm not above getting sick. I'm not the first to get sick, and I'm not going to be the last."

Tina wanted to understand what Connie was saying, but it hurt too much. She shook her head in denial.

"Tina, you've known me for a long time. Don't let these last few years be the only memory that you have of me. We've had some good times. Let that stand for something."

Connie let go of her hand and Tina made her way to one of the sofas.

"You don't even have children."

"I've lived a full life. I have no regrets. Look at all of you. You are my legacy. I love all of you. I feel blessed for that, let alone all of the other wonderful things that God has done for me."

The first part of the evening had been tense. Connie's circle of loved ones were in denial. She had done all that she could to prepare them for her final days, but now that her death was imminent, they weren't ready. Each wanted to cling to a little more time and a few more memories. Connie wanted to help each of them through this trying time, but she knew they had to find the way to their own peace. She turned to Karen. "You keep trusting in the Lord. He's going to keep you well."

It was Tina's turn, and Connie passionately told her, "Tina, girl, I love you."

Tina was shaken by Connie's proximity to death. She mouthed the words, *I love you* back to Connie.

"I know that all of that toughness in you is just for protection. I know how vulnerable you are inside. You are going to mess around and let God get hold of you, and that's going to be the end of that."

Tina smiled past the tears.

"Johnny, you're all right with me. You have been a good friend to my Tyrone. I want to thank you for that. From time to time, can you check in on him?"

He nodded in affirmation.

As much as each person in the room wanted to change the subject, Connie was determined to let this moment of sharing be a positive and unhurried time for her. She felt complete looking around the room. To see her loved ones filling the place made her life seem worthwhile.

Tyrone was struggling through every word. Putting on a brave face wasn't so easy for him.

"Can I get coffee for anyone?" he inquired.

Karen jumped up and said, "Tyrone, let me get that."

"Thanks, Karen. I appreciate that. In the meantime, I will get out a deck of cards. Any takers?"

Johnny and Karen leaped at the opportunity to change the tone of the evening. Tina declined. She was still feeling sorry for Connie and for herself.

"Okay, that leaves the two of you and me and Connie. That's four. We can play spades." He dumped the cards out of the box onto the tabletop. "Oh, I forgot; Connie can't see that well," Tyrone remembered. "She won't be able to read the cards." He gathered the cards together and was planning to put them away.

"No, no, Tyrone, don't put the cards away." She grabbed his arm. "Get Tina. The four of you can play. I can sit back and watch."

"You sure, honey?"

"Positive. Besides, I'm tired now. It won't be long before I have to go rest anyway."

"I don't feel like playing," Tina said.

"What, you scared that I'm going to beat you?" Johnny asked.

"Please, that's the least of my worries."

"Prove it, " Tyrone insisted. "Men against the women."

Tina sighed. "Fine, I'll play, but don't think that you're winning anything in here. We're going to beat you bad, right, girl?" She gave Karen a high five to seal the challenge.

Connie appreciated the people closest to her. This was the first time in nearly four years that they'd all sat together and had fun without Johnny and Tina hurling bitter words at one another and making everyone else uneasy. Bantering and jokes were the only words tossed around the table. Laughter reigned during hand after hand of cards being dealt. Connie was at ease in her chair, knowing that all was well with her loved ones.

CHAPTER 41

Connie was having a rough night. Her breathing was strained with hollow snores. Each breath sounded like her last.

It didn't take Tyrone long to wake up. He had been sleeping lightly for the past two weeks, ever since the doctors said that there was nothing else medically they could do for Connie. It was in God's hands.

"Connie, baby, wake up." Tyrone nudged her.

Her body was trembling in a seizurelike fashion. She gradually opened her eyes, only for them to roll back in her head.

The doctor had explained to Tyrone that Connie might have a series of seizures and possibly strokes. He knew that any one of them could be severe enough to kill her.

"Connie, Connie." He gently held her.

The trembling slowed, and she opened her eyes wide enough to see Tyrone.

He bent down so that she wouldn't have to strain trying to talk.

"Connie, can you hear me?"

"Yesss," she slurred.

"I need to get you to the hospital."

"Nooo!"

"Please Connie," Tyrone agonized through his teary, bloodshot eyes, "let me take you to the hospital. I know that I promised to let you stay at home. But Connie, please forgive me. I don't think that I can do it. It's so much harder than I thought it would be."

Connie had a way of making his worst fears melt with her reassuring words. Her body had become sick and weak. Her mind was still trying to function. Connie had spent the past year preparing him for this moment when she would be at this final crossroad in her life. Yet she knew that her loving husband needed her now more than ever before to help him get through. She took his hand and placed it across her cheek.

"Sweetheart, I don't want to go to the hospital." Her words slurred, but she continued to force them out, trying to make them clear enough for Tyrone to understand. "They can't do anything for me. We know that. It would make me happy to be here at home with the man that I love. Remember, honey, that's what we talked about."

All of the earlier conversations and preparation that they had discussed about how he would react when her time came meant nothing. Tyrone quickly realized that thinking and talking about being strong in the midst of a loved one's death was dramatically different from actually doing it.

"Okay, okay, I know. I'm going to get it together. Just give me a minute."

The recent growth of the tumor had severely impacted her rational abilities. When she did speak, half of it made sense and the other half sounded as though she was talking out of her head.

Connie stroked his face. None of the pain and suffering that she'd endured with the tumor compared to the agony she felt seeing Tyrone so helplessly brokenhearted. She wanted to console him. She prayed for God to give her the words and soundness of mind to express her feelings.

"My darling, my wonderful husband, my hero, I don't want you to be sad."

Tyrone wiped the drool from her lips before she continued.

"If you're sad, I'm going to be sad. I don't want that to be your last memory of me."

Tyrone felt selfish and guilty for wanting Connie to stay around, even if it meant her having to linger on with a compromised quality of life. Nothing else mattered so long as she was alive. He considered stealing away for a few minutes to call her doctor and visiting nurse, but with a heavy heart decided against it. Having people poking and prodding Connie in the final moments was against her wishes. Tyrone had promised her that he would let her die at home in peace. It was a difficult promise that he wanted to keep.

She was finally able to rest after a heart-wrenching night of suffering and seizures. The constant pain was finally gone.

Tyrone was overcome with a sense of helplessness. He sat on the side of the bed gazing at his wife of eight years. He gently stroked her face, feeling the warmth lingering in her body. In spite of her hair loss, weight fluctuation, and immobilization, he always saw her as the same vibrant, mesmerizing, and humble-spirited woman that he'd met in the beginning. Perhaps that was what he loved about her most. She never lost her radiant spirit even when her body and mind began to fail her. He thought about all of the times that she could have opted to be a bitter and mean woman in light of her battle. Yet she never considered it an option. To Tyrone, she was like a walking testimony and it had made him a better person.

He sat on the edge of the bed for a little while longer, trying to hold on to the moment. He finally felt that it was time to call the visiting nurse and have her come over. He was glad that the nurse had explained the process to him weeks ago. He hadn't been eager to hear it at the time. Tyrone was relieved to know that the nurse would make the necessary calls to Connie's doctor, the coroner, and the undertaker. Most of all, he was glad to know that she would tidy his wife's body. Regardless of how strong Tyrone wanted to be, he knew that holding her lifeless body again would be too much for him to endure.

While Tyrone was waiting for the nurse to arrive, he remembered that Connie had prepared information for the nurse ahead of time. He stood and took the long, slow walk to the desk drawer and pulled out the folder of items Connie had left. His face lit up seeing the note stuck inside.

My darling, dearest Tyrone,

I love you. I am leaving this note because I know that it might be difficult for you right now. I don't want you to be sad, but I know that you probably will be for a little while. But don't stay sad too long. There's no need for tears. We had a wonderful marriage. I am so blessed to have been with you these past eight years. I truly have no regrets. I am grateful to you for taking care of me while I was sick. I know you'll never say it, but it was a real sacrifice for you. Even if you hadn't told me a million times how much you love me, I would have known it from all of the things that you did for me. You are a good man and an even better husband. So, sweetheart, in time I want you to get on with your life. Don't sit around moping about me. I'm at peace, and that's where I want you to be.

Mr. Tyrone Sims, you are truly my soul mate, and I'll love you for another lifetime if it's in any way possible.

Your loving wife,
Mrs. Connie Renee Sims.

He pressed the note tightly to his chest, feeling that somehow, if he could just press it hard enough, the words would leap from the page and engrave themselves in his heart. He flipped through the other pages in the folder and found a list for the nurse and another for him.

Isn't that just like her to leave me a list of things to do so that I wouldn't have to try to figure it out on my own? What am I going to do without her?

He sat at the desk, folded his arms, laid his head down, and wept. He cried two years' worth of heartache.

After nearly twenty minutes, he opened the folder containing his list of to-do items. The items read:

Tyrone, if any of this is too difficult for you to handle right now, let Johnny and Karen know. I've already talked to them, and they're going to help you do whatever needs to be done. You won't be alone.

1. *Call the nurse. She'll make all of the appropriate calls for you, including the one to Dr. Moseley (all of the phone numbers are on the next page).*
2. *Call Tyrone and Karen, because I don't want you to be alone. Tell them that I love them.*
3. *Call Tina next, because she'll have a fit if she has to find out any other way. Tell her that I love her too.*
4. *Whenever you feel up to it, call my sister Dee in Philadelphia. She'll contact the rest of the family for you.*
5. *Perhaps Karen can call Soror Dorothy for me. Once somebody gets in touch with her, she will let the rest of the chapter know. You know that whatever help you need, my sorors will be there for you.*
6. *See if Karen can call Pastor Hill and let him know.*

7. *When Johnny and Karen get there, give her the instructions on page four. She has agreed to coordinate the funeral with my sister, Bonnie, so that you won't have to.*
8. *Don't forget to say a prayer. You're going to need God to help you get beyond all of this. Sweetheart, I must admit that I feel like the fortunate one. It would have been so hard for me if you had gone first. I'm not as strong as you are. I couldn't have imagined living without you. Still, I want you to be okay, and you will be.*
9. *After the nurse gets there, I want you to get something to eat. Then I want you to get dressed and get out of the house for a while. Go for a walk, or for a drive, or anything that will help you find some peace. Push yourself if you have to, but please go out. It won't do you any good to just sit around the house.*
10. *Always remember that I love you and that you did the right thing by letting me stay at home. I just couldn't go back to another hospital. Thank you for that.*
    I love you.

Tears filled his eyes as he remembered his wife. He laid the list on top of the folder and went to the phone to call the Clarks. It was three-thirty in the morning, but he dialed the number without hesitation. Johnny and Karen were family.

The phone rang and neither rolled over immediately to pick it up.

"You have reached the Clarks. To leave a message for Johnny, press one, for Karen press two . . ." was the only voice that Tyrone heard.

Johnny was roused, but not in time to get the call before it went into the voice mail.

Of all the calls on the list, this was one Tyrone needed to make. He tapped the reset button on the phone and then pressed redial.

Johnny glanced at the clock when the phone rang again. He figured that either someone was crazy for calling so early or that it must be important. He grabbed the phone with a tinge of sharpness.

"Hello?"

"Hey, partner."

"Tyrone!" Johnny popped up in the bed, expecting to hear serious news.

"Yeah, buddy," Tyrone said, rubbing his hand across his face, "it's me." He paused before sharing the news.

Johnny waited patiently for Tyrone to speak.

"She's gone, Johnny."

Johnny sat up on the side of the bed with both feet on the floor. He searched for the right words of comfort, but didn't find any that adequately conveyed his feelings for Tyrone's loss.

"I'm sorry, man. What can I do to help?"

"Nothing right now. I have a list of calls that Connie left for me to make." He chuckled. "Man, can you believe that she left me a honey-do list?" He put every effort forward to squeak out a little humor.

Both men laughed, remembering how many times they had joked about the list of items Connie would give Tyrone. Each list started off with the heading *Honey, can you do . . .*

It wasn't long before Tyrone's laughter turned into crying.

"I can't believe that she's gone, Johnny. After all of this time, she's gone. What am I going to do without her?"

"It's going to be hard, Tyrone, but you're going to get through this, man."

Karen had been awake for a few minutes but didn't disrupt the conversation. She knew that Tyrone needed to talk with Johnny more than he needed to hear from her. She rubbed Johnny's arm to let him know that she was awake and listening.

"It's harder than I thought, partner. Even though she was sick for two years, I still wasn't ready for her to go."

"I don't think that you can ever be ready for something like that," Johnny speculated.

"I guess not. I remember all of the times she was suffering with pain. Being in limbo was a killer, I can tell you that. Many nights I thought it would be better for her to pass and be at peace rather than stay here and suffer through the pain and sleepless nights. I even thought that a part of me would be relieved when she either got better or died." He contemplated the thought in momentary silence. "I was wrong. I would rather have had her with me, sick as she was, than to be without her now."

Johnny provided a listening ear, with a few agreements thrown in to let Tyrone know that he was still on the line. Johnny knew that his friend wasn't looking for advice. All he needed was someplace to start emptying out the grief in his heart.

"I should have done more for her."

"No, Tyrone, you can't say that. You did all that was humanly possible for Connie, and she knew it. You went farther and longer than most could have."

"Yeah, but there were times when I was drained trying to take care of Connie and keep up with work and everything else around here. I'm not going to lie, man. It was hard."

"I know that feeling."

"Yeah, well, I feel bad about it."

"Don't. It's like you told me months ago: you're only human. There is only so much that you can do."

The doorbell sounded, followed by a banging knock that could be heard faintly in the bedroom. Tyrone stood up.

"Hey, Johnny, that's probably the visiting nurse at the door. I have to answer it."

"All right. Karen and I will be over in a few minutes."

"No need to do that. It's too early in the morning for you to be coming out."

Johnny ignored his comment and reconfirmed, "We'll see you within the hour."

"Okay, chief. Thanks. That means a lot to me."

The doorbell rang again. This time Tyrone hustled to the door yelling, "I'm on my way. Just a minute."

CHAPTER 42

The Michigan wind whisked through the collage of orange, brown, and yellow leaves that dangled from the ends of the supporting limbs. Some weren't able to withstand the pressure and gave way from their life source, fluttering to their demise. Those that endured were a vibrant display of beauty.

It was Karen's favorite time of the year. The leaves had always caught her eye, but they didn't have much other meaning before. She had begun to see life in its simplicity following her relapse of cancer in the spring. She sat on the park bench reading a book that the marriage counselor had recommended. It was a little nippy out, but the brisk air felt good. She was glad to be alive.

She looked up from the book and gazed into the distance. She often found herself reminiscing about her girlfriend. Certain smells, songs, or places would prompt a memory without warning. She took the knuckle of her index finger and brushed away the tears forming in her eyes. It had been barely two months since Connie had passed. Karen knew that it would take time to make the adjustment of living without Connie, someone who had been like a sister to her. The best Karen could hope for was to one day get to the point where she could reflect on a memory of Connie without swelling with tears. She stared at the leaves and reflected how they were the most beautiful right before they died. She picked up her book and continued reading.

"Oh, my goodness!" All of a sudden she jumped up from the

bench, anxiously grabbing her belongings. It dawned on her that the new housekeeper was meeting her at the house around two o'clock.

It didn't take her long to zoom around to 712 Morning Glory Circle. The housekeeper was standing in the driveway, as Karen had figured. She pulled in and hopped out.

"You must be Karen," the housekeeper said.

"Yes, I am. I apologize for being late. I lost track of the time."

"No problem. I've only been here a few minutes."

"Good. Come on in, Leslie, and I'll show you around."

"By the way, the directions were perfect, and you were right. This is the only house in the area with the tall black wrought iron fence. That made it easy to find."

"I knew that it would." Karen waited for the garage door to open, revealing an empty room, with the exception of a few boxes and a workbench. "Come on. I'll take you in this way."

"A three-and-a-half-car garage—nice!"

"Yeah, it was nice when we had three cars. We recently sold one of them."

"Must be nice to have all of this space."

Karen grinned. "Actually, we're trying to get rid of some of this space. That's why we're moving to a smaller house in Southfield."

"I can't imagine giving up this beautiful place for a smaller one?"

"Sure am. Don't get me wrong. This place has been wonderful for my family, but it really is more house than we need. My husband and I decided that less is more. Less house, less maintenance, and less expenses. That means less stress and less work."

"I wish you could convince my husband to do that. It seems like the more we work and get, the more he wants. He's never satisfied," Leslie stated.

"Oh, trust me, I know all about that. We dug ourselves into a big hole. Thank God we finally woke up and started to change."

"Well, maybe my husband needs to get a dose of whatever it was that caused you and your husband to change."

Karen smiled and told Leslie, "No," shaking her head. "I don't think he wants to go through what we've gone through." Karen gave Leslie a peaceful and cheerful look. "Just pray that you and your husband will have God's wisdom. There are some lessons you'd rather not have to go through the hard way, like we did. Come on, let me show you around."

* * *

Johnny was continuing to transfer some of his workload to his assistant. His goal was to get his travel down to no more than five nights away from home a month and no more than one late night a week. He had learned how much of a difference his presence made with the girls. He was also learning how fulfilled it made him feel as a father.

"Excuse me, sir," Sonja interrupted. "Mr. Richter wants to talk with you on line one."

"Thank you, Sonja. I'll take it. Oh, and could you please close my door?" Johnny pressed line one. "Well, hello, Al. I wasn't expecting a call from you. What's cooking?"

"What's cooking, John, are your second- and third-quarter numbers. I don't know how you did it. Your production levels were twenty percent over plan with a thirty-five percent increase in quality levels. Congratulations, big guy."

"Thanks, but it wasn't all of my doing. I have an entire staff of people that made it happen, like Jeff and DeWayne."

"I know that you have a great team, and that's also to your credit. John, the bottom line is that you got the job done with whatever limited resources you had available. You continue to be the kind of leader that Tennin Automotive needs. In light of your performance, I have some good news for you. I wanted to tell you in person, but there's no way that I can get out of this meeting in New York with the Wall Street analysts. But I want to thank you for your efforts and be the first to congratulate you in your new role as senior vice president of manufacturing."

"Senior VP! Are you talking about a promotion?"

"I sure am. I'm taking all of the production operations off of my plate and handing them over to you. You've proven that you can handle the level of responsibility."

"I don't know what to say."

"And you will be entitled to a hundred-thousand-dollar annual salary increase with ten thousand additional shares of stock. The stock is currently trading around forty dollars a share. Hopefully it will still be worth something after I finish throwing my two cents in with the analyst." Al chuckled. "So what do you say?"

Johnny took a deep breath and sat back in his chair. He didn't know what to say. Less than a year ago he would have jumped at the additional money, recognition, and responsibility. That was when getting ahead still meant everything to him. But now all he could do was reflect on the struggles that he and Karen had gone through over the recent years. Through all of the sickness and marital disputes, money hadn't bought him any extra happiness or Karen any more health. He shook his head, realizing that the peace he was now enjoying hadn't cost a dime. He had reevaluated what was really important in his life. Johnny wasn't quick to give an answer about the promotion. After all, he was trying to wind down at work, not gear up.

"I say thank you for the offer. I was not expecting any kind of promotion. This comes as a nice surprise. I do have questions regarding roles, responsibilities, and my operating budget."

"Of course. I can address all of your questions when I get back in the office on Monday. Have Tammy put you on my schedule, and we'll talk then. I don't want to waste any time on this. I want to get you transitioned into the new position in plenty of time to get the projections together for next year."

"Will do, Al. Thanks again, and have a safe trip back."

"Thanks, John. I'll see you Monday."

Johnny hit the button that released the speakerphone. He sat back in his chair again, twirled his pen, and pondered the offer. The promotion put him in an awkward position. Turning down a promotion at this point in his career would be damaging. He knew several other managers who had turned down promotions and ended up getting blackballed or labeled as a nonteam player. In each case the men were slowly phased out of their jobs and the company. After being with Tennin Automotive for over eighteen years, he didn't want to look for another job. There might be an alternative. He called Karen to share the news of his promotion.

Karen was showing Leslie around and going over what she wanted cleaned before the realtor put the house on the market. She heard the phone.

"Excuse me, Leslie, I need to get that." She grabbed the cordless phone from the kitchen to find Johnny on the other end.

"Hi, Karen."

"Hey, I'm showing the cleaning lady around."

"Oh, I forgot that she was coming. Don't forget to let her know that we're interested in hiring her for regular service after we move to Southfield."

"Oh, trust me, I am not about to forget that. So how's your day going?"

"Great. Al called me a few minutes ago and offered me a promotion and an extra hundred thousand a year, plus stock valued around four hundred thousand dollars."

"Oh, yeah?"

"Yeah, how's that for a surprise?"

"What did you tell him?"

"I haven't told him anything yet. I wanted time to think it over and to talk with you first."

"How do you feel about it?"

"To tell you the truth, Karen, it sounds perfect. The catch is that it will be more work and responsibility than I want on my plate. These past few months have been good for me. I like not living at the office anymore."

"So are you thinking about turning it down?"

"I don't know. That might be hard to do. What I'm thinking about doing is taking seventy-five of that hundred thousand dollars and hiring a second assistant. With two assistants, I'll be able to keep my workload down to a reasonable level. And I'll still be able to get a raise and an assistant without impacting my own operating budget. After giving the seventy-five thousand a year away, I will still end up with about two thousand more a month. With the eighteen hundred that we're saving each month by getting rid of the car and getting the smaller house, we should be in good shape. When I think about it, this is a real blessing."

"You're right, it is a blessing. What about the stock options?"

"Shoot, I'm not crazy. I'm taking that money. I still want to retire early, and that will go a long way toward helping the cause."

"This is good news."

"I still have to present my plan to Al. We'll see what happens."

"Sounds good. We'll just have to pray that God gives you favor."

"Well, I'm going to pack up early this afternoon. I would like to meet with Tyrone this evening, if it's all right with you."

"Sure, go ahead. Give him my love. Are you going to Floods?"

Karen remembered the other times she had gotten sick. Johnny would drop his shenanigans and rush to her side. Each time she accepted him. Shortly after the crisis was over he'd return to Floods and pick up a few stray women. Four years, round and round they went with the scenario like their dog chasing his tail.

"Oh, no, not Floods. I've paid my dues at Floods. It's time to move on. I think we might catch a game of pool at Dave and Buster's."

"Go ahead; I'll be fine. Tina's coming over later to tell me about this guy she's been seeing. She's finally thinking about getting serious with someone for the first time since she got divorced. Can you believe it?"

Johnny chuckled and said, "That ought to keep you busy. Tell her that I said to go easy on the guy."

"I will," she said. "See you later, Johnny." Karen prepared to disconnect when she remembered something else. "Oh yeah, I almost forgot. The counseling session has been changed from next Tuesday to Wednesday at five-thirty P.M., and my appointment with Dr. Costas got moved to the slot on Tuesday. Are those times going to work for you?"

Without checking his schedule Johnny quickly answered, "I'll make them work. Go ahead and confirm them both."

"You sure, Johnny?"

"Your health and our marriage come before this job. If I had to, I could get another job. I can't get another you."

The past flashed before him. He recalled how close he and Karen had been during her illnesses. He was supportive and she was receptive. After the battle was over, intimacy was great. But it wasn't long before she would lose interest in sex and eventually cut him off. He would plead with her, each time less and less, before heading to Floods and a finding a few comforting female friends. Johnny promised himself that he was through with that cycle. This time was different. It was reassuring to know that Karen wanted him. They had had more intimacy in the last four months than they had in the past four years. He didn't know a lot about having God in his life, but from what he could tell, it was already better than what he had.

Karen blushed and grinned from ear to ear. It was wonderful having the couple back that she remembered from nearly twenty years ago. It felt good being in sync. She was flying high like a butterfly that had finally gotten some wind under its wings.

"Have fun with Tyrone, and I'll see you later."

"I love you, Karen."

"I love you too, Johnny."

MAKES YOU GO HMMM!

Thought-Provoking Questions for Discussion

Now that you have read *No Regrets*, let's talk about some of the issues addressed in the story. Grab a glass of your favorite beverage, a few snacks, a couple of your reading buddies, and strike up a discussion with the following questions in mind. Have fun.

1. Tina and Connie had different views on what Karen should do about Johnny. Tina said to leave him. Connie said to try to work it out. Do you agree with either of them? What would have been your advice?
2. Under what conditions, if any, should married individuals seek advice from single people? What about Karen getting advice from Tina?
3. Close friends share all kinds of information, including some secrets and marriage "stuff." Is there any marital- or relationship-related information that should be kept in the strictest confidence, not to be shared outside of the marriage with even close friends and family? How much of Johnny's business should Karen have shared with Tina?
4. What are the red flags/warning signs associated with a marriage headed for disaster? How do you recognize them? How do you correct them? What signs did Johnny have? What should he have done about them?
5. How and when do you forgive a mate or loved one for hurting you? Is there ever a time when enough is enough? Are there any conditions by which you can't or won't forgive someone? Can you forgive without forgetting? Do you think that Karen should forgive Johnny for seeing another woman? Is Karen an innocent victim? How did she contribute to the marital breakdown?
6. What help can God provide in a troubled marriage or in tough financial times?
7. How do you shield children from the struggles and issues that

occur with their parents? How do you keep them from feeling like they have to take sides? What could Karen have done to improve the relationship between Johnny and John Erick?

8. Can someone find compatibility in a mate who does not have the same educational, professional, or religious aspirations? How significant was the fact that Karen and Johnny were at different places spiritually and professionally?
9. What is the best way to handle financial issues in a relationship? What could Johnny and Karen have done differently?
10. If a person tends to be mean, nasty, whiny, or clingy during their serious illness, how tolerant should the caregiver/friend/helper be? Is there a limit? If there is a limit, what do you do if it's reached? Did Karen drive Johnny to a limit?
11. How do you handle a close friend who cares for you but also either envies you or is quick to give you hurtful information, primarily out of spite? What was the key to Karen and Tina's friendship, recognizing their extreme personality differences?
12. What was it about Big Mama that enabled her to befriend Johnny in the hospital, even after he told her off?
13. What about Connie—do you think that she was in denial about her illness? What about Tyrone—do you think a man can change so dramatically for the "right" woman or for any other reason? Do you think that Tyrone will remarry after Connie?
14. What are the various ways to check for breast cancer? Which have you done personally? Karen got breast cancer in her early thirties, although most mammograms aren't recommended till age forty or fifty. How early should you have a mammogram done if you don't have a family history of breast cancer?
15. What does the dusty Bible metaphor on page one represent?

Dear Readers:

Thank you for reading *No Regrets.* I hope that you enjoyed the story. While it is meant to entertain and encourage, I hope that it also enlightens you about breast cancer awareness as well as other prevalent forms of cancer. There is a war against cancer, and we have the power to dramatically improve our ability to win by equipping ourselves with knowledge and increased awareness. Visit your local library and the multitude of on-line sites for more information.

Drop me a line at my Web site, www.patriciahaley.com, and let me know your thoughts about the story. Keep reading! I look forward to hearing from you!

Patricia Haley